Praise for Ciar Cullen's *Lords of Ch'i*

6 Wands "From page one I was riveted. …There is non stop action and sexual tension that will have you turning page after page. When I reached the end I was frustrated that it was over so soon. Jet is one sexy hero and Silver is not your typical heroine. She is smart, beautiful and doesn't pull any of those too stupid to live acts. I highly recommend this book." ~ *Enchanted Ramblings*

5 Hearts "Ciar Cullen draws the reader into a wonderful fantasy world of elves, clans and danger. In an adventure that will thrill the reader, characters that will sear the heart and emotions that grip and squeeze, Ms Cullen leads her reader down a wild ride that will leave her breathless. …This reviewer hopes that soon there will be more stories from this wonderful world." ~ *Love Romances*

Lords of Ch'i

Ciar Cullen

A SAMHAIN PUBLISHING, LTD. publication.

Samhain Publishing, Ltd.
2932 Ross Clark Circle, #384
Dothan, AL 36301
www.samhainpublishing.com

Lords of Ch'i
Copyright © 2006 by Ciar Cullen
Print ISBN: 1-59998-286-2
Digital ISBN: 1-59998-037-1

Editing by Angie James
Cover by Anne Cain

First Samhain Publishing, Ltd. electronic publication: August 2006
First Samhain Publishing, Ltd. print publication: November 2006

Dedication

Many thanks to Angie and the staff of Samhain Publishing for their wonderful support and guidance. This story is for my teachers and friends in the martial arts.

Prologue

Unified Year Thirty-Eight

Jetre scowled at his classmate, Kilé, the brilliant beautiful boy who infuriated him simply by breathing. Kilé always spoke eloquently of Wu Xing, the organization of the universe, and his desire to find his true nature. It annoyed the hell out of Jetre.

Sissy, ass-kissing, Master's pet.

Master Guo rapped Jet on the head. "Jetre, stop daydreaming! Kilé completed his assignments magnificently. I suppose a winged Pteran ate your essay again? Or perhaps it fell into the river on your way to class?"

Jet ignored Guo's reprimand and, reaching up, grasped one of her hands and rubbed the sensitive spot in the wrinkled flesh between her index finger and thumb. A flicker of intense pain and then blessed relief crossed her face. Her energy flowed properly, and the agony plaguing her arthritic joints dissipated.

"Do not try to avoid punishment with your healing skills, little one." An affectionate twinkle in Guo's eyes softened her scolding look. "Now, expound upon your current understanding of Wu Xing. Be precise, focus." Guo absently straightened the deep-blue sash that marked a Master and fretted with her many long, gray braids as she paced.

How many times had Master Guo told him to focus? Jet bit back a smart comment, knowing to utter it meant grueling evening hours of extra work, time away from his archery or staff practice, plus a mighty beating from his father. Keeping his face as blank as possible under Guo's close examination, he stood to recite the credo of the Unification.

"All the universe is the product of the magnetic forces created when the Five Elements interact. Metal, Wood, Earth, Water, Fire…"

Guo frowned. "Must you always name the Destructive cycle? Again, but name the cycle of Creation, in the reverse order."

Jet sighed dramatically. "Metal, Water, Wood, Fire, Earth." The other students giggled, and Jet snickered and surveyed his classmates, appreciative of the attention.

"In the age of human destruction, after the last great climate change, only a small percentage of the all the races survived. They wisely turned to the Way, the ancient philosophy of Wu Xing." He tried to sound as bored as possible as he stared idly at the marble ceiling of the dojo's classroom.

"Our greatest purpose is to learn our true nature and element, and to embrace the teaching each brings in battle and in creation. Dissidents, fearful of change and the mixing of races seek to distort Wu Xing, control others, and pirate the remaining resources of our land."

Guo stopped pacing and nodded in mock approval. "Superbly quoted. However, we speak of your calling—to become a great Master and help lead the Unified clans. You mimic the great teachings with disdain."

"But the clans are not unified." The children all gasped at his courage, his foolishness for uttering the truth. "I am Wood, all my folk are Wood. We are nothing like *him*, like Kilé. None of the Wood Clan wants this Unification. I bet the Metal don't either." Jet pointed to Kilé, noticing with satisfaction that the blond sat upright in surprise, looking fearful for a moment. Lowering his voice—aiming for drama—Jet watched his classmates hang on his words and relished the feeling of power, of attention.

He nodded in Kilé's direction in the serious manner of adults he'd witnessed at Council meetings. "We'll be enemies."

Kilé turned away with a smirk, and Jet wondered how he hid his hatred so easily.

Guo growled in frustration and threw her book on Jet's desk. The children jumped at the noise as Jet regarded her calmly, expecting her outburst. "This is not about war. This is about peace, about plenty, about healing and harmony. You've learned nothing." She turned to the rest of the children and waved her hand impatiently. "All of you, dismissed. Take to the field and practice your weapons. I expect perfection in your forms in one hour." The children stood and filed out of the room, snickering and whispering.

"Jetre, stay behind." Guo's low voice sounded threatening. Jet looked again at the ceiling in frustration, already imagining the sting of his father's hand on his naked buttocks. The man would admire his son's tirade, but would feel compelled to punish him. Masur always complained his children forced him to the beatings, but Jet knew he enjoyed inflicting pain.

The only escape was to appeal to Guo's soft nature, hidden under her hard exterior. Jet tried a smile.

"Jet." She drew his name out, lips turned down in disapproval, narrowed eyes bringing deep furrows to her brow. "Don't even entertain a thought of trying to charm me." She sighed and took his hand, leading him onto the balustrade of the huge marble building. Jet peered on tiptoe over the railing to the practice grounds in the central courtyard. His classmates worked diligently on their weapons forms, wielding long and short swords or small scythes. A few twirled wooden staffs. Jet picked Kilé's long blond hair out from among the flowing and blurring of arms and weapons, and watched his expert sword thrusts with reluctant admiration.

"Enough jealousy. Sit with me." Guo patted the stone bench. Jet climbed into her lap and wrapped his arms around her, laying his head on her shoulder. Guo smelled of ripe apples and spices—how he imagined a cozy, safe home would smell. Jet's chaotic home smelled only of his father's drunken fits and mother's anguish.

I wish you were my mother. I wish Master Tsien were my father. Please let me live here, let me stay with you.

"Boy, why must you fight me at every turn? We have been together for five years, since you were barely able to hold a weapon."

9

"Five and a half years, Master. They brought me on my fourth birthday. The year of the Unification."

"You speak of the Unification as if it were a terrible plague upon the land. It's our only hope for survival."

"Tell my parents. You know all the clans meet in secret, planning against one another. Why do you pretend you don't? You and Master Tsien, the whole Council, teach us to love one another, to work together. When we go home for the festivals, our parents talk of nothing but their hatred for the other clans. They'll be at war before I'm your age, before I'm half your age. You know it, you and Master Tsien and the others. Don't you?"

Guo sighed deeply. "We do all we can, Jet. We placed our hope in our youth, but we can't fight your clan leaders, your traditions. I understand all too well. Before I renounced my clan affiliation to join the Council…"

"You were Fire." Jet pulled away. He looked into the old woman's pale green eyes and rubbed his hand on her wrinkled, brown cheek, which was a shade lighter than most of Fire clan. "I can't change my clan, and I can't change who I am. I am Wood, and I will never be anything else."

Master Guo groaned. "Yes, we've established that. Your nature matches your element, indeed—stubborn."

"Do not forget benevolent." Despite his heavy heart, Jet flashed his winning grin and Guo let a small giggle escape. He kissed her cheek and laid his head back on her shoulder. She caressed his long, dark hair and playfully flicked at his slightly peaked ears.

"I'm your favorite, aren't I, Master Guo? I know you won't answer, but it's true."

"You're right, I won't answer."

Jet thought seriously for a moment, not wanting to hurt the woman he loved deeply. "Master, I know you want the best for the clans. The world isn't behaving the way the Masters intended. The Way, Wu Xing, won't bring the clans together. It's too late."

Guo sat up straight and pulled Jet's chin up to meet his eyes closely. "Young man, you must attend to me now, lock onto my words."

"Yes, Master, I'm listening." A hand of fear clutched at his gut and reached towards his heart as Guo's foretelling energy filled the air around them.

"You are right in what you say. I have seen a time when the clans lose their way, and the warring of a bygone era returns. During your lifetime, Jetre, not very long from now. Power corrupts. You and the other devotees will learn how powerful you are and use this knowledge for harm." Guo pushed at a lock of Jet's hair and searched his eyes closely. "You understand the minor territorial battles of late threaten to escalate into something more devastating?" Jet nodded emphatically. Indeed, he thought of little else, heard little else discussed at home.

"Boy, I want you to understand you will have a role to play, an important one, once you have taken your oath." Guo held up a crooked index finger. "If you demonstrate strength, knowledge, and wisdom enough for the oath taking."

"I will take the oath, have no doubt."

"I'm not sure you quite understand the sacrifice at your age. Celibacy is not for the faint of heart."

"I won't care about stupid girls."

Guo laughed heartily. "My boy, unless you become a lover of men, I guarantee, you will care dearly about stupid girls. I'm even more certain they will care desperately about you. The oath won't be kind to you."

"Sex. Big deal. I still don't understand the point of the oath. Not that it will bother me much, as I said." Jet wondered nervously if indeed it would be a big deal. He heard the older boys whisper about fucking with such passion and awe—maybe it was a big sacrifice?

"You will understand better when you reach the appropriate age. Let me try to explain in a way you can understand now. Sexual passion is a powerful force, and few are immune to its pull on their intellect and energy. As a clan leader, *one devoted to the Unification and peace,* you will need to exert immeasurable control of your energy and the energy of your entire clan. Sex disrupts control. The oath acts in two ways to strengthen you—you conserve all of your Ch'i, losing none to the vicissitudes of young romance, and you show your clan your unparalleled self-discipline. And self-discipline is…"

"The basis of self-knowledge, yes, I know."

"Your clan will respect you for it, Jet. Don't mock the oath."

"Well, how come you all thought this up now? Doesn't seem fair my father and Kilé's father and Paulo's all got to do whatever they wanted, and we have to train and take the oath."

"Firstly, you imp, the Council has yet to determine which of you will take the oath and lead the clans into the new era."

Jet sighed and held up his hand, counting the names of the five most accomplished Wu Xing practitioners. "Me, Kilé, Paulo, Iain, and Bourne."

Guo growled and pulled at Jet's ear. "Don't let your other classmates hear you dismiss them so easily. In any case, the Council deems it wise to create a structure of training to serve all of Isla for millennia to come. Of course, your clan must also approve the Council's choice of lord."

Jet held back a sputter of laughter. Wood clan already inclined their heads when he walked the streets of Traier, acknowledging him as their future leader.

"Yes, Master. I know. If my clan deems me worthy, as you say, I will rule Wood. You know also I will rule all the clans."

Guo gasped. "What makes you think that?"

Jet shrugged. "Dreams. Daydreams."

"Or simply your hopes?"

"No, the deep knowing, Master. I've seen it in my meditations. I'll lead Wood to victory over the rest."

"You have very special gifts. You could work to strengthen the Unified territories. Don't be a fool, boy. The warlords will rise and fall, do not be among them."

"It is my destiny. If you've seen the future, you know I'm speaking the truth, Master."

Guo sighed and leaned back on the bench, looking deflated.

"Remember, you can change destiny."

"I do not wish to."

In fact, I can't wait to kick Kīlé's ass.

Chapter One

Twenty Years Later

Jet pulled up the collar of his long coat and loosened his hair from its leather binding to give him additional warmth against the biting wind. He didn't bother muffling the sharp tap of his boots on the glistening street or mask his presence under the ghostly lamplights, although he knew an enemy tracked him.

A snowflake hit his cheek and he looked up, straining to remember what his mother said about snowfall. Yes, that lovers should kiss at the first snow of the season.

Jet groaned inwardly. *Lovers. What is it to have a lover?* All he knew of passion was one aborted attempt at a quick coupling the night before his oath and the obscene entertainment his beloved cousin orchestrated to keep him from going insane—or to drive him insane. The press of warm soft lips on his, the scent of perfume, the feel of full breasts against his bare skin—all so long ago he wondered if his memory tricked him. He couldn't even remember the girl's name, the only one he'd ever held in his arms.

His father had beaten him to within one breath of his life for attempting to cheat the oath that night. Lue, his mother, had cleaned up his blood, pulled him in close, and whispered ancient fairy stories as if he were five instead of sixteen. He pushed the memory aside. Lue's stories told only of snowflakes and faraway places and heroes—none taught him about death. None prepared him for her assassination and the gaping hole it left in his soul. Why didn't parents teach children how painful life could be?

And the guilt. No one explained the guilt.

He missed his mother deeply. It was his father's death, however, that plagued him, and not because of loss. Did anyone grieve for Masur? The man had been a monster. No, his father's death came as a blessing, for Jet now controlled the clan. There would be no more confrontations over the man's horrific treatment of his wife, of his children.

Still I must play the grieving eldest son and hunt down Masur's assassin.

Brushing away the familiar hauntings of the past, he reached out to the only other soul on the dark, silent street. Belanor was in lockdown, the barren town speaking more to a recent defeat at his clan's hands than the cold of winter. Supplies were scarce in Metal territory, the clan afraid now to venture beyond its borders. Why did this Metal warrior venture out to the gray cobbled streets, to the gray air? Only an assassin on official Metal clan business would be allowed to roam at this hour.

His pursuer emerged from behind the cover of a large stone column.

Don't they understand my power? How many more will they send?

Jet picked up a mental glimmer of bronze wire wrapped around long female fingers. *The fool intends to cut your throat.* Why would she imagine herself strong enough to subdue him? He turned suddenly to face his would-be killer, who stopped cold several yards away.

Jet masked the shock of the sight of her, the instant tremor she sent through him, even at this distance. Metal clan, as he suspected, but quite lovely, with white-blonde hair sheered into a short cap, eyes reflecting the glistening snow, tall and slender. She stood erect, her hands tucked inside her cloak sleeves.

Confusion, fear, and something else he didn't recognize—perhaps regret—all flashed across her lovely face.

"Sympathy for one's victims weakens you, betrays your intention. Your Master has been remiss in your training." Jet spoke in the ancient Metal tongue, noting with satisfaction her surprise and quick intake of breath.

"Sympathy, Lord? Hardly." Her strong, steady voice surprised him.

"You're Metal clan."

Her cool energy hinted she might be full-blooded Metal, without a drop of the Elven blood, or the blood of the night-black shifting Were, or the lithe water clan. Few Trueborns survived into the post-Unification era. Was she of the ruling family?

"Yes, Lord, I'm Metal clan."

"Surely you realize I won't let you harm me?"

"Aye." She shrugged, her breath turning to mist. The snow fell more earnestly now, and Jet glanced up at the rare sight.

"At least the snow will whiten this ever-present gray of your clan. Your town deadens my soul, Metal. Doesn't it deaden your spirit? Must everything be gray and stark? Your hideous buildings block the stars. How can you tolerate it?"

Why are you chatting with her as if this were a chance meeting with a friend? Are you that lonely, Jet—that hungry for the sound of another intelligent voice?

"Your disdain for our culture is well known, Lord. I have no answers for you. I understand Traier and its people are more bonded to nature. That is as foreign to me as Belanor is to you. We yearn for pre-Destruction comforts."

Jet laughed lightly. "Yearn away. There's not enough ore on Isla to arm all your clan members with long swords, is there? Enough chatter. It seems you aren't very concerned about your imminent death?"

She shrugged again. "You started the chatter. I care about my death, but I'm helpless to change it."

"I see. They will kill you for failing to kill me? You'd rather die at my hand, imagining me to be a gentler executioner?"

"You've earned that reputation, Lord. I pray I've not been misled." The woman laughed wryly, and Jet wondered again at her amazing composure.

Take care, Jet. Do not underestimate this one. The danger is in her charms, her face. A face to bring any warrior to his knees.

Except for a Wood Elf sworn to purity.

"Your name?"

"Silver." She smirked. "I changed my name in adolescence in hopes I would become a Metal warrior, follow in my brother's footsteps, and perhaps become a trifle less of a burden to my family."

Burden? How could this beautiful woman burden anyone? The strong energy she emanated filled the air between them, danced with his in the snowflakes.

"Ah, it might have been worse, Warrior Silver. You might have picked Bronze. Or Iron. Doesn't exactly roll off the tongue. Not such a bad choice for a child to make. What name did your parents give you?"

"Atra." Her eyes glimmered briefly in what at a distance looked like amusement and Jet found himself smiling despite the gravity of their situation.

"The pre-Destruction ruler? You didn't fancy being named after a ruthless despot?" She smiled back, bringing a quick finger of warmth to the energy between them, a brief flicker of lightness to a bleak night. *A bleak month. A bleaker year.* Jet pushed down the ache and longing threatening to intrude on his control whenever Fate dangled something tempting but unavailable before him.

"I may have been a trial to my mother inside her womb. I asked many times why I should carry such an accursed name, but the woman would only mumble unintelligibly. My suspicion is I didn't quite listen carefully enough as a fetus. She desired a different child."

"A male? An elf perhaps? Or did she crave the Were-child? She might have mated differently if she wanted a different child."

Silver's laugh matched her energy—light and sparkling, and drifting gently on the cool breeze swirling the snow along the sidewalk.

"Was there a time before the Melting when men and women chatted on the streets at night as if there were nothing more urgent pressing for their attention? What do you think, Warrior Atra? Would we have become friends had we been born in another age? Should we pretend to live in that time, or would you like to go back to trying to kill me?"

"I apologize for wasting the great lord's time with my dull, unimportant tale."

"Ah, but you want to talk to me. And you care how I view you—I see it in your eyes, feel the plea pouring from you. Isn't that water under the dam, as your clan says?"

"Over the dam, under the bridge, Lord." She winced at correcting him and he saw a flush sweep to her cheeks. *Lovely. And pale.* Jet imagined the creamy whiteness of her flesh hidden under her heavy cloak.

He walked slowly towards her. Silver looked for a moment as if she would try to flee, and Jet shook his head subtly.

"Don't."

He watched resignation take hold. Averting her gaze, Silver studied the ground and kicked at a pebble with her black boot as a child would. The gesture charmed him. *Don't underestimate her. She knows of your oath, and she knows she's beautiful.*

Finally standing toe-to-toe with Silver, Jet lifted her chin with a gloved finger. A flash of heat spiraled through his chest when he looked into her eyes from such a close distance, and his blood stirred at the images he saw dancing there. Her projections were unsubtle yet stirring—her tongue licking the head of his cock, her mouth caressing him into ecstasy, seducing him to submit to her insatiable appetites, binding him with ropes of promises and chains of pleasure beyond his experience. Frenzied couplings, skin burning with excitement, mouths locked in desperate kisses, whispers of forbidden acts, teaching him the passion denied him. And Mikalis with them. How could she know about his cousin?

A flare of anger mixed with compelling lust. Jet pulled a sharp short blade from his cloak. "That's not impressive, Metal. A very obvious ploy. You think a silent promise to suck my cock will save your life? They've tried this before. While the last whore-assassin wasn't as lovely, you overestimate the value of your allure."

But you would like to fuck her brains out, and she knows it. Are these your visions, Jet?

He waved his blade an inch from her face.

"I have no idea what you're talking about. I object to the label of whore. Assassin will do." She bit her lip nervously, her chest rising and falling quickly with her shallow breathing. He smelled a hint of dark, spicy perfume waft on the freezing air, and it brought up an ache for the loss of Master Guo.

"I won't waste more time with you."

A tear slipped down her cheek and she brushed it away quickly. "There's nothing for it, Lord Jetre?"

He shook his head slowly and pressed the blade against her throat as he pulled her head back by her short blonde hair. The smallest trickle of blood traced a dark, sluggish path down her neck, nearly freezing on her skin. She clutched at his coat to steady herself.

"If I vow to tell you everything I know, all the plans of my clan?" Silver clenched her jaw so tightly her face trembled. "If I offer myself to you to in total servitude?"

"If you'd betray your own, you'd betray me more easily. Do you think I'm an imbecile?"

"The Lord Cirin sent me, knowing you'd defeat me easily. He didn't want my blood on his hands, the death of another of the Metal ruling family. The clan members grow restless, call for changes, an end to the corruption and assassinations. Cirin disbanded the Metal Council. This is his way of killing me without casting suspicion upon himself. Let the great Lord Jetre take the blame. I didn't come to follow orders. I would have fled the territory. I came to find you."

Jet arched a brow and stared more deeply into Silver's eyes. "You're lying. Why would you risk certain death? One falsehood and it's over."

The sight of her pupils dilating in fear quickened his heart, and he realized her terror excited him, the smell and taste of her dread stirred his heart and groin. *What ails you, Jet?* He'd killed women, but never wanted one to fear him like this. One flick of his wrist, and her life would flow onto the sidewalk. *It's because she's the enemy, nothing more.* The lie crept into his gut. *What's this pull she has on you? It's because the end of the oath draws near. You think constantly of sex.*

Jet moved in a step and brushed his finger along the line of her jaw. Silver's lips quivered and she panted out her words. "I want revenge for my brother, Kilé." She gasped as Jet pressed the edge of the icy blade against her cheek. "I sought you…" She slowly pushed the blade away from her face with a trembling hand. "I sought you to help me prove Cirin's guilt and restore my family to the chair of Wu Xing Metal, if any besides me survives. I followed you in peace, despite appearances. Teach me to defeat the man, and I'll do us both a favor. I'll ensure an alliance, and you'll have one less territory to defeat."

"Who would you see in the chair? Yourself? How long did you train?" Jetre snorted. In fact, he thought a woman would fare well on the Metal throne, but Silver was far too old to begin the aggressive preparation needed to control the Ch'i of a clan.

"I'm too old, your elder by two years."

"Who? Your sniveling little brother, Desmen?"

Jet saw Silver's fury at the mention of the coward who abandoned his element in the face of battle. He knew her family—even her entire clan— never spoke his name.

That was a low blow, Jet. She brings out pettiness in you.

"Since you continue to mock me and have no interest in my plan, I'll keep it to myself. Get it over with, Lord."

"Plan? Some plan. Sneak up on a clan lord who can pick thoughts from the air, feel a threat looming from miles away? You're not impressive, Silver."

"How does a Metal warrior get the attention of the Lord of the Wood? Was I to invite you to tea? Tap on the gate of Traier?" She cocked her chin up in a haughty fashion, but Jet caught the tremble still in her voice.

"You have my attention for a moment. Tell me why I should listen to you." *Give me some reason to let you live a while longer, to look at you a bit more.* The urge to touch her cheek where a small beauty mark broke the serenity of her porcelain skin pulled at him and he fought to keep his arm still, fought everything she evoked in him.

"I'll tell you all I know if you show mercy and let me walk away tonight in good faith. Allow me to join you at Traier. I'm a sitting duck here. If they learn of my betrayal…" Silver winced in dismay.

"You aren't in much of a bargaining position." Jet allowed himself to wipe the blood from her throat with his gloved thumb, sliding his hand from her hair to the nape of her neck. He stepped in close enough that her breath warmed the skin left bare at his throat. Her eyes grew wide and she parted her lips slightly.

An invitation? How could she think of anything but death? A kiss. What would it hurt? She'd be dead in minutes, couldn't tell anyone.

Silver licked her lips in nervousness, and Jet's sense and control slipped away. *One kiss after ten years.* He leaned in slightly, angling his face to capture hers, meeting her shocked gaze. Her sudden intake of breath made him pull back.

By all that is sacred! Do you know how to kiss, Jet?

It couldn't be difficult, no different than when he was sixteen, huddled in the hay with the buxom girl…why, he'd watched Mikalis kiss a hundred times during the orgies in which Jet's only role was voyeur…

A faint whimper from Silver brought him to his senses and he stood tall. Silver lost her balance and fell into his chest. Steadying her with an arm around her waist, he took deep, calming breaths, and finally let her go, pushing her away gently.

"Come to Traier on bended knee, Warrior Silver, and I'll hear your case. But prepare to captivate me with your plan and tell me all you know of that backward clan of yours, or die by my hand, which may not be as gentle as you imagine. You'll gain admittance with this symbol." Jet took off his long black glove and held out his hand. Silver stepped back, shaking her head.

"Convert, now, here with me, or die. It's your choice." *Choose life, woman. Choose my clan.*

She closed her eyes and shook visibly. With a deep breath, she pushed back her cloak sleeve and turned her pale wrist towards the light from the gas lamp above.

Jet clasped her wrist and pressed his palm to it. She paled at the pain, but didn't pull away. Energy soared through him for a moment, as did her anguish—a brief thrill at the contact of their life force. Heart pounding and cock throbbing at the exchange, he turned quickly lest the woman catch a glimpse of desire on his face or in his mind. He hurried down the street towards the road to Traier, to his army. Her crying tugged at him, but he assumed a fierce look, needing to regain control. He turned back suddenly and pointed to Silver.

"One week, Trueborn. The mark on your wrist will destroy you within a week if you don't seek my audience. Is that understood?"

Her mumbled curse rang out clear in the cold air. "Fucking asshole."

Jet turned away and smiled. *Extraordinary woman. I hope she makes it. What will I do with her if she does?*

They never told you when you took the oath of chastity about the loneliness. He had prepared for the years of sexual frustration; however, the masters never trained the oath takers for the isolation and bitterness. Had Kilé kept his vow—died chaste? And the others? Surely not Paulo.

Jet picked up his pace, headed towards the edge of town and his adolescent haunt, Perinor, the drinking hole of the chosen boys. *Liquid courage, that's what Kilé used to call the brew.* And the blond had been terribly fond of the liquid courage, but it evidently hadn't saved him. *Was Kilé truly dead, his exquisite sister a fugitive in her own town? What of Paulo and Fire clan?* Jet laughed lightly at the thought of the dark, sarcastic boy. Paulo had avoided drink completely, complaining it wreaked havoc on his shifting abilities. They had all known better though. Paulo didn't trust the others, didn't trust himself to inebriation, despite his incredible strength, intellect, and talent. And those vile Pteran beasts he trained to do his bidding.

Those were the days, when the five oath takers formed an uneasy alliance, hating one another as future enemies, yet clinging to one another.

For only they understood the inevitable foul era descending upon Isla. And no one on Isla knew what it was to be a grown man with the weight of the world on your shoulders, the lives of your people in your hands, and the isolation from any form of comfort. The constant need for the appearance of strength was suffocating. What must it be like to be comforted, to be held, to be needed for anything but your power and position? He might never know. At least he'd finally know the warmth of female flesh, the release inside a willing partner. The thought made his legs ache, his whole body shudder in anticipation.

One week, Jet. One week and any of the clan is yours—young, old, female, male.

Silver fell to the ground the moment Jetre disappeared around the corner. His essence lingered, a faint warm shimmer in the glistening, swirling flurries. The searing agony of his seal on her wrist pounded through her body. Pushing down pain that turned her stomach, she pressed her branded flesh into the snow, but it brought blessed little relief.

Tears slipped down her cheek at the greater pain—that she bargained away twenty years of training and her sworn life oath. Jetre ensured she could only turn to him, to Traier, branded a traitor.

Does it matter, now? You had nowhere to go anyway. And you've probably delayed your death by a few days only. For Jetre wouldn't listen to her pitiful plan, or even if he did, he'd dig to the truth of her intentions very quickly. She'd underestimated his psychic abilities and would likely pay with her life.

"Well, I hope you're satisfied, you imbecile. You caught the attention of the great Wood Lord."

Jetre—the reality of the man overwhelmed her. Her brother Kilé had reviled the gifted Elf Lord. Whenever Kilé spoke of Jetre, fire burned in his eyes, and now Silver understood the jealousy stoking that fire, the envy that had tortured the proud warrior. Many of the Metal died in failed attempts on Jetre's life. In desperation to overthrow the ever more powerful warlord, Kilé had done the next best thing—cut the hearts from Jetre's aging parents. *And no doubt Jetre would have killed me if he knew.* Did *he know who killed his parents?* Perhaps Jetre wanted her at Traier to execute her in a more public fashion?

Silver laughed wryly, despite the pain searing up her arm. How could you admire your clan's greatest enemy, your brother's nemesis? While Silver had expected the lord to be powerful, large, strong, and arrogant, she'd never pictured the *man*. Her clan spoke only of his talents rather than his presence, his appearance, his raw appeal. It had taken all of Silver's powers not to cry out at the sexual images swirling between them.

Had he said she was responsible for the visions? They were his thoughts, his fantasies. What about the oath? How could a man with those thoughts be chaste?

He almost kissed me. A shudder rippled through her at the memory of the exquisite man leaning an inch away from her face, dark eyes staring into hers, the scent of male power, of exotic forests, emanating from him.

Jetre left her lost, vanquished, wanting nothing more than to fall prostrate and beg for conversion and sexual servitude. Shame burned at her cheeks as his poison burned her wrist.

He's your sworn enemy, and you would beg to be his whore? Jet said she was to his taste, hadn't he? Did she imagine it?

The pain in her wrist gradually subsided, replaced by a terrible ache clutching her entire arm. Silver examined the willow branches etched onto her skin forever, or at least until the funeral pyre would melt the flesh off her bones. She wondered what it meant to be of the Wood. Well, she would learn soon enough, reaching Traier within the week, or a little over a day if she managed to steal a horse.

Silver walked through the light snow, pulling her hood up back over her head, shivering as a cold breeze picked up. Her thoughts were for Jetre only. She stopped in mid-stride for a moment, closing her eyes to better recall his features. Long, black hair, slightly peaked ears betraying his clan's heritage, deepest brown eyes made more exotic by the dark kohl of the Wood warriors, high cheeks and full lips. And a thin scar marring one cheek, the remnants of his ordination ceremony. To her utter dismay, she longed for the moment when she would lay eyes on him again.

The branding—it scrambled her senses. He'd burned more than willow branches onto her wrist.

"Kilé, forgive me for a woman's weak spirit."

Watching the lamplight grow blurrier in the thickening snowfall, Silver made her way down the street towards the desolate outskirts of Belanor and the start of Mashran village, hoping to find warm shelter in a barn. The reality of her homelessness suddenly hit her. *Fool. Belanor hasn't been home for months. Cirin took that, too.* No matter, life had never been kind to Atra SanMartin, and the cruelty was nearing a quick end. Perhaps there would be some peace after the Lord Jetre slit her throat? She'd believed strongly enough her Ch'i would survive long after her body turned to dust, but somehow with the moment at hand, she wasn't so stalwart in her faith in Wu Xing.

Before Jetre killed her, she would do her best to convince him to help overthrow Cirin. Perhaps she could persuade Jetre to speak richly of her deeds to the Metal clan, to tell how she gave her life to rescue her people from a vile coward.

Chapter Two

Silver sensed his presence before she saw him and opened one eye. No more than ten or eleven, the slender boy with long, coal-black hair and faintly peaked ears no doubt belonged to Wood clan. As he bent over to examine her bag, a priceless, emerald necklace bounced against a bit of pale skin left bare beneath his filthy cloak. The boy tucked the gem back under his shirt.

"My good man."

The boy jumped, but didn't cry out.

Silver sat up and brushed hay from her coat and hair. The boy looked as if he'd bolt as he backed up slowly, inch by inch, weighing his chances of escape.

"Oh shit."

Silver knew he recognized her for a warrior. "That's fairly base talk for a Wood Elf, isn't it?"

"Oh shit. Don't kill me lady, I only needed a little...something...some food or drink..." Silver knew he planned to run, but as he backed up, he tripped on a coil of rope and fell, scrambling frantically.

Silver held up her hand. "All right, dear, let's start over. First, relax." She tried a soothing voice, but saw instantly it wouldn't work on the strong-willed child.

"Leave me alone, lady. I didn't take anything."

Silver arched a brow.

"Okay, I thought about it." The boy held up one finger. "Only thought about it, mind you."

Silver laughed and a sly smile crept to his mouth. *He's used to charming women already. He'll be a heartbreaker someday.*

"Let's make a deal, my friend." She held out her arm and flashed a brief glimpse of her new brand. The boy gasped and his big brown eyes grew huge.

"Who did that? Only the Lord Jetre can do that. Tell me."

"I think you're the one with the explaining to do. Calm down, young man. I can wield a nasty blade, and I suggest you mark your tongue and tone. Now, come over here."

He didn't move.

"All right, tell me your name."

"Petrov. Petrov."

"Petrov Petrov?"

"No, only one Petrov. Are you stupid or something?"

"You're obviously fairly stupid. As well as ugly." Silver tried to keep a straight face as she watched the gorgeous boy's cheeks flame red.

"Ugly?"

"Is that why your parents kicked you out? Because you're ugly?" Silver waited patiently for the inevitable reaction. His face fell.

"They didn't kick me out. They're dead. Because of Metal assholes like you."

Silver turned her wrist to him again.

"Because of Metal assholes like you. I don't know where you got that fake brand, but you're not Wood, never were, never will be...you're a Trueborn Metal bitch..." Petrov broke off as a tear slipped down his cheek.

Silver went to him slowly and he backed up a step.

"Asshole Trueborn."

"Ugly Wood Elf." She stepped forward quickly and pulled him into her arms. He stood stiff as wood, his back muscles taut, all of him ready to flee, to spring into action. Sobs sputtered up again, and finally his body moved in concert with his spirit—shattered. *He's recently orphaned. I hate this fucking war.* She caressed his silken, black hair.

"Let me go. I never cry. You're pushing bad Ch'i into me, aren't you?"

"It's all right, Ugly." Silver softened her voice, trying to imitate the tone mothers took when soothing their children, and held him tighter. As his sobbing gradually subsided, Silver led him to the loft where she had slept. Petrov sidled up to her and tentatively allowed her to pull him into her arms.

"Who are you?"

"I suppose I'm your new friend. My name is Atra SanMartin, but you can call me Silver."

He snuggled against her and a final sob escaped. "If you tell anyone I cried, I'll have to kill you, Metal. I know your name, your family. You're Kilé's sister. I'll betray you to my lord."

"It's a little late for that, Petrov." The pain in her wrist flared and Silver realized Jetre's promised poisoning moved in her blood. One week. Now the fate of a war orphan rested on her shoulders. Metal or Wood, these homeless children burned a hole in her heart. She couldn't—wouldn't—see this child go without a home in the cold of winter, even though winter lasted a few weeks only.

"Petrov, we're going to Traier, where you'll be among your kind. I'm not sure I'll be able to stay there, but they'll give you shelter and food." *Perhaps even love.*

Petrov eyed Silver curiously for a moment and fell into deep thought, his brow wrinkled, eyes narrowed to dark slits. "I'll finally see my real father."

"What do you mean, your real father? I thought you lost your parents to the conflict?"

"My real father abandoned me when I was a baby. The Lord Jetre."

Silver's blood ran cold. Surely the child was fantasizing, his grief taking a common course. Didn't every child fantasize about having different parents? She certainly had wanted a warm mother instead of the stern bitch who treated the hounds better than her children.

"Do you understand the oath of the lords, Petrov?"

"Of course, I'm not a baby."

"You must know Jetre never seeded a child, at least since the oath-taking."

Petrov snorted. "Someone should have told my mother. Do the calculation, woman. I am the correct age."

Silver nodded slowly, realizing Jetre's ten-year oath could easily have fallen after the conception of this boy. *Why, the lords' oaths are soon ended.*

"And where is your mother, Petrov? Who is she? What makes you think Jetre is your father?"

"My mother is gone." He sounded weary, and Silver wondered when the boy last slept in the bed or ate a hot meal.

"Why did we meet, Petrov?" He already slept, exhaustion and perhaps relief at her company lulling him. She wished for the same relief for herself. Silver opened her coat and pulled the boy in close, throwing her arm over his chilled wet cheek.

❋ ❋ ❋

"Whiskey." Jet threw a thin square piece of bronze on the heavy oak bar of the Pelinor. The smell of dozens of candles, stale ale, and smoldering oak in the rough-hewn fireplace brought bittersweet memories of his youthful mates flooding to his mind and bringing pangs to his heart. He'd been to the Pelinor many times since, but the pull of the past had never been stronger. *Why, Jet? It's the oath. Aren't you ready to let go of the past?*

"Whiskey? Since when did you start drinking Trueborn brew..." Raimondo growled and threw his hands up in surrender when Jet held the dagger to his throat.

"Calm down. I don't know how the hell you pull that fucking thing out so fast, but it's losing its effect, you do it so much..."

Jet pressed the dagger against Raimondo's neck again.

"Okay, maybe it's not losing its effect." Raimondo poured the deep-golden drink into a short glass. Jet pushed the glass aside and grabbed the bottle, carried it to a corner table, and sat with his legs propped up.

"Raimondo, did you hear about Kilé? He was always your favorite, wasn't he?"

"Now you compete with a dead man? Aaayee! You were always the most jealous of the boys, needing everyone's attention. Let me tell you something, *Lord.*" Raimondo wiped his hand on his filthy shirt before pointing it at Jet. "You may be the strongest of the five, but you aren't the smartest. I don't get this shit from Paulo."

"Paulo comes by? Does he speak of me?"

"Aaayee! What an ego." Raimondo turned his back to wash mugs and looked over his shoulder and chuckled. "Of course he speaks of you. Can't wait to slit your throat. You know Pelinor and all of Mashran stays as neutral as possible. Don't pull me into this shit. Council had their heads up their arses when they put this plan into action. Clan lords indeed. Five boys who couldn't hold their drink and grew to men who still can't."

"Certainly Kilé can't. Imagine it would pour out of his wounds." A deep swig of whiskey burned Jet's mouth and throat, bringing a blessed distraction. He closed his eyes and pushed down the images parading in a constant rhythm through his mind. It always started with the sight of his mother's funeral pyre, followed by his father's. He'd hear Master Guo's crackly voice call to him from her deathbed. "You're bound for notoriety, my love. You'll either be the greatest ruler in the world, or the most-loathed despot of this age. I think I'm glad I won't be alive to see it."

Which are you, Jet? Neither. At least not yet.

Chilled air brushed Jet's face as the door opened. A howl of wind pierced the quiet tavern, and he smelled the particular musty scent of a horse master, and smiled inwardly. He spoke quietly from his table.

"Horse Master. Join me in a drink?"

"All of Traier is looking for you. It's four in the morning. Your generals are camped out in the goddamned snow, and you're suckling on a bottle of...what the hell is that shit?"

"Nice language. Sit your fat ass down here and update me." Jet opened one eye and regarded his baby sister with a scowl.

"You're so damned happy to see me you can barely contain yourself. Stop with the dark dramatic look." Jaine tapped him on the head and leaned in, kissing his cheek. Jet couldn't repress a grin—she affected him strongly, more than he'd ever let on. Jaine quelled a bit of the emptiness, the heaviness. He pulled her into his arms and squeezed the breath out of her, ruffling her short dark cap of hair.

Jaine examined him closely for a moment.

Watch it, Jet. You're supposed to be untouchable. You never show affection like this.

"Lord Jetre, spit it out. Where have you been? Whoring your way through Mashran while your soldiers freeze their asses off?"

"How droll, Jaine. It's taken you ten years to make fun of my chastity? I wonder if all the lords put up with such horse shit? I imagine Paulo would slit his sister's throat for such impertinence. Have you managed any chastity during this campaign? Keeping a few of my generals warm, perhaps? Managed to keep your hands off Mikalis? He is blood, you know, although I imagine that wouldn't stop either of you."

Jaine punched Jet in the arm and he laughed.

"Mikalis is too busy with his harem of pretty boys and girls to be bothered with the likes of me." She pulled a candy from her pocket and offered it to Jet, who simply raised a brow in refusal. She shrugged and popped the sweet into her mouth.

"As for your generals—they are pigs. They have the manner of pigs, the look of pigs, and the smell of pigs." She cocked her head to one side and winked. "Except perhaps for one..."

Jet bit back a retort, pretending not to suspect Jaine's undying affection for his greatest general, his truest warrior, his only friend, Artier.

"Can you refrain from speaking with your mouth full of taffy? It's very unbecoming."

Jaine grabbed the bottle from Jet's hand and took a deep swig, spitting it out almost immediately. He patted her back until she waved him off as she coughed.

"Fill me in, Horse Master."

"Damn. That's evil stuff. All right, I'll fill you in if you first tell me where you've been."

"I don't remember having to report to you."

Jaine rolled her eyes in impatience.

"All right, if you must know, I had one of those feelings." Jet waited in resignation, knowing her reaction in advance—motherly frustration.

"Oh, honey, not that again. They're gone, and no *feeling* is going to bring them back. The rumor is that Kilé is dead and Cirin took over Metal clan. Cirin claims Kilé killed Mother and Father. That doesn't quite matter does it? Water under the bridge."

"I think it's over the bridge, and under the dam." Jet caught Raimondo's amused look.

"Mind on your chores, proprietor."

"Do you know what a dam is, Jet? Aaayee! Idiots, all five of you."

Jaine shrugged in confusion. "Anyway, there's nothing left for you to do. Time to move on. If you haven't noticed, we're at war."

"War? This isn't war, Jaine. It's a series of pointless assassinations and skirmishes—posing, posturing, positioning for power. The lords are megalomaniacs, me included. We're vying to rule a thin strip of land so bereft of resources we've been tossed back to the days of our earliest ancestors. If pressed, none could name a valid reason for the fighting, except mindless fear, bias, and greed. The worst part is each of us knows it, deep down."

Jaine took his hand and laced her fingers in his. Her grasp always sent the warm yang coursing through him, comforting his blood, making him feel more whole. "Such a serious lecture from the great clan lord. I think you're lecturing yourself, Jet. Why? Finish it. Make peace with them—with Earth or with Metal, and the others will follow suit."

"There's no ending it. No one will surrender first. I will not—they can't be trusted. They'd slaughter all the Wood living at Traier and vanquish those .outside the town walls in days. I must simply wait for the right ally, a man or woman of vision, one who understands the cycle fully. I'm young; I'll outlive most of them. You're younger—you and Pete will live to see us prevail. I've seen some of it."

"You won't live to see any more if you keep roaming unfriendly territory in search of Mother's murderer."

"And Father's."

Jaine scoffed. "It's me, honey. You're not searching for Father's murderer. None of us are sorry Masur is gone." Jaine wrinkled her nose in disgust. "Come on, let's go. The soldiers are growling like hungry dogs, frustrated, aching to get home. A few of them even worried about the whereabouts of their lord. Let's put their minds at rest. This winter is cold and I want to go home."

Jet wondered briefly about winters lasting for weeks, even months. How did their ancestors withstand the cold?

"When were you last at Traier?" Jet cursed himself for not being able to ignore the question prickling at his brain, the woman who made his skin tingle in premonition

"Yesterday, looking for you."

"Did a newly-branded warrior approach for an audience?"

"No strangers, no. Who do you mean?"

"A would-be assassin. I spared her, branded her, and ordered her to Traier. She claims to have a plan for overthrowing Cirin."

"She's Earth?"

"No, she's Metal. Trueborn, I think." Jet turned away, lest his sister read anything in his eyes. *What are you afraid she'll see, Jet?*

"Trueborn? Not a bit of mixed blood? You spared a Metal attempt on your life for information that is no doubt a plant?"

"We'll see. Keep your eye out for her."

"I see." Jaine drew out her words and Jet looked sharply at her.

"You don't see at all."

Jaine shrugged. "Have it your way, oath taker. How much longer—let's see." She scratched her head in mock befuddlement. "Oh, one week, is it? I don't suppose this Trueborn Metal branded assassin is attractive at all? Haven't I heard you speak of how lovely you think the pale bitches are?"

"You irk me, Jaine. You truly do."

Jaine laughed and kissed her brother. "Let's saddle up, Lord."

Jet groaned and took another swig from the bottle. *Silver. You'd better hurry, or you'll die.* He shrugged and stood, pulling his coat around him tightly. The woman didn't matter. She'd have nothing to offer, at least nothing to help him take the first steps towards a republic. He'd turn to the next battle, and surely forget about her by the time it ended.

❋ ❋ ❋

Silver stirred at the feel of moist lips on her cheek and opened one eye to find Petrov smirking at her.

"Wake up Metal. There's a break in the snow. Time to hit the road."

Silver groaned. "It's light already?" Pain shot through her arm as she sat up. The brand on her wrist now looked puckered and infected.

"You'd better get to Traier soon or that stuff will kill you."

"Thanks for the encouragement." *What I wouldn't give for a hot shower, a warm bed and a clean memory, with no Jetre or war or child to care for.* "Let's not worry about me. My concern is to get you to Traier."

"I care for myself, Metal." Petrov scowled and folded his arms across his chest petulantly.

Silver arched a brow at the boy. "But I bet you're no fighter, eh?"

"I'm master level with the staff and knife, if you must know."

"Good. I must know. Because we might meet with trouble on the road." She touched her finger to the boy's nose and searched his deep-brown eyes for answers. "And you, my ugly friend, are to flee at the first sign of trouble. Can't have the blood of a Wood Elf on my hands. Wouldn't go over too well at Traier, and I'm in trouble enough."

"You're the one who needs my protection. And stop calling me ugly. I'm gorgeous, at least, that's what everyone tells me. I may be as handsome as Jetre some day, and I'll have all the women in the world to choose from."

Silver snorted and ruffled his hair. "I imagine you will." He did resemble Lord Jetre. Could he actually be the son of the great one? The lord was a filthy, oath-breaking devil and would be cut down by his own people if they knew... Perhaps she had a bargaining chip, she wondered?

"Come on lady, let's get moving. Here." Petrov plopped a canvas bag in her lap and she peaked inside at the dried fruit, nuts, and sweet cakes.

"You stole this."

Petrov shrugged.

"Good boy. I don't suppose you'd be able to steal a..."

"The horse is tethered out back." Petrov rolled his eyes. "As I *said already,* we have to *move* before the owner of this farm discovers us."

Silver chuckled. "Yes, sir. All right, staff master, give me a private moment and I'll join you."

Petrov grinned and scurried out the door. The freezing cold water she scooped up from the barrel stung her skin, and she dried down quickly with her scarf. She dressed and hurried outside to find Petrov already mounted, bareback, on a handsome chestnut.

"Someone is going to be very angry about losing this horse." Silver rubbed the creature's neck. "Move up."

"No way. You'd better stop treating me like a child. I'll be insufferable elsewise, Metal. I'll take the lead position."

"Elsewise isn't a word, boy. Fine, but you won't be able to see over my head. Move up."

"Bitch." Petrov inched forward and the horse turned and snorted, uneasy with the strangers and the cold. Silver reached up to Petrov, who pulled her up with the strength of a grown man. She grabbed the reins from his hands, handed him the satchel of food, and secured one arm around his waist.

"I don't need your help to stay on a horse, damn it."

"I imagine you don't, Ugly. I want to hold you, nevertheless." Petrov turned and looked into her eyes, searching for her meaning, trying to read her energy, feel her thoughts. She blocked his probe quickly. "Simply so you can shelter me from the cold a little."

"You know what I think, Metal? I think you enjoy my company, plain and simple."

"Time will tell, my boy." Silver gently kicked the horse with her heels and ducked as they emerged from beneath frozen branches onto the open field. She stopped for a moment to get her bearings, and headed north to Traier.

"Nothing like heading north in the winter."

"Jetre also complains of the cold. At least I've heard it said about the lord. Since he is my father, I do follow the tales of his comings and goings. He's the Lord of my Element…" Petrov's voice trailed off uncertainly.

A chill of premonition washed up Silver's body and met the chill of the frosty fingers of morning wind. *Who is this boy?*

"Well, if we are lucky, we'll see your great lord before nightfall." *And Mother help me, I want to see him again. Perhaps I'll get my kiss before I die.*

Chapter Three

Jet rubbed the fog off the window with his shirtsleeve and peered towards the southern pass. A few warriors huddled and chatted, no doubt sneaking sips of liquor from their canteens.

"The fools will freeze if they fall asleep."

"What the hell's wrong with you?" Mikalis threw his hands in the air in frustration. The young woman sucking on Mikalis' cock eyed Jet with practiced flirtation, brushing her huge breasts with her hands and moaning dramatically.

Jet returned to the mass of large cushions thrown about the floor and nodded for the trio to continue. "Yes, yes, very nice. Carry on."

Mikalis arched a brow wryly and sighed.

Brendal, is that her name? Pretty. The young soldier behind her opened the bindings of his pants and rubbed his shaft in preparation. Brendal moaned again and cried out in earnest as he pushed his huge member into the cleft of her buttocks and worked her. Mikalis lay back and motioned for her to lower herself onto his erection. The young man withdrew from her and looked rather lost as he watched the girl ride Mikalis in a frenzy, screaming and arching to the ceiling, calling curses and prayers, huge breasts bouncing. The young soldier rubbed himself quickly to release, eyeing Jet uncertainly.

"What's your name, Warrior?" Jet suppressed a laugh.

"Alain, Lord."

"Thank you, Alain. You are dismissed."

He nodded and quickly withdrew from Jet's quarters. Jet turned back in time to see Mikalis face him, eyes latched onto his as he groaned in release. He pushed Brendal off quickly and patted her ass.

The girl looked from man to man, clutching a cloak to her breasts. A tear slipped down her reddened cheek.

Mikalis threw an arm over her shoulders and retrieved a few Metal clan bronzes, pushing them into her palm. "There's no need for tears, my dear, you did well. Run off now. Perhaps you can meet up with Alain."

Brendal threw the coins to the floor in disgust. "I'm not your whore. I came to please my clan lord. Evidently women don't much please him."

"Really?" Jet stood and the girl scurried backwards in horror, covering her mouth.

"I'm sorry, Lord Jetre. I did not mean...I only meant..."

"Goodnight."

Mikalis hurried Brendal on her way, pulled on his britches, and poured wine for Jet.

"*Lord*, it's come to this. You're bored with sex."

Jet scowled and took a sip of wine. "Has it escaped your notice I'm not the one having sex?"

"Come on, Jet, I've never failed to entertain you. It's a wonder you have a hand left from pulling at your own knob. You hurt our little Brendal's feelings tonight. Not to mention Alain."

"There's nothing little about Brendal. She hopes I'll name her as my mate, doesn't she? Ridiculous."

"But you won't say who you intend to name?" Mikalis reached to Jet's hair and pushed an errant long strand behind his ear. It annoyed Jet and he slapped his hand away. A twinge of regret hit Jet at his cousin's hurt expression.

Returning to the window, Jet took in a deep breath, wondering how to broach the delicate topic without hurting his friend, his most trusted scout.

"Mik, Brendal was wrong about me. You know that by now, don't you?"

Mikalis snorted and Jet turned back towards him, surprised to see his smile. *We could be twins. Sometimes it's like looking in the mirror. Our energy is different, though, and he is a lover of men.*

"I know what you're thinking, Jet, I know you very well. Pretend all you like. I've watched you grow hard at the sight of men fucking more times than I can count."

"I regret these...games. I appreciate your efforts, but it hasn't been healthy, for either of us."

Mikalis sighed dramatically and stood, pulling on his shirt. "You simply fear the bond these years have created between us. You fear how much you rely on me."

"I fear nothing except the prospect of the coming battles. I don't fear for myself, but for the clan. If you don't know that, you don't know me at all."

"Horse shit, cousin. You're afraid of the end of your oath. I know why you won't name your mate. Do you even know yourself?" Mikalis picked up the bronze coins Brendal had cast to the floor and twirled them between his fingers. "I suppose these are mine. I've been your whore for years."

"Enough. You have your orders. I expect a report on Paulo's whereabouts within two days' time."

Mikalis made an exaggerated salute, turned on his heel, and nearly bumped into Artier, who stood in the doorway, disapproval etched across his rugged face. Mikalis puckered a kiss at Artier and Jet groaned aloud.

"One of these days I'm going to pull Mik's heart out with my bare hand and shove it up his ass. Except he'd probably find some way to enjoy it. I wish you'd stop these games. It's unnatural."

"It's over." Jet walked back to the window and glanced nonchalantly at his guards again. *Where is she?*

"Art, next time you're giving the troops a hard time, make sure they understand about alcohol thinning the blood and stopping energy flow—very chilling. Especially for those fighting the yin imbalance. It's quite unhealthy in winter."

"You sound quite the father and healer today. Concern for the health of the soldiers." Artier slapped Jet on the back jovially and Jet nearly hit the ground from the huge man's pat.

"That's my job. I'm always concerned for the enemy's fodder. What else will I throw before them if my boys and girls all die of cold and disease?"

"Try your ruthless leader talk on someone else. Now, tell me what's eating at you and why you're suddenly obsessed with the southern pass?"

Jet sighed and pushed back his hair. *What would Art think? That he had lost his hold, his grasp on the clan's energy slipping through his fingers? Worried for an enemy, a pitiful woman. But it* was *cold.* He considered baring his soul when Jaine burst through the door.

"Don't you knock anymore, Jaine?"

"Shut up, Jet. Just shut up. It's Pete."

"Pete?"

"Yes, are you deaf?"

Jet's heart sunk and a familiar anxiety clutched as his heart. "How long?"

"No sign of him since you went to Mashran on your 'hunch'. Since right after the last skirmish."

"Why the hell didn't Master Culran keep him under lock and key?"

Jaine threw down her saddlebag in disgust. "He's as talented as you were at his age. Maybe more so."

Art clasped Jet's arm. "I'll go. He's probably still in Mashran, looking for you."

Jaine paced quickly, slapping one gloved fist into the other hand. "He's looking for you all right, Jet. We've told you to either stay at Traier, or take him along, because he won't be apart. He won't stand for it."

"Take a ten-year-old into battle? Brilliant. You claim to care about your brother?"

"Stay at Traier, where you belong. None of the lords put themselves in the way of their enemies like this. I think you have a death wish, brother. It's likely to kill Petrov instead. Great way to honor your mother, by killing her baby."

"Pete's resourceful, and likely somewhere in Traier, simply looking for attention." *Please, someone protect him.*

Art shook his head in dismay. "It's not like you to ignore a truth, Lord. What have you taught me? To face the darkest…"

Jet stopped him with a look.

"Shut up, both of you. I'll find him myself."

Art and Jaine groaned together. "The point is for you to be safe, brother." Jaine turned to Art. "He's a fucking idiot. You get through to him. I've tried for twenty years."

Jaine turned on her heel, kicked up her bag with the toe of her boot, caught it, and stormed out of the room.

"Jaine and I will go for him. Stay here, don't make it worse."

"Get Mikalis, take him along…his tracking skills…"

Art rubbed at his chin, and Jet knew he struggled with how to refuse his direct order. "Your cousin can take another route. How's that for a compromise?"

"You won't even ride at his side?"

"I don't trust him, Jet. There, I said it. Strip me of my rank, execute me. I loathe the man. Man?" Art spit in derision. "Boy. He's frozen at fifteen."

"True, however, he's a great scout and a devoted warrior. We'll talk of him later. Pete comes first."

How did you let this happen? He wanted to put his fist through the wall, settling instead for pounding the oak table.

"Damn him, what was he thinking? Well, let me at least try to locate him for you. It's hard when he doesn't want to be found."

Jet pulled a long woolen cape around his shoulders and sat before his shrine, a simple altar adorned only with the symbol of his clan and a single green and silver candle. It took moments for his breathing to calm. He reached into the cool air for the energy of his beloved brother—a shimmering, yellow light, the color of the first spring flowers.

If he lives to see spring, it will be a miracle. The little shit. Running away, defying my orders. I'll kill him if I get my hands on him.

Jet sighed and calmed himself again, emptied his mind, reached out for Pete. *Boy, where are you? I love you.*

The shock of what he saw set his heart racing, his nerve endings tingling. Pete rode atop a tall horse, chattering away with Silver. She hugged Pete from behind, pulling her cloak around him affectionately, pressing her lips to his forehead. *It couldn't be. Did Silver cloud his vision somehow?*

"What is it?" Art's voice came from very far away.

Jet waved him off and sank again into the depths of clarity. *What does it mean?* Pete continued to jabber away, no doubt telling lies and asking a million questions.

Jet stood and slowly smiled.

"He's all right?"

"He's on his way home. I think he tracked me to Mashran, and now he's spying for me. I love that clever boy, more devious than I ever was. He'll be a great leader some day, if he's not assassinated first."

Art sighed in relief. "I'd watch my back if I were you, Jet. He might be after your place sooner than you think. Who's he spying on?"

"On a Metal warrior. It's not important." *Why, Jet, why does it feel like everything depends upon it?* "Go, tell Jaine. Don't let her leave Traier unnecessarily."

Art saluted, fist to chest, and bowed quickly. He hesitated, as if to speak, but turned and left.

The relief of solitude filled Jet's senses—the freedom to reach out to the vision of Pete and Silver, a chance to lay eyes on her again. She wouldn't die before reaching Traier after all. He sighed in satisfaction and watched the pair chat, watched the woman laugh, her lovely lips curve and her dimples spring to life in her cold-flushed cheeks. Jet groaned when he saw her bring a flask to her lips and hand it to Pete.

"That had better be water."

Without warning, his groin warmed and his cock stiffened as the recurring image of Silver's tongue licking him to ecstasy intruded on his meditation. He stood and grabbed his heavy practice staff and knives, craving a good workout, some way to rid his body of the tension thoughts of his new prisoner brought.

❀ ❀ ❀

Pete shuddered at the potent brew. "What is that stuff? My brother drinks this shit."

"Your brother?" Silver pulled Petrov's chin around to see his expression. "What's this about a brother? Are you playing me for a fool, Ugly?"

"I haven't seen him in many months."

"I see."

The truth hit Silver in the gut in a split second of ultra-knowing. The boy wasn't the lord's son, nor even a boy who wanted to be his son. His *brother*. Their energy was similar, and their look was similar. This boy wasn't the distillation of Jetre's energy, however, but its near twin.

Petrov poked at her mind for suspicion, probably wondering if she was on to him. Silver blocked him and quickly picked up the conversation and the pace. *What's his game? Surely Lord Jetre didn't need to send a child on a warrior's mission. He could have killed her at any time.*

"Petrov, tell me of Traier, of your clan and your lord. I'm anxious to know what I'm getting myself into. Is there some horrid initiation ceremony I'll endure before being taught the great secrets of the willows?"

"I think the branding satisfies the initiation requirement. You're mocking my clan, aren't you? We don't have tree secrets, we're simply in touch with nature in a way your kind doesn't understand, never did."

"Oh, some of us did, very long ago. We lost the knowledge of nature, you are correct. We spent our time trying to hold back the great tides, the great melting, the destruction we exacted upon ourselves. Some believe it was merely a natural cycle, and we were not to blame. I suppose it doesn't matter now." Silver shook her head at the real tragedy. "Petrov, try to imagine days when winter was not a week long, but many months—indeed, in some places, almost an entire year cycle of snow and cold…"

"I know the history, lady. Pounded into my head with a stick, let me tell you."

Silver laughed. "I suppose you do, perhaps better than I. Go on, tell me what you know."

"That's for our lord to tell you. I don't know what he plans for you. I simply want to be with him again."

"Your father."

"Right. He'll never leave me behind again."

"I see."

But her thought was lost in the next split second as she sensed the horror winging its way from above—a Fire-sent Pteran, mottled, sickly-brown and black, jaws opened wide, teeth like small knives gleaming in the sunlight, clawed wingtips ready to tear into flesh. It headed straight for the boy. He saw it too, and they struggled to protect one another and to draw weapons against the beast, but too late. Silver murmured a prayer of thanks that Petrov was smaller and weaker than she as she threw him to the ground and turned her right shoulder towards the coming attack.

The flap of a huge wing sent a rush of warm, fetid air past her face and she reached out an arm to pull Petrov back to the horse. The boy extended his metal staff fully and was ready to do battle. As if in a dream, Silver wondered why it was difficult to stay upright on the horse. Glancing down, she saw a crimson circle slowly broaden around the projectile the pteran spit into her flesh. The chilling call of the reptile above her pierced through the cold air and from far away, she heard her name repeated again and again. The boy, screaming to her. Silver's world spun away in blissful, pain-free peace before she could call to Petrov.

Chapter Four

The whispers around her bed gradually grew intelligible as Silver's head cleared. She kept her eyes shut and spied on the strangers. Not all strangers exactly—she recognized the Lord Jetre himself, and Petrov—thank the Mother—was alive. Her heart pounded quickly and her throat burned as they discussed her fate in whispers.

"This is the Metal warrior you scoured the countryside for, Jet?"

Jetre ignored the man and barked his instructions in a low tone. "Give her a bit of the yin cooling mixture, and a good deal of water—tepid, mind you, not cold. Keep it quiet and dark, and get some of those damned furs off of her or she'll fever up again. There's probably a trace of the poison left in her, although I sucked what I could from the wound. My branding weakened her before this attack." The foreign lilt of his voice wafted through the air and sent a thrill through her. *You've grown sick with this man's poison.*

"She'll live of course." Silver heard the nervous question in Petrov's statement.

A woman spoke. "Pete, it's a little puncture. Weren't you listening? She'll have a small scar and no doubt be pretty sore at you. Why the hell did you put yourself at risk to guide a capable warrior? A woman whom the lord, your brother, is likely going to execute in any case?"

"Dunno. Seemed like the thing to do at the time."

"Fucking simpleton."

Jetre growled at the pair. "We'll talk privately of your ridiculous behavior these last months, Pete. It's going to stop. Oh now, don't start."

Silver's heart went out to the boy, whom she heard sobbing. How could the great lord not see what was crystal clear to her? The boy grieved and wanted his brother's love. Perhaps the lord was *that* cold. He knew, but wouldn't console the boy. Petrov obviously wanted his parents back. *And your own brother took them, Silver. Sliced their hearts out while they lived.*

The woman cooed at the boy. "Come here, Petie, let's get you washed up—you have the bitch's blood all over you."

"Don't call her that. She…she took the dart for me."

"A Metal warrior shielded her sworn enemy from a Fire Pteran? Sweetie, that dart probably had her name on it. Pterans don't often get it wrong."

"This time one did. She saved me." Petrov's tone was final.

"You're sure? How can you know?"

"He knows," Jetre muttered. "Leave her. Art, repeat my instructions to the healers. Don't let them treat her elsewise. I'm to be notified the moment she wakes."

Petrov sniffled and sat on the side of the bed. "I'm going to stay."

Silver heard their footsteps and a door shut and slowly opened one eye. Petrov smiled broadly.

"She's awake." He brushed his small, calloused palm along her jawbone and nodded encouragingly. "You okay, lady? Can I get you some water?"

"You're a lying little bastard, aren't you, Pete?"

"Sure. You knew that." Petrov grinned and Silver shook her head in wonder. A smile to charm the devil himself.

"Yep, that's what Jet says. He says, 'you may not be the devil, but you're definitely one of his emissaries.' What's an emissary?"

Silver laughed and then winced as the motion sent a sharp pain down her arm. "Stop reading my thoughts, it's rude. I don't have the energy to block you right now. Yes, I know. You're a rude, lying little bastard."

"You're still hurt. I'll get Jet."

"No, I'm fine." Silver trembled at the thought of confronting the compelling lord.

"Don't worry, lady. I won't let him kill you, I promise. Not since you tried to save my life. At least, I'll try."

"Who were the others, Petrov?"

"Pete. No one calls me Petrov anymore, except in ceremonies. You heard Uncle Art—he's not my real uncle, more like Jet's friend and a general in his army."

"The woman?"

"Jet's woman."

"Jet can't have a woman."

"In about one week he can. Jaine is his woman. I wouldn't cross her. In fact, I'd avoid her completely. She's evil. Makes you wash, read books and do lessons. Horrible person."

"You think she'll make me read books and do lessons?" The boy's lie rang out, and Silver knew the woman must be a sister or cousin.

"No, I think she'll try to kill you in your sleep. Cause of the way Jet looked at you. She didn't like it, I could tell."

"How did he look at me?"

"Like he wanted to fuck you. When we stripped you down for him to examine at your wound."

"Watch your mouth. Why did you have to strip me down to look at my shoulder?" Silver moved in the bed and realized she was naked under the covers. *Jet undressed her? Surely not.*

"I think they were checking for weapons."

"I see."

"You didn't have any."

"I know, honey." Silver tried to smile at the odd little elf, the small, impish likeness of his handsome brother.

"And I'll be even more handsome. And all the girls will want me, like they do Jet."

Silver laughed weakly. Pete surprised her by climbing into her bed and stretching out along her side, rubbing her cheek in what she supposed was a Wood gesture of affection. He laid his head against her good shoulder and she reached across painfully and caressed his silken black hair.

"I hope I can keep you, Silver."

Silver sighed. *I hope so too, boy.*

"By the way, I killed the pteran. You would have been proud."

"You're an extraordinary little warrior, but you know that."

"Yep. Everybody says it." Pete grabbed her hand, and his cooling, healing energy flowed from his palm into hers and up to her wounded shoulder. His brows drew together with his fierce concentration, and she decided not to question his healing. It was too wonderful to have someone care.

Chapter Five

The Holy Glen. Traier lived up to its name, Silver thought as she looked out the window and surveyed the circuitous, shaded streets and paths, the buildings built so closely that second-story walls formed canopies over the streets, windows of buildings opposite one another nearly touched. Huge vines covered nearly every wall, vines that would flower magnificently in a month. It was like a man-made forest—dark and green and earthy. She couldn't quite tell where trees ended and buildings began, where streets stopped and natural paths took over. Traier smelled of spices and musty, decaying leaves and incense, but most especially, of ancient magic.

Silver awakened at dusk with Petrov gone, the room empty, and her shoulder pain free. She assumed she was a prisoner, but had found the heavy oak door not only unlocked, but unlockable—it merely swung on its hinges with a push. Of course, she thought. All of Traier remained secure from without, and there were no threats from within. The sensitive elves would detect any danger and handle it with deadly speed and accuracy—a short blade, a touch of death points by trained fingertips. Legend held the Wood knew a thousand ways to kill without a weapon. It was also said the powerful Jetre could kill with his mind, and she didn't doubt the legend. How had her brother Kilé managed to assassinate Lue and Masur?

A bang at the door interrupted her musings. A pretty female elf kicked the door open with a high boot. She carried a bundle of clothing in her arms and a leather flask by a cord between her teeth. Her eyes were dark as night, her hair short and messy, her skin still tan from the previous summer. She spat on the floor at the sight of Silver and threw everything onto the bed.

Silver pulled the cover she used as a wrap more closely around her and moved away from the window, wondering how to respond to this woman's insult.

"I am Jaine Artraud, the Lord Jetre's horse master. I am second in command of the cavalry. I hate you and your kind, and would enjoy watching your torture and slow death. These things are for you to wear for you audience with Lord Jetre." Jaine nodded to the bundle on the bed. She picked up the flask and walked towards Silver, who backed up a few steps.

"Be still. Drink this."

Silver shook her head and Jaine groaned. "Listen, idiot, I'm not here to simply poison you. I could kill you with both hands tied behind my back. Drink the shit. It's the lord's healing mixture."

"You're his sister. You're Petrov's sister."

"I am cursed to be the sister of the two biggest idiots on Isla. Egomaniacs, both of them." She ran her hand through her short hair and flopped back on the bed, kicking the clothing into a messy heap. "Honestly, I'm not sure which of them is worse—Jet has lost some of his childishness, but he's still very compulsive and quite the jokester."

"Jokester? The Lord Jetre?"

Jaine ignored her. "He's a bit more sober because of the whole rule-the-world thing, of course. He won't admit to it, claiming he'd like peace for Isla. Bah. Men!"

Silver stared numbly at the lovely woman, wondering why she confided the secrets of the ruling family.

"And Petrov? He's the same?"

"Trying to pry information from me, eh, Trueborn? Well, I wasn't born yesterday, you know." Jaine sighed and sat up. "Here's the thing." She held up a gloved hand. "Pete desperately wants to be like Jet. Jet's powerful, intelligent, worshipped by his folk, but Pete is completely uncontrollable and very ambitious. Everything Pete wants to be, Jet already is. Pete doesn't understand if he waits sixteen years or so, Jet will pass it all to him. And in his twisted child's mind, he thinks if he can somehow get Jet to love him enough, all his dreams will come true."

"Why wouldn't the chair pass to you? Why are you unfit to take on the role?"

"You're rather rude. Are you insinuating I don't have the ability to rule Wood?"

"No. No, I didn't mean…"

Jaine winked. "I don't. My powers are somewhat mediocre. That's why I'm the horse master. Oh, you're rather slow, this should be fun."

Jaine pointed at the clothes.

"Put this shit on. Evidently you're to dress like a whore rather than a warrior. I do apologize, woman to woman. Prisoners don't wear warrior garb. Of course, the men do make the rules around here. Jet's quite fair minded when it comes to female warriors, actually. I'm the first female horse master ever. Jet doesn't mess with all the traditions. Have to keep the idiot populace happy. Couldn't shake things up too much, nooooo."

Jaine went to the door and turned suddenly on her heel. "I didn't like the way he looked at you, Metal."

"Pete told me." Silver held out her wrist. "I'm no longer Metal."

"Well, we'll see if that took or not. He's not done that before, you know. Not to an enemy. What transpired between you?"

"I tried to get his attention with an assassination attempt. It worked. We chatted for a few moments. I wanted him to kiss me, which did not work."

"No?" Jaine laughed loudly and clapped her hands together. "He claims to be immune to the charms of devious women. I always thought it horse shit. Guess I underestimated him. Well, I don't know what the brand means among Metal, but among Wood…"

"It means I converted, yes?" *Dear Mother, what did I let him do? Perhaps I should have let him kill me.*

"Yep, converted all right. Sworn to protect and serve. You're one of his inner circle. Can't fathom what he was thinking."

"He's not going to kill me?" The air rushed back into her lungs and her knees wobbled with relief.

"I'm going to beg him to, but my guess is it's unlikely. You'll simply die in the next battle protecting him, unless you're very, very skilled." Jaine winked again and turned her wrist to show her brand. "I've avoided the grave. No doubt you're bright enough to have guessed that on your own. Now drink my brother's vile potion and get your pale ass to the lord's quarters." Jaine was halfway through the door when she turned yet again.

"Thanks very much for Pete's life." Jaine banged through the door. A cool gush of air rushed in behind her.

Silver sat on the bed and picked up the flask. "What I wouldn't give for a strong whiskey right now." Her hand trembled as she uncapped the flask.

Silver pinched her nose, warding off what would surely be a horrendous taste, and downed a half cup of the liquid. She nearly spat it out in surprise.

Liquid gold, the old Trueborn style. She sipped a bit more and savored the tingle on her tongue and the warmth as it moved from her belly to her limbs. Hadn't Jet ordered some damned Elven cooling mixture for her?

Jaine. The woman must have given her the liquor. As a gift? Why? The answer pushed through her door and grinned. Pete.

"Hey Lady, you're looking better. Come on, hurry or you'll miss the feasting. Get your meeting with Jet over so we can have fun tonight."

"Feasting?"

"Sure. They just returned from Kor-Mashran. A victory over Earth. Feasting." Pete rolled his eyes. "Don't the Metal celebrate victories?"

Before Silver could answer, Pete ran to the bundle of clothes on the bed and sorted through them quickly. "Whoa, this is odd."

"Prisoner garb, Jaine said."

Pete looked at her oddly. "Sure, prisoner garb. We do right by our prisoners."

"And she said I'm now chosen, a bodyguard. Is that true?"

"Sure is." Pete held out his wrist to show his brand. "I haven't quite figured out why Jet branded you." Pete shrugged. "You don't have a man back home? No Metal husband or anything?"

"Nope."

"Good. When I'm a little older, you can marry me. I can have a betrothal ceremony in three years if Jet agrees. We can mate before I have to take the oath at sixteen."

Silver muffled a laugh with a cough. "We'll see, Pete. Now sit here and tell me why you tricked me and followed me to Traier? What were you doing in Mashran, alone?"

"I don't want to talk about it. Come on, get ready." Pete sorted through the garments again and shook his head in dismay. "Go to Jet. Just find the highest point in Traier. See ya later, Metal."

"Okay, Ugly."

Silver picked up the dress that intrigued Pete and spread it out on the bed. The deepest-green velvet—almost black—with dozens of pure gold clasps down the front and embroidered leaves of gold and silver along the sleeves and neckline. It looked like the gown from a Trueborn fairy tale. *Prisoner garb, indeed.*

She slipped the gown over her head and fastened the few clasps open at her bosom. It fit like a soft glove, like a warm hug. It must be enchanted with some Elven energy, she thought. Silver stepped in front of the mirror. Jaine was right—she looked like a whore, her breasts pushed high by the cut of the bodice. She never wanted to take the dress off.

The Traieren hated her. Not even the cold wind eased the burning of her cheeks as she made her way through the narrow streets. She bit back epithets she longed to spit at the Traieren, but knew to do so might mean her death.

Trueborn. Metal. Bitch. Whore.

The whispers from matrons leaning out windows, children playing in the narrow streets, soldiers drinking and playing quartzbox chess on small tables near tavern windows—it ended only when she climbed the stairs to the high quarters of the lord and the crowds thinned out.

Jetre's quarters weren't quite a palace, she thought, noting the building looked simply like a larger version of all the other houses in Traier. It was a mansion, and a lovely one, with vine-covered walls and turrets, ribbon-like banners of forest green and silver flapping gently from the upper floors, cut glass windows—some with colored figures painted onto them. Two guards eyed her curiously as she entered the main courtyard, nodding for her to continue. Sconces fastened along the inner walls flickered and cast shadows on an extraordinary garden.

This must be the most glorious spot on Isla.

A lovely stream, gurgling and shimmering silver in the dying light, wound through the courtyard amidst fountains, benches and ancient white gnarled trees. Flowers coaxed from bulbs during the short winter flared red, pink and burgundy from beneath crystal terrariums large enough for a person to enter. The smell of dark, rich earth mixed with the fragrance of sweet herbs and exotic flowers. Hyacinths—the flower always smelled of decay, with cloying sweetness. Silver bent to smell a cluster of the blossoms and jumped when a warm hand touched her shoulder.

"Warrior Atra SanMartin." The man's deep voice penetrated her entire being.

She stood quickly and turned to face one of the largest men she had ever seen. The stranger at her sickbed.

Silver bowed her head, knowing this must be Artier, Jetre's second-in-command. His battle skills legendary, he was responsible for the deaths of most of her comrades, either directly or by his strategy.

"Indeed, that is my name and my function."

His face was friendly and calm, with deep-blue eyes sparkling from beneath silver brows. He wore his long silver hair pulled into a tight knot and a long robe of deep gray silk shimmering in the dying light. Artier looked more like a priest of old than a warrior. And Silver thought he looked a bit older than he actually was—he might be as young as thirty.

"You all read minds, General?"

He shrugged. "Those closest to the lord do, of course. We are the best trained. I'm sure it's the same at Belanor among Metal? The most gifted surround the lord?"

"It was so, although with Cirin in the chair… I haven't been among them for many days, so I can't say who surrounds the new Lord of Metal." Silver bit back the anger that choked her each time she spoke about Cirin.

"Ah. I'll leave it to the lord to discuss with you. You do ken one goes to the lord on bended knee, and you are his prisoner still, despite the branding?" Art eyed Silver's garb. "And despite the odd choices he seems to be making these days."

"Aye, he made it quite clear he holds my life in his hands. I know my place. I don't yet know my destiny." Silver looked at the man for some indication of her fate, but his expression remained calm and unreadable.

"Go. Jet's not a patient man." Art bowed his head briefly, pointed to a second inner gate, and turned towards the path to town, leaving Silver to deal with her nerves alone.

Silver wound her way through the gardens to a low gate and passed through to find a dozen guards standing casually along the stairs to the main building entrance.

"I have an audience with the lord." Silver proudly noted her voice remained steady. The men barely took note of her, an intentional slight. She pulled herself upright and marched up the stairs to the huge wooden door. All of her composure failed her. *Was she to knock, to enter unannounced?* Silver looked over her shoulder to find the men staring at her. They quickly turned away and feigned disinterest again.

"Damn it!" She slowly pushed the door open. Gardens within gardens, she thought, as the moist, warm air in the entry hall caressed her face. Colorful birds flitted from tree to tree and the last bit of sunset cast a pink hue on the hall through the skylights above. Another flight of steps and another door. She found another empty room, this one darker still, lit only with a half-dozen burning sconces and filled with huge, heavy wooden furniture. It looked like an audience hall, but the judge wasn't about. To one side, another threshold opened onto what looked like living quarters, and Silver tiptoed to peak inside. Jaine was asleep on a long, cushioned bench, curled up into a ball, snoring softly. Silver cleared her throat and Jaine opened one eye sleepily and sat up.

"I'm not sure what to do."

Jaine smirked at Silver's awkwardness. "I don't give a damn what you do. I'm hungry. You'll be late for the feasting if you have to wait for the lord. And you do. Have a seat. One of us guards him at all times, and it's your turn. The glorious one isn't ready for you."

Jaine stood, stretched and strode out, leaving Silver alone again to fret, every nerve ending in her body screaming for her to run.

A heavyset, older woman startled Silver by pulling aside a thick velvet drape and beckoning. "The lord's just finishing up. He says for you to enter." Only a few candles burned in tall wooden holders, and the lush quarters came into view slowly as Silver's vision adjusted to the low light. Dark-green drapes, wooden sculptures, paintings of exotic lands filled with lush greenery…and the Lord Jetre, naked, stretched out face down on a cushioned table. The masseuse moved to the end of the table, pressed deeply into Jetre's foot and slowly worked her way up his calf.

The sight of him mesmerized her. His smooth, hairless skin stretched taut over bulging muscles, tight buttocks, an incredible broad back, strong arms—she'd seen nothing like it in her life. Jetre's head was turned away from her and his long hair cascaded over the side of the table in midnight waves. The masseuse eyed Silver with a quick smirk, and she realized her mouth hung open.

Silver quickly fell to one knee and cast her gaze to the floor. She heard a rustle and looked up to see Jetre staring at her now, chin propped on one hand.

"You're supposed to wish me long life and peace, Atra." One side of his mouth curved up in a smirk. Silver tried to keep her gaze averted, although she couldn't help watch the hands of the woman as they massaged Jetre's buttocks.

"Long life and peace, Lord." Silver barely heard her own words, cleared her throat, and tried again.

Jetre laughed. "Come near, sit by the fire and we'll have our little chat."

The magic and joy in his laughter stunned her. Which was he—the harsh master who drew blood from her neck and sent her to her knees with his branding, or the sensuous, lighthearted creature laying naked before her?

Silver worked her way slowly to the fireplace and sat on a huge cushion on the ground near the table on which Jetre lay—still naked. The masseuse glanced at her briefly again as she kneaded Jet's hard muscles.

Jet's long hair shimmered in the candlelight as he turned his head to face her. His dark eyes surveyed her intently, and Silver knew he read through her thoughts. She tried to block him and saw a flicker of amusement cross his face again.

He'd now see it all. She thought he was the most exquisite creature, male or female, she'd ever seen—no, even imagined. His eyes flared and she knew he caught her lusting for him. A sly grin came to his lips.

"When we last spoke, you expressed an interest in an audience with me. Welcome to Traier, Warrior Atra."

Pull it together, Silver.

"This isn't quite what I envisioned, Lord Jetre, when I asked for an audience. I imagined you'd at least be clothed. I expected shackles for myself, a guard, a bit of ceremony, perhaps even a bit of torture. I even envisioned a public execution. Not a gorgeous gown and your healing energy."

A flash of amusement twinkled again in his eyes and Silver's nerves relaxed slightly. Perhaps he didn't mean to kill her. Perhaps he had a plan for her, one she could live with.

"Marie, leave us. Atra can finish up here. I'm sure her training extends to energy flow."

"No, I'm not trained for that." *Oh, Mother, he means for me to massage his naked body?*

Marie bowed quickly and trundled out of the room, leaving only the sound of a crackling fire, the smell of dark incense, and a tinkling of wood chimes from far off.

Alone with him. Oh, Mother, alone with him. What will he do? Heat rushed to her cheeks and she looked in horror at Jet's midnight eyes, searching hers intently. *For what?* The silence hung in the room like thick smoke.

Jetre finally moved, pulling his hair off of his neck into a bundle and pointing to a leather cord on a nearby table.

Silver couldn't move.

"Oh, come on, I'm simply asking you to bind my hair. That's not difficult, is it?"

"No, sorry." Silver jumped up and handed him the cord.

"Do it for me. My hair won't burn your hands." He rolled his eyes and she wrapped the cord around his hair and tied a knot with shaking fingers. *He's wrong, his hair will burn my hands. Looking at him hurts.* Silver tried desperately not to let her eyes wander from his face.

"Lord, you've made your point. Can you put some clothes on?"

Jetre laughed. "What point did I make? You like the sight of naked men? You like it immensely? I can smell the musk of your desire, Warrior." Jet took in a deep breath, held it for a moment, and exhaled slowly. "It pleases me. You might want to mark your tone a bit."

Silver looked down and shook her head. "Am I supposed to become mad for you before you kill me, or whatever it is you intend? Surely an elemental lord doesn't need stroking." *Is this his punishment? How can one so powerful be so petty?* She stood as her fury built. She took in a last look at the glorious sight of him and turned her back.

When he finally spoke, his voice was soft but determined. "A Wu Xing lord receives no kind of stroking. He forswears one kind, and does not need the other. Look at me when I speak. I've executed my own kind for such an offense."

No he hasn't. He's never harmed a soul except in battle. I know it.

Jet stared intently at her as he reached for a cloth and sat up, draping the fabric over his lap. He looped it into a wrap and stood, moving to a low divan.

"Do you feel well, Silver? Fully recovered from the pteran attack? I understand from Pete you warded off a dart meant for him?"

"I don't know. Why would Fire attack a boy?" Silver realized immediately how naïve she sounded. "Of course, they knew what I didn't—he's your brother."

Jet nodded seriously and Silver saw pain flit across his face.

"And you hate that he's a target because of you."

"Your analysis—while correct—is a bit inappropriate. I asked how you feel."

Silver nodded. "I'm fine. Hale and hearty and stuffed into a gorgeous gown and a bit cheerier than I might be because of a flask full of whiskey."

Jet threw his head back and laughed heartily, and Silver smiled with him, despite her anxiety. He laughed openly, freely. His eyes caught the firelight and twinkled.

"Sit near me. Get used to me. You no doubt know now from Pete or Jaine you're one of my chosen warriors?"

"I don't understand any of this, Lord. You spare me, I assume for information about Metal, possibly for information about your parents' assassin. Why the honor? Because of Pete?"

"It is not an honor unless you act honorably, Silver. You're simply in the circle of my closest companions. The why and wherefore will become clear in time." He shrugged. "Actually, I'm not completely sure of my own plan yet. You may have a role to play."

"A pawn in reserve?" Silver tried not to sound bitter, reminding herself he was sparing her life.

"Precisely."

"You know Metal will do nothing to save me, would barter nothing. Cirin has no love for me."

Silver sensed Jet probing gently but firmly into her mind. *He knows it all; why must you explain anything? What power.*

"I was one of three choices for leadership of Metal with Kilé's passing and no one trained by the Council—by the Masters—was available. I'm certainly the most unlikely candidate. Less skilled than the others, but closest to the chair by the strictest code of familial succession. I understand Wood, and indeed Earth, do not consider heredity when choosing a lord?"

"Wrong." Jet nodded impatiently, motioning again for her to continue.

"Among Metal, parentage plays a role, but not the strongest. Cirin killed my cousin, Bartoc, and I fled before he killed me. We discussed this on the street in Belanor, didn't we?"

"You're skilled and intelligent enough to have escaped; you can't be so weak. Although I'd have found you in minutes."

"Cirin evidently doesn't have your power, any more than Kilé did. You don't need to be highly intelligent to flee once you learn one of the lords targets your entire family for assassination. I regret I didn't have time to warn my cousin Bartoc. I regret his passing."

"Interesting, and as you say, pretty much as I thought. I hated your brother when we were children and never grew to like him. He acted as he saw fit to further the cause of his people, no more or less than he should."

"I'm sorry about your parents." Silver whispered, searching for something else to say, to redeem her family, her brother. Jet's veiled grief escaped for a moment into the air, creating a mist of still and quiet. "Kilé spoke of you often, and I always thought he was a bit obsessed with you. I never quite understood it. I see now jealousy drove his hatred. Does your energy control surpass all the other lords?"

"That remains to be seen."

"No, it does not. I see you mock me. If you're the most powerful, why haven't you vanquished your enemies?"

"Ah, with a wave of my hand?" Jet snorted and played with a strand of hair.

He seems disturbed somehow. Ill at ease. That can't be it—something else is at work here.

"We'll discuss all this further. Your life is spared for now. I will spend time with you, listening to all you know of Cirin and his plans, of my parents' murder, of your brother, Kilé."

Kilé, I miss you. I wish you were alive to rescue me. There's no one left to care. Don't cry in front of your new lord. He must know you for a strong warrior. One tear traced a crooked path down her cheek, as it did the night Jetre held a knife to her throat.

"You weep for your brother?"

"For all of us. For you and Pete and Jaine. And for myself."

"Ah, a woman tired of war, tired of loss. Would you live in a different world, Silver? What vision do you have?"

"Unfortunately, Lord, I have no vision. I see no end to this senselessness. I believe the universe may have intended for us all to die in the last age of ice. Certainly this Destruction is unnatural in every way."

"Spoken like a true revolutionary. A little blasphemous during these times. Smacks of softness towards enemy clans, of betrayal."

"Don't you want Pete to grow up in a more peaceful world despite your grand aspirations?"

"My grand aspirations? What do you know of me? Nothing. Simply that the great Wu Xing lord was bred to perfection. A fighting machine, exquisite in his power, exquisite in his beauty. What makes you think the great Jetre wants peace? Don't you Metal quake at my name?"

"Sarcasm isn't your strong point, Lord. I'm not sure if you're ridiculing me, all the clans, or yourself."

"Ah, well said. I suppose all three. Do you know what it is to be a killing machine with a conscience, Warrior? To lead your people into battle for scraps of land and bits of metal and wood, knowing nothing permanent will come of it? To lead empty horses back through the gates, and hear the sobs of widows and widowers, of orphans? And to have to rally them again within days to do it all again?"

His eyes flared in anger, and she knew it wasn't at her, though his rising harsh tone sent shivers along her spine.

"Why not end it?"

"Because people are frightened, weak. They need something to rally around, to keep them separate from those unlike them. They only understand the ease of hate, not the work of peace. They would revolt against any move towards peace."

"That makes no sense. Their loved ones are dying. They would embrace peace."

Jet arched a brow wordlessly and Silver reluctantly admitted to herself his argument was sound.

"Kilé might have surprised you had he lived. He grew to hate the killing and his position. He once told me these conflicts were designed merely to keep the lords in power. The clans wanted resources, and they used the gifted as pawns. Kilé would have listened to you."

To her horror, another tear slipped from its prison and before she wiped it away, Jetre brushed the tear with his thumb and sucked the drop off. Silver started at the odd gesture.

"You grieve badly for Kilé."

"As I said, for all of us, especially the young. For Pete."

"Don't fear for Pete. I won't let anyone harm him."

"Aye, not even a Fire Pteran?"

"Pete's impetuous, like I was at his age. Part of it is his grief, but it will pass."

"I like your brother. He certainly worships you. In fact, he is starving for your affection."

Jetre's eyes glimmered in annoyance, and she bowed her head. "I beg your forgiveness. As a lord's sister, I became accustomed to speaking my mind. I forget myself."

She looked up again, and a shock of electricity ran through her at Jet's intense stare. He looked from her eyes to her lips, and let his gaze wander to her breasts, pushed high by her gown. His eyes burned as she he assaulted her senses.

"You're rather strong-willed, Silver. I don't buy your apology for a second. And I think I rather fancy that about you. You'll make a good bodyguard. What do you think of the gown? It's been in my family for many generations."

"Lord?"

"Yes?" He continued his sexual appraisal of her and her breathing quickened in longing. She let her gaze wander down his smooth stomach to his rigid cock, straining against the black silk wrap. *Surely he can hear my heart, it's so loud.*

"Do you like what you see, Silver? You can't seem to pull your gaze away for long. Do you know the whole time we've spoken, the whole time you've cried over the conflict and your brother, you've filled the room with your lust. You've stared at my mouth and my chest, my stomach, wondering how it would feel, how it would be between us. Am I wrong?"

"You are quite wrong, Lord."

He laughed a little and motioned her to come closer. "I'd like a closer look at you in my ancestor's garb. You must admit, it suits your figure, which is…" Jetre took in a quick breath. "Adequate."

"Adequate? My figure is adequate? Why are we discussing my body? Your oath, your…"

"Have I broken my oath, Silver?" He worked his fingertips from her collarbone across the swell of her breasts. His touch blazed a fiery trail across her skin and his energy seeped into her veins. *Which burns,* she wondered—*the touch of an elf or the touch of a lord?* He slowly unfastened the clasps of her dress until he exposed her breasts. His calloused fingers and palms brushed across her skin like a kiss as he cupped one breast in each hand. His moan stirred her to quivering. He caressed her as if he'd found a priceless treasure he'd sought for a lifetime. Silver fought the sensations he evoked, but surrendered and cried out when he rubbed his thumbs on her nipples.

"Jetre."

"Yes?" He continued his slow circles. "You find this unpleasant? Should I stop?" Jetre looked at her from beneath his dark lashes as he leaned in to suckle on one breast. His hot mouth assaulted her senses, his tongue darting across her nipple, his lips pulling and pinching. A low groaning sound came from far away, and Silver realized in shock it was her moan, her lust filling the air. She laced her hands in an errant strand of his luxurious hair and pulled it towards her face, smelling his scent—dark spices and male magic. When he moved to her other breast, the new pleasure sent her to the brink of orgasm, and he kept her hovered there for minutes. He broke away suddenly and looked into her eyes.

Silver panted, aching, throbbing, ready to push him to the ground and assault him. "You're no virgin."

"How dare you. Do you understand how you insult me, Warrior?"

"I honestly couldn't tell you what I think right now if my life depended upon it."

Jetre arched a brow. "It will come to you."

Silver's hands shook at the conflicting, overwhelming emotions consuming her. This man, this gorgeous man, her sworn enemy, now her master—was he seducing her? No, simply playing with his prisoner. No more, certainly. A tiny dagger of regret pierced her heart. Silver shuddered, the memory of his mouth on her still making her tingle, still making her throb and moist and ready.

What I wouldn't give to lay with him, to feel him inside me... She cursed to herself. Too late, he heard it.

"Tell me, let me hear what you want." His voice grew low and languid, his eyes nearly hidden beneath his black lashes. "Tell me what kind of lover you imagine me? What draws you? My look? My manner? Or my power?"

All of those. None of those. Don't let him hear any more. Thoughts poured out, desire and longing overwhelming her, betraying her.

You're the most beautiful creature. Take me now or leave me be. I don't want to feel this way.

"Yes you do." His voice was such a low whisper Silver thought she might have imagined hearing him speak.

Jet sat up straight, eyes now wide, spell broken. "I'm not one to take advantage of my position with a woman, with anyone. You aren't required to placate me in a sexual way." Jetre snorted. "Perhaps that's only my ego. I couldn't stand the thought of forcing myself on a woman. I've always assumed no woman would reject me, which is quite disturbing. Perhaps you don't want me?"

Silver groaned. "Don't mock me, Lord, you read my thoughts clearly enough. It's bad enough that I've betrayed my kind. Don't make me betray myself."

Jetre ignored her words and stood, pulling the cord from his hair.

That's his way? Play with me for a moment, send my world reeling, and dismiss me like a scrap of garbage.

"You'll help me dress now, and we will eat and drink with the soldiers and their families. I intend to speak to the crowd of your presence here. Some of it will annoy you, badly, especially when I speak of your brother. Try to show restraint. Understood?"

"Yes, Lord."

He turned and nodded. "Silver, in private, you may call me Jet. I'm a little less formal than most of the lords." He held out a finger. "In private, mind you."

She nodded. "Jet." She tested the nickname on her tongue.

"One thing." Jetre turned away again. His voice was quiet and Silver struggled to hear him. "Was it right? Did it feel right, what I did? When I kissed your breasts?"

It was the last question she expected from him, the most amazing thing. The great Lord Jetre, wondering if he had given her any pleasure. *How to answer him?*

"Because my ten years end in a matter of days." He pushed his hand through his hair and laughed at himself. "I don't want it said the oath made

66

the lord incapable. How embarrassing. Is this your nature—to bring out the inner truths of a person?"

"How will I protect you from the women who will storm your quarters when your oath is complete? They'll be more dangerous than Fire and Metal combined against you." *And how will I bear to watch it?*

Jet laughed. "As appealing as that picture might be, I must pick only one. The second part of the deal." He shrugged.

"I see." A small knife poked at her heart unexpectedly. No doubt the woman would be Wood and was probably already betrothed to the lord. An elf, of course.

"You didn't answer my question." Jet toweled down and Silver turned away. From the corner of her eye she saw him step into his dark leather pants and pull on a thin, collarless, long-sleeved, black shirt. He went to the dresser and placed a kohl stick against each eye, blinking and wiping the excess from his cheeks.

"The woman will be quite fortunate, Jet. I hope that satisfies your ego."

He inclined his head and smiled very subtly. "It does. Might I practice on you again some time?"

Silver closed her eyes. The pain came in very faintly, like the smell of a coming summer rain shower on the breeze. She wanted her sworn enemy, and she meant nothing to him. A plaything, a practice toy. *Well, there are worse fates than being the whore of such a man.*

He pointed to his tall boots and Silver brought them to him, helped him push into them.

"You did something terrible to me when you branded me, Jet. I know you did. You say you wouldn't force a woman, but you charmed me in some way."

Jet looked up at her, puzzled. "Nonsense."

"I don't believe you."

Jet pointed to the dresser and his heavy, white-gold pendant, the Wu Xing symbol of his clan, the symbol of the Way of Ch'i. Silver brought it to him and fastened it around his neck. She bit back thoughts of Kilé and how she had fastened his pendant many times.

"Not many call me a liar without punishment. If Jaine or Art were here, you'd already be bleeding."

"Yes, my lord. Based on my brief encounter with your formidable sister, I believe you."

"Now my hair."

"What about it?"

"Brush it." He rolled his eyes at her.

"This is fucking awful, Lord."

"You'll get used to it."

Silver went to the dresser, grabbed a brush, and pulled a cushion behind Jetre's. She brushed his beautiful hair, wishing she could bury her face in it.

He turned suddenly and grabbed her by the neck. "I heard that."

She cried out softly, even though he didn't hurt her.

"They'll have to wait a few minutes more."

Jet caught his breath. *No. You won't stop at her breasts. How did this happen, damn it? You want a Trueborn, this one. So badly you can taste it. Is it because you want to fuck Kilé's sister? For revenge? You've become the man Guo warned about.*

"Never mind. They'll be furious. Don't want to keep a warrior from his ale."

Jet looked at her flushed cheeks and sparkling gray eyes. Her hair was mussed, and he wanted to muss it more for no reason he understood. His eyes fell to her wonderful breasts, the globes he'd feasted on. He longed to rip the dress off her and devour all of her.

The burning he'd pushed down for all of his adult life flared before his eyes in the face and body of this pale warrior.

"We're ready to go? To the feast?" Silver started to stand and Jet pulled her back down.

"I haven't quite decided." He lowered his voice and pushed a tone into it he knew would excite her. He saw her breathing quicken, her breasts rising and falling. "I might like more of those. The feel of them in my mouth. I'm so used to my cock aching for release, I've almost stopped feeling it. You made me feel it again."

Silver closed her eyes and bit her lip. "Don't you...find release? Alone, I mean? That is not prohibited by the oath, I believe. I certainly caught my brother in the act more often than I wished."

Jet snickered. "What's your guess? It doesn't quite have the effect I'm craving these days. Although I wouldn't mind having you catch me 'in the act,' as you say. Would you like to see me pull at my cock and cover you with my essence?"

Jet pulled away her dress, kissing her neck and moving slowly to her breasts. Silver arched and moaned as he nibbled and sucked, and the sound pounded to his cock. He met her moans with his own. *Don't kiss her mouth, Jet. The danger lies in her lips.* He was still pondering what it would be like to kiss her when Silver shook beneath his grip. She clutched at his arms, digging her nails into his flesh, shuddering and crying out his name. He watched in wonder as her cheeks flushed and her eyes grew misty.

"You're awfully easy to arouse, aren't you?" Jet watched her gradually come to her senses.

"Not typically." She clenched her teeth and gazed into his eyes.

"Not sure you're the best woman for me to learn on." Jet turned away, wondering how she'd respond to his taunt. It bothered him he cared.

"Kiss my ass." She stood, fixing her dress.

"Next time, if you're a very good prisoner." Jet smiled to himself. *Fun. She's fun. What's this game I'm playing with her?*

"Prisoner? I thought I was a Wood-chosen, special whatever."

"You seem rather angry all of a sudden. What's eating you?"

"You were."

"Oh, my, this is interesting. You're getting a bit caught up in me, aren't you?" A wave of pleasure washed through him, made him feel a bit adolescent. *You're ready to giggle. Put a stop to this.*

"I don't know how the hell you've led this clan since you were a lad, because you're about as immature as little Petrov, and about as subtle."

"I've heard it all before." He dismissed her words with a wave of his hand. "You won't win at this game, Warrior Silver. I'm immune to insults regarding my immaturity and manner." He paused a moment to let her calm down, to give himself time to steady his energy.

"Ready to meet the grand folk of Traier? I'm sure they're on the edge of their seats, waiting to learn what you're doing here."

"As am I, however I need a private moment to freshen up."

He bit back a groan at the images still invading his peace. *One more bit of play, perhaps?* "Yes, I smell it on you. What I did to you. May I feel how wet I made you?"

"It would be against my will."

"I'm teasing, Silver. Remember, we're flirting?"

Jet winked at her and caught the tiniest smile pull at her lips. *I like her very much. The people would never accept the sister of Kilé. Nor would I. But for play...wouldn't it be amusing to have the woman fall in love with me? Kilé's sister? If only Kilé were alive to see it.*

Silver looked up at Jet suddenly and he wondered if he had let his mind wander, let his thoughts slip into the air. Perhaps she was stronger than he originally suspected. She looked pained.

"Finish your ablutions in that room and hurry."

Silver nodded curtly and walked proudly to the room. Yes, she heard him. Oh well, her feelings were inconsequential.

Chapter Six

Silver swore from that moment on Jet would touch her only by force. Her mind raced as they took the winding path away from Jet's keep and towards the Great Hall of Traier.

Silver started when Jet pulled on her elbow and stopped her. His eyes burned with intensity. "It's not quite like that."

"Like what?"

"I'm unlikely to throw you to the dogs without a thought."

"You are likely to do what you will with me, with no concern for the effect it has on anyone but yourself. I heard you, and you know it. I'm simply a plaything, no, more—I'm especially valuable because I'm Kilé's sister. I believe you would actually enjoy my distress. Do not touch me again, Lord."

"As you wish." Jet nodded curtly. "You will no doubt be relieved to learn I announce my betrothal choice this evening. Surely your mind will rest, knowing I'll be occupied with a wife within the week."

"I don't care who you name as a mate. I care that we take down Cirin. It's the only reason I sought you out—the only reason I'm here. Whether the Metal power goes to you or another, I don't care." Silver wanted to slap him. *Tonight?* She wouldn't look at the woman, couldn't bear to see her.

"Liar. I'll take Cirin down, as you say, with or without you and your pitiful little plan, which I have yet to hear. And you will look to see who I'll be fucking every night for the rest of my life. You won't be able to help yourself."

"Why would you care about making me jealous? We spent a few inconsequential moments together. Do you honestly think all it takes to win a woman's heart is a lick of her breasts? You do have much to learn, Lord."

Silver saw her tiny arrow hit as the slightest hint of confusion passed across his face. She'd guard her thoughts, her body and her heart, and concentrate on her cause, Jetre be damned.

"Dishonor me in front of my people and I'll slit your throat without a second thought."

I don't believe you. She didn't bother guarding her thoughts.

❈ ❈ ❈

Cirin bit back his surprise and veiled his face with the cold, impassive mask of disinterest he wore in public. The messenger trembled visibly despite Cirin's noncommittal response to the letter.

"Read it for me, slowly. I cannot conjure one word of the scribble that serves as your script." Cirin thrust the page towards the young woman and turned his back on her, gazing out the arched window, across the plain covered with a light blanket of new snow. He knotted his hands behind his back, lest he clench his fists in anger before his companions.

The messenger cleared her throat softly. "Lord Cirin. You no doubt believe the Warrior Atra SanMartin dead by your orders. However, one of my scouts saw her within the week riding towards Traier in the company of Petrov Artraud, brother of Jetre Artraud. I leave you to your own conclusion regarding this unexpected development. My scout, who stands before you and who was alone and inferior in skills to both SanMartin and the younger Artraud, wisely opted for a pteran attack. Young Artraud killed the pteran, and I assume SanMartin, while wounded, survived to reach Traier. Whether she lives still is beyond my knowledge. No doubt Lord Jetre extracted information from her regarding whatever she knew of your clan's current plans.

"I send you this information as proof of my good faith, the last such gesture. If you refuse me now and decline an alliance with Wu Xing Fire, I will take my offer elsewhere. Respond to my messenger, Warrior Senta."

Senta looked up nervously and nearly whispered. "Thus ends my Lord Paulo's letter. What are your instructions?"

Cirin turned quickly and forced a brief smile. "Why, you'll stay the night, won't you, Senta, while I ponder your lord's offer? Dreia will show you to the guest quadrant." Cirin watched anxious relief sweep across the lovely woman's face. He made a mental note to visit her that night, to have his first taste of Fire flesh. Cirin nodded and the woman followed her guide quickly from his audience chamber.

Cirin flopped back into the chair and rubbed energy points on the fleshy pad of his palm to ease his growing headache. He knew how urgently his generals wanted to speak, but knew also they would wait for a word from him.

"Guntar, spit it out."

"It's a true tale, I feel it soundly lodged in my gut. Atra lives in the company of Jetre." Cirin groaned in concurrence and nodded for the graying warhorse to continue. "She's of no consequence. Jetre knows your strength, your numbers and your weaknesses. The woman has no information of worth."

Jeannette scoffed at the old man. "That's not quite the point, is it, Guntar? You're correct, the woman, as you call my dear friend, is of no import. However, the point of the letter is a very unsubtle threat, is it not? Despite his claims of good faith, Paulo fishes for the best offer, the soundest alliance. He wants to ride in the wake of the winning clan. I suggest you take him up on the offer, Cirin."

Although Jeannette made sense, doubt crept into Cirin's heart, and he knew well enough to pay heed to his intuition. "Paulo might turn one hundred eighty degrees towards Water for his useless alliance against Jetre. Or perhaps he intends to bow to Jetre before he slits his throat. The arrogant elf has something on us all. Masters Guo and Tsien taught him more than the others, more than Kilé, I know it. I'll wager he understands the cycle of Creation."

"Impossible." Guntar growled. "The Cycle of Creation withered in antiquity and no one has the knowledge to use it."

Impossible? Unlikely, surely. Cirin knew to underestimate Jetre was to write a death scroll for oneself.

Guntar cleared his throat and Cirin nodded for him to continue. "Jetre is the force to reckon with, no doubt. I assure you Paulo is not a match for a Metal Lord, as least…not for Kilé."

Cirin arched a brow. "You play a dangerous game, Guntar. And your thoughts ring out quite clearly. I'm no Kilé, didn't have his lifetime of training. I had training enough, old man. Kilé wasn't all that difficult to murder, was he?"

Jeannette clenched her jaw. "No one is difficult to kill when you barter your soul away. You did not fight him. An assassination is no proof of strength, and no other lord would stoop to such a coward's choice."

Cirin stormed to Jeannette's chair and slapped her. She cried out and Guntar rose uncertainly to aid the woman. "You will always be Kilé's whore in your heart, won't you, Jeannette? It's perhaps time you retire from my service."

"Leave me, all of you." Cirin turned back to the window in fury, his grip on the clan loosening by the hour. *In their hearts, they're still loyal to SanMartin. Well, Kilé wanted peace, and there will be no peace. Let them think their hero was a vile assassin. Let them think he murdered Jetre's parents. And let Atra SanMartin rot in the dark mist with her new Wood Lord.*

Chapter Seven

The scents of sweet pipe smoke, fragrant candles, roasted vegetables, spicy grain, and dark ale filled the Great Hall of Traier. A few thousand men and women ate, laughed, and drank with abandon. Song broke out here and there—drinking songs, Silver thought, victory songs. The hall itself arched like a cathedral of wood, towered above them, a web of intricately carved wooden beams. High along the walls, silver inlay told a story in Elvish script Silver couldn't read. Ancient, the place looked as ancient as Isla itself. No doubt generation after generation of Elven lord entertained his folk in this grand fashion.

Silver stood behind Jetre in the darkened entrance and surveyed the happy scene in awe. The Traieren were nothing like her clan. *When did you last dance, Silver? When did you last sing, or tell jokes, or pull your dress down off your shoulders to tease a man?* She watched one pretty young woman do exactly that, coyly easing her blouse down low enough to show her ample breasts. The object of her flirtation pulled her onto his lap and kissed her passionately while the rest at their table pounded on the wood and let out cheers.

I don't belong here.

"Well, you're here now, so tough it out, Warrior." Jet turned and looked at her closely. "I'll warn you again, this may not be pleasant for you, but you'll endure it as one of my chosen. You're not to speak to the people, but you may speak to my family, and to Art. If you refrain from insolence, perhaps I'll reward you."

"Reward me? By ceasing the lectures?"

"By kissing you. It's what you crave more than air or food or water, isn't it?" Jet's gaze lowered to her lips and he pursed his in amusement. His anger was gone, his mood lighter in the space of a few minutes.

Heat suffused her cheeks and Silver groaned inwardly in frustration at how easily Jet dismissed her protests.

I mustn't give in.

"We'll see about that, my dear."

Jet raised his arm and held his palm towards the crowd. He closed his eyes and the air around him moved subtly. A shimmer of green and silver energy spiraled into the room, and at once, everyone rose and bowed their heads.

A deep voice emanated from the front of the room and Silver recognized it as Artier's.

"Greetings to our lord, Jetre Artraud. We thank you for the blessing, we thank you for the feast, and we welcome you to your rightful place among us."

"Long life and peace," the crowd intoned loudly in unison. All eyes looked towards the lord as he prodded Silver in the back to move towards the front of the hall. Like a sleepwalker, she numbly put one leg in front of the other. The crowd's whispers came as if from far away. Some spoke in the Elvish tongue in low tones, some hissed at her like forest creatures. She reached deep into her center for the quiet spot of Metal energy and with tip of tongue to roof of mouth brought forth a circle of energy to quiet her mind. The Wood Elves must have sensed her deflection of their taunts, for the chatter gradually subsided. By the time she reached the lord's table, the Great Hall fell completely silent.

Jet nodded for her to take one of two empty seats between Petrov and Jaine at the huge, ancient oak table. She sat close to Pete, only to see Jet scowl and motion with his eyes for her to move next to Jaine. Pete sniffed in annoyance.

Jaine grasped points on Silver's wrist tightly, and a wash of cool energy pounded up her arm. She hissed lowly in her ear. "Mistake number one."

"How was I to know?"

"Your position requires you to know. Open yourself up to the lord's wishes. He sends them out for you to hear, but you aren't listening. Pay attention."

"Fine. I'm simply dying to know how to please the Lord Jetre."

Jet motioned for all to sit, but remained silent. He surveyed the crowd slowly, and Silver suspected he sorted through the mood of his people before offering his speech.

He bowed his head and the crowd burst into applause, some rising to their feet again and cheering.

"What's going on?" Silver whispered to Jaine. Jaine shook her head in warning and held a finger to her lips. "He honors the clan greatly by bowing to them."

Jet motioned again for the crowd to sit and held out his palm, sending another shimmering trail of energy into the room.

"My blessings." His clear, baritone voice cutting the silence like a knife.

"The victory at Kor-Mashran shines like a beacon for generations to follow—your bravery proven for all the clans to witness." He reached for a goblet and raised it high. All followed suit. "To the fallen. We drink their blood in gratitude. The blow to Earth was substantial. To many more such victories, brave warriors."

Jet drained his goblet. Silver looked into the deep-red liquid and shook in dread. Jaine leaned in. "It's not actually blood, you idiot."

Silver's hand still trembled as she drained the goblet. Sweet, dark, spicy wine sent heat and pleasure through her veins. *That's what he'd taste like. Sweet, dark wine.*

Jet turned to her suddenly and Silver looked at the table. Had he heard her thought? Had he pushed the thought into her head? This was humiliating.

"And now, to answer the question ringing through our hall." Jet gestured to Silver and motioned for her to stand. Jaine poked her in the side and she popped up, waiting for the worst.

"Atra SanMartin stands before you."

Loud hissing filled the room. One woman held a hunk of bread as if she would hurl it at Silver, but Jet motioned for silence.

"Metal, indeed. You know her brother Kilé rots in hell with his kind. Atra is branded Wood, sworn to protect me."

The crowd gasped in unison and muttering broke out in spurts. Jet again held up his hand.

One old man stood and bowed his head before speaking. "Lord. The rumor spins through the streets of Traier, indeed through all the territories— Kilé killed Masur and Lue. This woman's brother killed your parents."

"No."

Pete pulled at her sleeve and stared at her in horror. "Is this true, Silver?" Tears welled up in his eyes and Silver had to turn away, the boy's small fist clenching at her heart.

Jet pulled Pete to his feet and held him from behind, wrapping his arms around the boy protectively.

"Kilé is innocent of that crime. His assassin, Cirin, circulated the rumor to further his own cause. I held no love for Kilé, but he was no oath breaker and never stooped to assassination. Cirin is guilty. Cirin is a marked man. By deep summer, Cirin will see defeat and I will lord over Metal as well as Wood. This woman, Atra SanMartin, will aid in the destruction of Cirin by telling us what she knows of her clan. Treat her properly, treat her as one of your kind."

Loud cheers of Jetre went up, the noise growing, pounding through the huge hall. A swooshing of blood pounded in Silver's ears as she took in Jetre's words. *Cirin? Her brother was innocent?* Tears of both grief and relief trickled down her face and she fell back into her chair. Jaine placed a tentative hand on her shoulder, patting it awkwardly.

Jet picked Pete up, hugged him tightly, and plopped him to his seat, motioning for the crowd to attend to him again.

"We'll feast until Beltane."

Jet took his seat and poured himself a second goblet of wine. He whispered to Pete, who was calmer, Silver noted, and turned to her and regarded her seriously.

"Warrior Atra, what do you think of Wood celebrations?"

"Are you sure, Lord? About Kilé?"

"Quite sure. My cousin Mikalis leads my spies, and I've never known him to bring false information to me. It doesn't bring your brother back from the dead, but you may put your mind at ease. I never thought Kilé a coward. I'm relieved in an odd way to know he was not. We did train together, and it would pain Masters Guo and Tsien to know...if they were alive." He shook his head sadly.

"Yes, Kilé was very fond of Master Tsien especially. I don't understand how your spy discovered this truth?"

Jet laughed. "He did. And you were the second spy, Silver. Your deep knowing doesn't lie."

"I didn't know about this. You're wrong."

"I am not. I see the truths you witnessed, but cannot see because you are blinded by fear. I read the vision behind the thoughts." Jet turned his back to Silver and spoke again in hushed tones with Pete.

Jaine's elbow dug into Silver's side and she sat up straighter, trying to hold onto composure.

"Well, Metal, good for you. How you ended up a hero tonight is beyond me, but I won't question the great Lord Jetre."

"You don't hate me nearly as much as you lead on, Jaine."

"A bit more than I lead on, perhaps." Jaine ran her hand through her messy hair. "Look woman, try to roll with it."

"It?"

"Jet's plans for you. Whatever they are."

Silver sighed. "That's the issue, isn't it? What are his plans for me?"

"I'm beginning to think they don't include torture. At least not the kind you imagined." Jaine laughed loudly at her own joke and lifted her goblet. "Come on, drink up. We've a free pass tonight. How about you and I go whoring around town? The generals are all puffed up with their victory. Should be fun."

"Whoring around? What the hell kind of place is this?"

"Jaine." Jet drew his sister's name out in warning. "Silver's guarding me tonight. They'll be no whoring around."

Art snickered into his goblet and stopped suddenly when he caught Silver's eye. "Yes, Warrior Atra, you have a question?"

"No, sir."

The wine gave Silver her only solace as the night dragged on. Jet pointedly ignored her, and Jaine, more drunk by the minute, rattled on about her escapades in and out of bed. Silver listened with half an ear as she watched an enchanting young woman approach the table. No more than twenty years old with long auburn hair and twinkling green eyes, she wore a seductive gown cut midway to her waist. Her eyes were locked onto Jet as she approached.

The girl curtsied. "My lord, is there anything you require tonight?"

"No, Aileen, but thank you." Jet propped his chin in his hand and surveyed the beauty. He glanced briefly at Silver and called the girl back. "On second thought, Aileen, I might not mind a bit of a shoulder rub."

Aileen squealed in delight, and to Silver's shock, sat in Jet's lap and kneaded his shoulders as she seductively flaunted her cleavage.

Jaine groaned. "Ugh, I detest her. If he claims her tonight, I'll be sick, right on this table."

"Claims her?"

"His oath ends soon. He's to name his bride before the night is over. The odds are now ten to one in Aileen's favor."

"Oh." Silver's mouth went dry as she watched the young woman run her hands through the lord's shimmering hair. Aileen brushed a bit of kohl from his cheek and ran her thumb along his jawline.

Jet leaned back in his chair and watched Silver, his eyes narrowed, his expression impassive. Aileen worked her way down to his neck and kissed it lightly. Jet squeezed her waist as she moaned and nibbled on his skin. Silver watched as she licked at the vein throbbing in his neck and saw him shudder, all the time keeping his eyes on Silver's.

What's this horrible game, Lord?

"Game? Whatever do you mean, Warrior?" Silver gasped as his answer slid silently into her mind.

"Aye, game. You're taunting me."

"How? The girl wants what you don't. A taste of me. What harm is she doing? Am I doing?" He moaned as Aileen sucked at his neck, surely hard enough to leave a mark. She ran her hand down his chest and pinched at his nipple. Silver glanced at the rest of their party, who ignored the spectacle.

Silver cast her gaze at the table, unwilling to watch further.

"Enough Aileen." Jet suddenly pushed the girl from his lap and she looked at him with hurt etched across her pretty face. "Take your table."

A clock chimed the midnight hour and Jet stood slowly. The room came to silence immediately and everyone waited with bated breath for him to speak. *This is it. His remarkable pronouncement. Let her have him.*

"My oath ends within one week." Cheers went up again and Silver closed her ears to them. "And I defer my choice of mate. Until the end, Jaine Artraud will stand as my bride."

The crowd groaned and booed.

Jaine? His sister?

Jaine spit out a mouthful of wine onto the table. "Not again. Get it over with, for Mother's sake."

"What does it mean, Jaine? Surely he's not choosing you as his bride."

"Holy hell! This irks me."

Art leaned across the table. "The lord must always choose a mate or a surrogate—each year at this time, we repeat the ritual, and always with the same outcome. Our Lord Jetre consistently abstains from naming his bride by choosing his sister as the surrogate. For appearances, Jaine must remain abstinent although we only hold her to that for a short while. Any longer might kill her."

"Fuck you, Jet!" Jaine threw a crust of bread at her brother.

Jet snickered at Jaine from beneath his dark brows and rose, grabbing a tired Pete by the hand.

Art reached across the table to Silver. "Silver, it seems you do not understand our ritual?"

"A fair assessment, General." But life came back to her limbs and air back to her lungs as she took it in. He hadn't chosen Aileen. Not yet. Perhaps there was another…

"Perhaps there is another," Jet mumbled. "Perhaps not. Warrior Atra, you have pulled the short straw. You'll guard me tonight and until further notice."

The blood in her veins turned to ice water. She needed tonight's torture to end.

❀ ❀ ❀

Why would anyone build a couch short of an average person's height? Silver squirmed and pushed at the cushions with her feet, struggling to get comfortable on the couch in Jet's outer living room. First too hot, then too cold. She'd almost drift off to sleep, only to hear a subtle noise and sit up, alert, blade in hand. The wind, the tree limbs brushing against the window, a mouse perhaps. And the whole while, images of Aileen kissing Jet's neck infuriated her. Images of Jet kissing Silver's breasts made her breathless. Finally she sat up and lit a candle. She'd find sleep when it came, but it would not be this night. *I hate him, I hate him. And his insane people and awful sister. Except for Pete, I do like Pete.* Her mind raced from one thought to the next, nerve endings lit up, heart beating rapidly.

"What the hell is wrong? Your energy is bouncing off these walls, making my ears ring. How's a man to sleep?" Jet stood in the doorway to his bedchamber, hands on his hips. He wore a thin-silk sarong draped low around his waist. He pushed his disheveled hair out of his eyes and sighed.

"Come in, let's cure what ails you."

"Nothing ails me. I can't sleep. It's not an illness."

"Yes it is. Sleep is essential to your good health. Let me find the energy block troubling you so we both can get some sleep."

"I think it's the terrible wine. I drank too much."

"Nonsense, you're not drunk at all. Your energy is disrupted, and we'll repair it now. That's an order."

"No." She shut her eyes for a moment against the amazing sight of him, his beautiful body, skin like fine velvet. She opened them to stare at the cords of muscle roping along his hips and pointing towards his crotch. He mesmerized her, and no matter how she sought her peaceful center, this man would push her off balance.

Jet laughed as he took two long strides to her side and guided her into his chamber. He pointed to the table on which she had first seen him earlier in the day.

"I'm not letting you massage me."

"It's not a holiday, Silver. I don't provide relaxing massages. I am a healer, the greatest among my clan, perhaps among all the clans. Now get on the damned table."

"I'm not taking my clothes off."

"No, you're not." He motioned again and Silver moved slowly to the table and crawled onto it, eyes squeezed tight as she lay on her stomach.

"Face up. Mother of us all, don't you Metal practice energy flow? I'm not going to hurt you."

"We practice Ch'i Gong for energy flow, not hands-on healing."

"Which explains why you're all sickly pale."

"Sickly pale?"

His light laughter danced around the quiet room and Silver smiled to herself a bit for falling for his joking.

She rolled onto her back and stared at the ceiling. A lizard looked down at her from a high beam, and she opened her mouth to tell Jet, but froze as his warm hands pressed along the sole of her foot with precise circular movements.

"Ouch!" He pushed on a sensitive area beneath the ball of her foot.

"Hmmn. Heart Meridian imbalance. Your diet will change immediately. Cooling foods and cooling drinks. Perhaps some of the Fire Pteran's poison still works through your system."

Jet worked his hands up the inside of her ankle and pressed on another tender spot. "Actually, it would be best if you were naked, but I'll respect your wishes and request you hike that dress up a bit."

"No."

"That's an order. I can do it if you like." He didn't wait, but pushed her long gown up her legs, stopping at her torso.

What does he think of my legs? Oh, Mother, I've never cared what a man thought of my legs.

"They're exquisite. Silver, relax. When I heal, I can do nothing but heal. Do you understand?"

"I think so. Yes, yes, I understand."

A tingling started in her lower leg, spread up her thigh and looped around her body as Jet pressed his thumbs into points along her leg.

"Ah, there we go. Feel the movement? Now the other." He moved to her other foot and repeated the process. A feeling of invigorating calm suffused her entire being, and she sighed loudly.

"That's good, keep releasing the tension. So much tension." He ran his palms up her legs in long, sweeping strokes and finally, pulled her dress down to cover her. He held his hands an inch over her chest and warmth spread in waves to her extremities.

"Relax a moment while I meditate." Silver turned her head to watch Jet sit before a small altar covered in Elvish script, topped with only a candle and a Wu Xing statue. He sat erect and still for no less than ten minutes, and Silver tried desperately to still her mind, to give him quiet. He suddenly clapped his hands and rubbed his palms over his face as if he were washing.

He sealed his own Ch'i, Silver knew from her own energy practice. The Lord of Wood couldn't afford bad energy to invade his system.

When he came to her side and looked down at her, all the calm disappeared. She struggled for anything to say to break the silence, lest her longing ring out again.

"You shouldn't sleep in your eye kohl, Lord."

"Indeed? I'll try to remember. I was tired and forgot. I won't let it happen again." Jet laughed and motioned for her to stand and join him near the fire.

No, not there. I must leave right away.

He held out his hand insistently and she moved towards him. "I wish I could get out of this dress..." *Oh, damn!* "I mean, I wish there was something else to wear."

"You'll come better prepared for your guard duty next time. And I know that blade isn't your first choice of weapon. Art will secure the weapons you desire. Speak with him."

Silver nodded and took a seat close to Jet on the floor. She waited nervously for his next pronouncement, but none came. He watched her patiently. *What do you want me to do?*

"You're relieved to learn Kilé wasn't an assassin?"

"Yes, Lord." Her mouth dried and she pushed back exhaustion and the tears that would no doubt come if they talked about Kilé.

"Jet."

"Jet. I'm grateful beyond belief to know this."

"And you're relieved I'm not going to kill you, of course. Still curious what your role will be, as am I. I've yet to hear of your masterful plan." He arched a brow and grinned slyly.

"Always poking fun. Jaine meant what she said about you."

"Unlikely. What did she say?"

"You're a jokester. I didn't believe her. But you have another side...one I didn't expect."

"One you like." The smile spreading across his face was relaxed, peaceful. "This isn't terrible, is it prisoner?"

Is it? Is it terrible or wonderful? There's no one to help me sort it out.

"Undecided, Silver? Do you think you'll come to loathe me or love me? Or do you already know?"

The brief touch of his palm to her cheek sent a rush of fire through her veins. And his eyes grew…what was the look? Surely not longing. But gone in an instant, replaced with amusement.

"I don't know, Lord."

"Jet. My name is Jet." And his thought slipped into the air in a moment of neglect, and Silver heard it loudly and clearly. *"I'm a man, damn it."*

"Which is it, *Jet*? Am I to worship the lord or the man? Your friends, your family—do they love you or would any lord do? I suppose even Aileen wouldn't suck your neck if you weren't lord?" The instant her words slipped out, she knew she was wrong, trying to wound him, distance him, now that she saw the tiniest hint of weakness.

Fire danced in his black eyes and he pulled back, smile gone, jaw clenched.

"Nice try. Save your analysis for Pete. I've lived with my destiny my entire life, and it doesn't trouble me."

"I don't believe you. I think you've spent all your adult life wondering if anyone knows or cares about the man who rules them. My brother wondered, I'm sure."

"Your brother didn't learn the lessons the masters taught him. A Wu Xing lord needs nothing but health and his skills to prosper. We rid ourselves of the need for attachment. At least I did."

"You don't care for your siblings? Your friend, the general?"

"Enough." Lying back onto the pillows, Jet laced his hands behind his head and stared at the ceiling. He watched the lizard hanging upside down on a beam.

Regret filled her, heart and soul. It was like baiting a boy. Didn't he know how fragile his ego was? Asking if she found him compelling, asking how she might feel about him in the future, trying to earn her jealousy with the chit. All the while not caring if she lived or died, but wanting only the stroking he claimed was immaterial.

It suddenly struck Silver she'd only ever known one man who opened himself up to love and caring. And now that man ruled Fire clan—Paulo Ramirez. Paulo hadn't rid himself of the need for attachment, that much was true, or at least had been many years ago when they were lovers. She covered her thoughts quickly, lest Jet pick up a hint she knew Paulo and become suspicious of her motives.

He didn't speak, but he didn't dismiss her. She watched his chest rise and fall, his beautiful stomach muscles ripple, the mound of his cock and his muscular thighs beneath the silk of his wrap, his raven-black hair fanned out over a red pillow.

What a beautiful, complicated, wounded man. The most powerful man in Isla. And I'm doomed to care deeply about him. An ache in her chest warned her she might not hold back tears if she thought too long about Jet, about her situation, about all the losses and all of her own need to belong. She'd never be enough for this man. She wondered if any woman would.

He startled her by speaking. "You're relieved I did not name Aileen as my mate tonight."

"Nonsense."

"Liar."

She looked at his neck, at the red mark where the woman had lavished all her attention. "You'll have a bruise."

"Would you be gentler with your new lord?"

"Stop teasing me. I asked you to spare me your...attentions."

"It's a simple enough question."

Silver stood, fury building. "I'll answer simply. No, I would not be gentler. I would bite into your flesh and suck the very blood from your vein to taste your magic. I'd suck on your cock until you cried my name and begged

87

me to stop, begged me to continue, begged me to love you. I'd secure your limbs so you couldn't fight the pleasure. I'd climb onto your cock and fuck you like a base animal in the woods. And when you were finished, complete, satisfied beyond imagining, I'd do it all again. You'd be damned to think of me constantly, want me completely—despite your immunity for the need of others." She stood over him and took in his shocked expression. "No, I wouldn't do what Aileen did. That, my dear lord, was an adolescent display by a girl. Child's play. I, for one, believe you have chosen poorly. But perhaps that is all Wood women have to offer. A kiss of the neck."

"Silver." His voice was soft and she turned to him from the doorway.

"Lord?"

"Will you at least guard me well?"

"Aye, Lord, I will. I'll do that much for you. Thank you for the massage."

"Healing."

She disappeared into the front room and Jet let a groan escape. Child's play, she called it. Everything he'd ever done with a woman was no doubt child's play to her. And she wanted him, desperately, and wanted nothing to do with him. It would be terribly unkind to use her attraction to him. *And you like her, don't you? Strong and stubborn and beautiful, very beautiful. Those breasts, the creamy pale skin and pale rose nipples, hardened under your tongue.*

"I'd suck on your cock until you begged me to stop, begged me to continue, begged me to love you." Nonsense. A Wu Xing lord begging for sex or love…the woman thought fairly highly of her skills.

Jet crawled into bed, throwing his wrap to the floor, reaching out tentatively to Silver's mind, but she was nearly asleep, no doubt a result of the energy work. He rolled onto his stomach and groaned at the brush of silk against his cock, the brief thrill of fabric against hungry, burning skin. *What would her hand feel like? What would her mouth feel like, her womb?* An ache built and Jet reached his hand down his torso to caress the pain away. He tried to think of Aileen as he made long strokes down his hard shaft, but Silver's words made it impossible. *Turn about is fair play, Jet. Be certain you can win this flirtatious war before going into battle.* He muttered her name lowly as his hot essence poured into his hands. Jet stared at the ceiling, noting the lizard staring at him.

"What do you think I should do, my green friend?"

Leave her be. The answer rang out in the night air, and Jet rolled back onto his stomach and fell into a troubled sleep. In his dream, a Fire Pteran tore at the neck of Pete, and the boy's blood filled Isla.

Chapter Eight

A small, calloused hand brushed Silver's cheek, suddenly splintering a dream of Belanor, of her parents and childhood.

Pete's big brown eyes glowed in excitement. He offered her a mug, steaming with a fragrant brew.

"Tea. Very good for you. The lord's orders." Pete nodded proudly as he handed her the mug.

"Why am I in my quarters? How…?"

"I guess Jet carried you here."

"All this distance without waking me? I'm some bodyguard." Silver sat up and quickly pulled the blanket around her neck, realizing she was naked. Jet stripped her naked before laying her in bed?

"I think it was very early this morning. Jet's at practice now. No doubt wanted you to recover a bit more, Metal. Maybe you drank too much last night?"

"No, no Pete, it's not that."

Pete narrowed his eyes and bit at his lip. "Stayed up all night with Jet? Only talking, right?"

"Nothing like that, sweetheart." She patted the bed and Pete sat near her as she sipped the sweet, spicy tea. "Evidently I'm carrying around some bad Ch'i. The lord worked on it for me. Feeling a little wobbly, actually."

"Well, shake it off, Warrior. I'm in charge of your training today."

"I thought Jaine lost the coin toss?"

Pete snorted. "She'll be out for another five hours. Pickled, utterly pickled. Elsewise she'd be here, and trust me, you wouldn't like her the day after a bender."

"I can only imagine. All right, leave me be a bit and I'll get ready."

"Meet me at the dojo, and hurry. Eat something, but only cooling food, Jet said."

Pete pointed to a plate on a little table near the window filled with fruit and some pasty-looking substance. Before Silver could ask Pete the location of the dojo, he scurried out of the room, whooping and humming in glee.

I do like that boy.

Silver wandered to the table, blanket pulled around her, and pushed the window open to a glorious day, full of the promise of an early spring. The sun already held warmth and Silver turned her face to let the rays kiss her cheeks. A sparrow flitted to her windowsill and cocked his head to one side as if examining the stranger to Traier.

"Hello, pretty fellow."

"Hello yourself, Warrior." The cocky voice shimmered faintly in the air. The sparrow flew off quickly and Silver caught her breath. The stress, it must be all the stress. Fleeing Cirin and meeting Jet and...too much in the space of a few days. She'd ask the lord for some more healing, perhaps some meditation to ease her spirit a bit. With trembling hands she ate the fruit and scooped a bit of sweet cheese into her mouth.

"Greetings." A sharp tap on the open shutter startled her. "Oh, didn't mean to scare you. Simply bringing a gift from the herbalist guild." The matron bowed her gray head and smiled, pushing a package wrapped in fine parchment into Silver's hands.

"Thank you very much." Silver wondered if she held an explosive device. She started to unwrap the paper and the woman put a hand on hers to stop her. "Nay, Warrior, our way is to wait until the giver is gone. Therefore you are not obliged to express false glee. Understand?"

"What a wonderful idea. In any case, I'm grateful." Now she really worried the woman was trying to kill her.

"I'm next." A younger woman pressed in front of the herbalist and Silver nodded her head numbly in greeting, pulling her blanket more tightly around her shoulders.

"I'm Valera, and this is a gift of the perfumer's guild. The guild being me, my sisters, my mother and grandmother." Valera winked and pushed a bottle of oil filled with flower blossoms into Silver's hands.

A dozen more visitors lined up and pushed gifts of every sort and shape into Silver's hands. She accepted them graciously, hiding her confusion best she could. Her final visitor wrapped loudly at the shutter.

"Are you dressed?" Art chuckled softly when he saw the table covered with gifts. He wore training garb, now more warrior than priest, his silver hair tied back and a leather vest over soft suede shirt and pants. Relief washed over her at the sight of a familiar face.

"I'm not quite dressed, but that stopped no one else. What a difference a day makes in Traier. Your kin are a bit unpredictable."

"We're eminently predictable, Warrior. The Lord Jetre dresses you in his family's colors, seats you to his right at a ceremonial feast, and names you his permanent bodyguard. Tongues wag, rumors fly, and before you know it..." He gestured to the table. "I believe you may now wander the streets of Traier without looking over your shoulder for an attack."

"What do the folk of Traier know that I don't? Nothing's changed."

"Everything's changed. In any case, I'm not here to wag my tongue with the matrons. You'll need arms immediately. What are your weapons of choice?"

"The sai foremost. The stars are my second choice."

"Indeed. The stars we'll need to manufacture, unless there are enough recovered from our dead soldiers."

His meaning took hold slowly, and she nodded. *Yes, you've killed some of Jetre's men and women, haven't you Silver?* It now seemed unnatural, abhorrent. Perhaps the son of the matron who walked past, or the brother of the man sweeping the street? War is unnatural.

"I'm afraid war is most natural for the likes of Trueborn, Elf and Were. I will have your weapons ready sometime today."

"General? My position as bodyguard—it's ceremonial? Surely the lord detects any threat long before his circle of protectors?"

"Quite true." Art leaned in the window a bit and spoke in a quieter tone. "I believe he wants the company." He inclined his head and left Silver to ponder his words. She pulled the shutters tight lest more visitors shower her with gifts and turned to unwrapping the packages on the table—dresses and shirts and underthings, shoes and a pair of soft leather boots, potions and lotions and foodstuffs, jewelry and even a bit of rouge. A change of attitude, indeed, she thought, and picked from the gifts a shirt and leggings, tall boots and an intricately carved belt.

The walk to the dojo differed substantially from the previous evening's walk to the lord's quarters. Children danced alongside her and pointed the way, matrons waved from their doorways; men bowed their heads and lifted their caps. One woman squealed and waved frantically, calling to her family. "Come look, she's wearing the blouse. She's wearing the blouse." The woman flushed as Silver approached her house.

"This blouse is your handiwork? It's lovely, and fits like a glove. Thank you very much, Lady…"

"Glory. Oh, call me Glory." The plump woman clapped her hands in glee and her blonde curls bobbed as she did. "Stayed up all night to make it, I did. Once I eyed your figure, so to speak. Quite a figure it is, if you don't mind me saying so, Warrior Atra."

"Well, thank you." *She stayed up all night sewing?*

"Warrior Atra?" Glory stepped forward tentatively and looked furtively from side to side. "Might you tell me if it's true?"

"I'm sorry, Glory. If what is true?"

"If you and the lord…you know…" Glory wiggled her eyebrows and puckered her lips in a mock kiss.

"Mother, no. Certainly not. Absolutely not."

"Oh." The woman looked crushed. "I heard tell you spoke to a sparrow this morning. That would mean you have a bit of the Elf blood, and of course, you'd be eligible and all... What a shame. The two of you look rather resplendent together."

"Resplendent?"

"Aye." The woman nodded proudly at her choice of words.

"Glory, someone saw me speak to a sparrow?" Her heart sunk. Now she'd get a reputation for insanity. An insane, resplendent Trueborn.

"Oh no, the sparrow told us. Does mean you have some Elf. Still, if the lord doesn't fancy you, it's water under the dam."

"It's 'over the dam' and 'under the bridge'."

"In any case, I suppose we're saddled with Aileen after all." Glory spat at the ground, cursing Aileen's name. "She's a nice pair of tits with an empty skull atop, if you get my meaning. We're not pulling for her in my household. But of course, Warrior, only one vote counts."

The sparrow told them? The sparrow told them?

A boy sidled up to Glory and blinked at Silver with huge blue eyes. Glory ruffled his curly blond hair. "Sunny, this is Warrior Atra."

"Are you truly Kilé's sister?" The boy sputtered suddenly and Glory slapped the side of his head.

"Yes, Kilé was my brother."

"And you'll help us kill Cirin? Truly? It's not a trick, Metal?"

"Back inside, Sunny." The boy turned glumly. "I'm sorry, he lost his father at Kronish. Not a big fan of your clan."

"Nor am I. At least I'm no fan of Cirin's." Silver turned her wrist to show her Wood brand.

Glory smiled. "Aye, you'll help us defeat the devil what killed the lord's parents, that's what I told my Sunny."

"Thanks again for the blouse, Glory. Please come visit me sometime? I know no one in Traier, besides the lord and his family." *Why, Silver? Why would you offer such a thing to this stranger?*

Because she seems kind, and good, and trusting. And you haven't met anyone kind and good in many months. Not among your own, at least. But she speaks to sparrows... She picked up her pace, anxious to question Pete or Art on the topic. *A bit of the Elf blood?*

✻ ✻ ✻

Her young guides huddled at the broad entrance of the dojo, watching the masters at work. Silver hid behind the onlookers—not ready, not willing—to face the formidable group. Not ready to face the powerful man who confused her, heart and soul.

Amidst a dozen warriors practicing forms and weapons, Jet instructed Pete in a complicated series of aerial kicks. Jet wore the baggy black pants of the practitioners, but no shirt. Sweat glistened on his tan chest and stomach, strands of his black hair fell from his braid into his eyes.

Art spotted her and motioned her forward into the huge building. Doors on each side of the dojo opened to the warm breeze, which carried the scent of incense from a shrine in the corner. One wall housed an assortment of magnificent weapons—swords, staffs, knives, nunchakus, and others Silver didn't recognize. A huge symbol of Wu Xing, Wood clan, covered a second wall. Jet's colors—green and silver—were everywhere—chairs, benches, cushions, banners, even a water barrel.

"Damn it, Pete! You should know this by now." Jet's voice echoed through the room, now quiet as the others stopped to watch the boy. Silver sat near Art on a bench and held her breath, praying for Pete to do well.

Pete executed one quick spin with a wheel kick, a second in the air, and a third...to land on his ass in the sand. Jet pulled him up with one strong arm.

"Again." Jet's order made Silver nervous, and she wondered how terrified Pete must feel. The boy brushed himself off and tried again, with the same result.

Jet pulled him up more quickly and Pete didn't bother dusting off the sand, but went right into the kick and fell again. His cheeks flushed bright red from his efforts and his long hair stuck to the sweat and dirt on his back.

"That was the worst yet."

Pete nodded seriously.

Silver turned to Art in horror, wondering how a master could take such a terrible approach to teaching. Her instructors had always been patient, always encouraged her.

"That's terrible," she whispered to Art behind her hand.

"Indeed. The worst sequence I've seen the boy execute."

Jet squatted next to Pete and grabbed his arm tightly. Silver stood, biting her tongue as she died to lash out, but Art pulled her back to the bench. Jet whispered something to Pete, who nodded fervently and fell to his belly. Pete pushed out a hundred perfect push-ups while Jet counted. When Pete finished, Jet pulled him up again.

"Petrov Artraud, what is your guiding principle?" Jet asked sternly.

"Never retreat in battle."

Pete bounced up and down a few times, shaking his arms and moving his head side to side to loosen up. With a bloodcurdling yell, he took three leaping steps and spun, kicked, spun in the air, and spun a third time, head over heels, without touching the ground. He floated, Silver thought. And landed in a perfect split with another yell.

"Better." Jet nodded briefly and walked to the water barrel, scooping a mug of water. He handed it to Pete, who panted heavily. Pete smiled in appreciation and gulped down the water.

"Ready? Ten times, until the sequence meets your own standards. If you need assistance, we'll try again tomorrow."

"Thanks, Jet." The brothers bowed formally to one another. Jet then ruffled Pete's hair and snuck in a quick punch to the gut, starting a playful battle that lasted only a few moments.

Jet's smile lit up the room, Silver thought, and she found herself laughing with the brothers and Art. *Who is this wonderful man? How many sides does he have?*

Art glanced down at her and Silver met his eyes. "All right, since you're reading my thoughts, perhaps you'll honor me with an answer. Lord Jetre is the most complicated person I've met. Do you agree?"

Art rubbed his chin in mock concentration. "No. I do not agree. Jet is the model of simplicity."

Silver sighed. "Now you tease me. You Wood clan are all very humorous."

"I do not tease you. As all the elements flow to create a whole, so does our Jetre. As yin and yang combine in a seamless circle, so does our Jetre. He is light and dark, wise and foolish, proud and humble, kind and ruthless, soft and hard...shall I go on?"

Silver shook her head. "I get the idea. But I don't think I'll ever understand him."

"Oh, you want to understand him?" Art laughed heartily. "My dear Warrior, you must let him in. He won't open the door first, trust me. I don't think you're quite willing to take the risk, are you?" He didn't wait for her answer, but stood and greeted his lord.

Jet ignored her presence and Pete joined her on the bench.

"Hey, Ugly, you were pretty spectacular."

"I was spectacularly ugly, you mean. I'll have it down by Beltane."

"What's Beltane?"

"Um, not sure. But it's on Monday. A very old holiday. People who knew about it died long ago. But we still call the first day of the month of May Beltane." Pete shrugged. "It's a day off from lessons."

"What did Jet say to you, before, to help you get the kick?"

"He cautioned me not to dishonor him in your presence. I didn't, did I?"

Pete's eyes searched hers for the truth and she pulled him in close, rubbing his damp back, taking in the sweet spiciness of the boy's exertions still pouring from him.

"You did not dishonor your lord. I think you're spectacular in every way."

I want to hate you, Jet, I do.

Pete grabbed a towel and wiped the sweat and dirt from his arms. "Now it's your turn, Silver. I'm to rate your skills and report to Jet."

"Wonderful." She watched Jet leave the dojo without glancing at her, and sighed in relief. At least she wouldn't have to prove herself while he watched. *He has little interest in you, anyway, Silver. Put him out of your mind for a while.*

"All right, Master Petrov, what would you have me do?"

Pete motioned for her to stand and walked to the center of the dojo. He bowed formally and she returned his bow, realizing suddenly the boy outranked her in every way. She stood at attention and waited for his instructions. From the corner of her eye, she saw Art and a growing crowd of onlookers jockey for position to watch.

"Your highest form. We'll start with the bo."

Silver's stomach clenched, and she pushed down the butterflies that hadn't plagued her since her training. The staff was her worst weapon, and she was to perform it before the Wood clan, renowned for their mastery of the bo, as they called it.

Silver bowed and caught the heavy staff Art threw to her. *You can do this, Silver.*

Pete nodded for her to begin. She moved through the form at a steady pace, struggling with each move to envision her opponent, to create a sense of realistic fighting, worried she failed miserably. When she bowed at the conclusion of the form, her cheeks flushed in embarrassment.

"Not terrible." Pete smiled and Silver blew a bit of air from her lungs. "Close to terrible, but not terrible."

"Thanks."

"I take it you wouldn't try to kill with the bo?"

"I'd run away."

"Good idea. The sai?"

"Yes, sir." Art handed Silver a pair of sai, tri-pronged short weapons. Silver weighed the sai, casting both from one hand to the other in confidence. "Very beautiful, very balanced."

"Very ancient. Begin."

Silver bowed, closed her eyes and took in a deep calming breath. The familiar feel of molten metal moved through her body and her energy rose each time she filled her lungs. And suddenly she was there, nowhere, out of body, out of time and place. For five minutes only, indeed, five minutes exactly, for she knew precisely how long the form took, Silver moved through the ancient path of Metal, leaping and lunging low, spinning the sai and plunging them into her opponents, crying out in victory at each thrust.

She bowed breathlessly and realized as she came back to her senses the crowd was utterly silent. She looked to Pete for some sign, some approval. A slow grin spread to his face and the crowd applauded loudly.

"Not bad." Pete laughed and slapped her on the back. He leaned in closely. "Holy Mother, you're amazing. Wait til I tell Jet."

"No need." Jet's voice sent chills up her spine. "My sai, please?" He approached the pair slowly, arms across his chest.

"Yours?" Silver handed the weapons to him and winced at the amusement in his eyes. *Oh Mother, he's laughing at the best you have to offer.*

"Mine." He motioned to Art, who handed him a bowl of throwing stars. Silver recognized most as those of her clan, knew they were recovered from bodies, not battlefields.

Jet extended the bowl, looking deeply into Silver's eyes. She took a half dozen in a practiced motion and waited for her instructions.

He waved the others away and moved very close, close enough that she smelled his unique, spicy scent, a muskiness filling her in a way she wanted to ignore. Jet leaned in, his long hair brushing her shoulder. Silver flinched, and he steadied her with a hand on her back. "Do not shame me in front of my people."

Jet walked to the far wall, yards away, where he stood against a wood plank bearing the wounds of many strikes.

No. He can't mean for me to do this.

Silver's hand shook and she fingered the stars nervously. She shook her head no, but Jet narrowed his eyes, a sly smirk spreading to his face.

"That's an order," his voice slid into her mind.

"Aye, Lord." Silver glanced at the crowd, poised in amazement at the scene. It suddenly occurred to her she held the life of the great Lord Jetre in her hands. One precise throw to his neck, and his life would flow freely onto the sand. *Why would he put himself in this position? What is he trying to prove? You could assassinate him now, as any of Metal clan would. And it would be a dishonorable trick. One Cirin would play.*

She turned her back to Jet and faced the crowd, saw the intensity of her own expression reflected in their nervous eyes. She inhaled deeply and spun to her target, releasing the blades in rapid succession. It took no longer than a few seconds. The crowd burst into applause again and rushed into the room to examine the achievement.

"I do believe I'm stuck." Jet laughed as he extracted one of the stars to free his long hair. When he stepped away, a perfect arch of stars remained, forming the outline of his head.

He threw one high in the air and snatched it as it came down, pushed it into his pocket, and left the dojo without pause.

Silver's legs shook and she reached out to the open air, struggling to find support, sure she would fall. Pete rushed to her and steadied her by her waist.

"Why did he do that, Pete?"

"I'm not sure. I get the feeling he's testing you."

"No kidding, you think?"

But for what?

Pete took her hand. "That's enough for today. Let's get out of here—I'll show you more of Traier. And we can go swimming."

"We'll freeze. It snowed two days ago."

"Nah, winter's over. Besides, I'll show you the hot springs."

"Whatever you like, Pete." Silver couldn't think for herself, adrenaline wearing off, headache looming, nerves frayed. *Why not let a ten-year-old plan your day?*

Chapter Nine

Jaine tapped her fingers on the table in a gesture that annoyed the hell out of Jet. "I haven't forgiven you, Jet. I was to have a date tonight."

"A date? That's what you call them? Mother help us. Surely you can go without sex for a week? I've managed for ten years."

"Managing less and less—that's my guess, brother. What think you, Art? Jet seems a bit testy these days?"

"Nonsense. He's always testy." Art leaned back in his chair and propped his tall boots on the round table.

Jet waved off the silliness and looked at Art and Jaine carefully. *I need them both very much right now.*

"Where's the woman?"

"The woman?" Jaine scoffed. "Now she's 'the woman'?"

Jaine poked him in the chest and he knew she caught him. "'The woman' is with Pete, who—by the way—is quite mad for her. You'd best speak with him on the subject. He's heartbroken enough these days."

"What do you mean? They're becoming friends. He's ten."

"He's ten going on twenty, like you were. And he's quite mad for her. Speaks of nothing else." Jaine insisted, crossing her arms in annoyance. "Can we get on with this, Jet? What's the plan?"

Jet nodded. Jaine knew his heart, too clearly. Silver distracted him from enormous issues that boded poorly for his clan. The victory at Kor-Mashran was a fleeting one.

"Mikalis brought in intelligence this morning—Paulo Ramirez sorties three days west on the coast, in Logan. A thousand soldiers."

Art rubbed the rim of his glass mug with a finger, calling forth a hum. "Shouldn't be too much of a problem. He's weaker than you. His soldiers are weaker than ours."

"He's weak, but he's no fool. And he has those blasted beasts."

Jaine stood and paced. "He can't mean a direct attack on Traier? He's on his way to Belanor, to Cirin."

"We can't be sure." Dread crept into his gut. "That could be as bad as a direct hit. Cirin would likely fall to Paulo. If Paulo can hold on to Metal, if he can win their allegiance, he has a chance against us. We'd be hopelessly outnumbered."

Jaine squatted near Jet's chair and grabbed him by the arm. "It's time. It's long past time. Take Belanor, head on. What are you waiting for? You have 'the woman,'—learn something from her instead of mooning at her."

Why are you waiting, Jet? She's right.

"He is mooning a bit, isn't he?" Art sipped from his mug but Jet caught his sly smile. "Shame she's not Elf. Suppose he's stuck with Aileen. But any port in a storm. Of course, it's a lifelong port. One dock only. I'd want to choose wisely. Shame, that. Not a bit of Elf."

"What's your point, Art? You're about as subtle as Pete."

Jaine sighed. "He's reminding you your time is up and Warrior Atra is off limits. Who's it going to be, Lord? I hate Aileen and will make her life a living hell, but of course, you can't take that into consideration."

"It matters not who I take, as long as she meets the requirements."

Oh, Mother. A thousand women from which to choose, and you're stalling because it can't be Silver? Because you want—what? A few more days with her, a kiss, a touch?

Art chuckled. "Though it's odd a Metal Trueborn would have the Hearing, isn't it?"

Jaine yelped. "What?"

Jet's heart raced.

"Silver was seen talking to birds this morning. Several witnesses, in fact, including the sparrow himself."

"Nonsense." Jet waited anxiously for Art to go on.

"Of course, she doesn't understand it. Must think herself daft. I wonder how many generations ago one of her ancestors mated with an elf?"

Jet's mind reeled. "That's why she hears me clearly, why I read her easily, much more easily than those outside Wood clan."

"She *hears* you? Oh, Mother of us all! She doesn't look like an ounce of Wood blood runs in her veins."

"Dismissed." Jet snapped and regretted it instantly. *You are testy.* He simply needed quiet, needed it desperately. Jaine and Art rose to leave. "We'll talk of Paulo later, after I've a chance to speak with Silver." The two nodded and left, talking lowly and snickering.

He breathed deeply, breathed in the new spring air and watched as a sparrow settled on the windowsill and cocked his head back and forth.

"Hello, Lord."

"Hello yourself. Are you the one…oh, never mind." The bird flew off and Jet rested his head in his hands. Seven days. No, six now. He'd choose a life partner. And within a week, he'd also battle Paulo or Cirin. It started. The first step towards full power. And the first step towards a republic.

Master Guo, I'll make you proud. I'll rule more wisely than you dreamed possible.

It might be easier to defeat a clan than to choose a wife, he thought. If she were truly Elf, even in the tiniest measure… But how could he mate with Kilé's sister, with a Metal Warrior? How could he not, he groaned, thinking of the brave, skilled, beautiful woman who now insinuated herself into every waking moment of his life, made his groin ache and his cheeks burn and his chest…made his chest tight.

I'm trying to ignore you, Silver. It's not working. Where had all the training gone, what happened to his calm center, his ocean of peaceful isolation?

❋ ❋ ❋

Jaine fell into step with Silver as she took the winding street up to Jetre's quarters.

Silver struggled to regain some composure after the summoning that had panicked her—a sharp tap on the door that woke her from a light afternoon nap. A skinny boy, around Pete's age, handed her the note. She unfurled the paper and squinted to take in the precise Trueborn lettering. Jetre's hand, no doubt, for he managed to make her language look like Elven script. The contents mystified her, excited her, terrified her…and angered her. The tone was unmistakable; there would be no questioning his directive. *He's your lord, your master, Silver. Did you expect an engraved invitation to dinner, some flowers perhaps? It's not about you, it's not about any feelings for you.*

"Warrior Silver—

Arrive before sundown for our meal. Prepare your things, for you will move into my quarters permanently this night."

The only signature was his seal in wax, willow branches and the ancient symbol for Wu Xing Wood.

"What do you carry to my brother, Warrior?" Jaine's voice grated on her nerves, loaded with insinuation and contempt.

"I'm tired, Jaine. Please, can we put the taunting off until tomorrow?" Silver pulled the heavy satchel of gifts further onto her shoulder.

Jaine grasped Silver's arm tightly to stop her. "Come, sit, and I'll keep the taunting to a minimum while you rest."

Silver sighed. "As you like." They sat on a bench carved into a massive fallen tree. Silver rubbed her hand along the polished wood. "Everything here fits. The Wood clan blends into the land, like it was born from the earth, from Isla itself."

Jaine nodded. "It was. So was your clan. You simply don't understand the truth of it. You find Traier beautiful. It is. And if you trusted me, you'd admit you find the people beautiful and kind. They are. And if you trusted yourself, you'd say you find Jetre beautiful. He's more than beautiful. If you tell him I said that, I'll kill you. But you won't say those things, because you're Metal, and you won't admit the truth."

"How dare you. You call me a liar?"

Jaine shrugged and pulled candy from her pocket, offering a piece to Silver. Silver declined and Jaine shrugged again, concentrated on unwrapping her treasure.

"I'm not going to waste my time chatting about your feelings. I don't give a damn about your feelings. I want you to stay away from Pete."

"Pete? Why?" Her stomach clenched in warning. "He's simply lost and wants a friend. Well, perhaps he's not able to distinguish between a friend and a...girlfriend. I don't understand how a boy his age has these feelings."

"You've a lot to learn, Silver. Stop thinking of Pete as a typical boy. He is, in many ways, but his spirit is very old. He's an avatar—he remembers. Do you understand? The boy remembers his lives. His soul knows what it is to love a woman. His body and mind simply haven't caught up yet. When they do..." Jaine whistled softly.

"And Jet? Is he the same?"

"Aye. And then some."

Jaine whistled a high note several times and a bluebird flitted from a high tree and landed on her arm. She held the bird towards Silver, who shuddered in alarm. *Not again. I'm starting to fear small birds.*

"You heard I greeted a sparrow this morning. Big deal."

"No, it's no big deal to greet an animal. The big deal is you heard him speak. Why don't you say something to my friend, here? I call him Bunky."

"Bunky?"

"Bunky, say hello to Warrior Silver."

Bunky hopped onto Silver's hand and looked up at her. "Hello, Warrior. I'm a bluebird. I'm a bluebird."

The blood in her veins ran cold and she gasped for air. Bunky flew off and Jaine cleared her throat dramatically.

"I have to run, have a date. Although Jet pretty much fixed it so I'm not getting any tonight, the asshole. Which brings me to my next point—my brother chooses a mate in less than one week. I do not want her to be an insipid, untalented, unintelligent slut."

"I'm sure the lord wouldn't pick such a woman." *Aileen. I hate her. I would like to press a knife into her stomach and turn it...*

"The lord *would* pick such a woman, because if he can't have an equal partner, he'll settle for a slave—one who won't nag and contradict him. You see?"

"Surely there's an attractive, intelligent woman in Traier? Some middle ground between Jet's equal and an empty-headed maid?"

"Many such woman. But you're the one on his mind, Metal. I saw it the moment we laid you into bed, when he sucked the pteran's poison from your shoulder, when he undressed you. Looked like he wanted to move his mouth a bit lower to suck on those nice tits of yours. I know Jet as well as anyone can, I suppose, as well as he lets us know him. But I know what I see in his eyes. He doesn't hide everything."

"Everything?" Silver's heart pounded and nerves tingled in hope and fear and longing.

"You've spent too much time with Pete. We're not giggling girls, Warrior. You know damned well what I'm getting at. The man's hard for you. Real hard."

Jaine stood and popped another candy into her mouth. "Like it or not, Warrior, birds spoke to you today and you heard them. You hear Jet's thoughts. Someone jumped off your family tree and slipped into the night to mate with a lowly Wood Elf. You're eligible. I can't say you'd be my first choice, but I'll take you over Aileen. And I don't want you to fuck it up."

"Eligible? How would I fuck it up? Wait, what are we talking about? I don't understand any of this." Eligible—the word spun in her head and settled in her stomach. *Eligible but not wanted. Or wanted? No, he wanted no one, he had said as much.*

"Eligible. What's the Trueborn saying? 'The way to a man's heart is through his stomach.' Well…"

"I know." Silver interrupted numbly. "It's a few inches further down."

Jaine laughed loudly and slung her pack over her shoulder. "Don't forget it. I suspect you have skills enough to satisfy a man who's been celibate for his adult life. Seduce him."

"Seduce him? Seduce a clan lord who still holds to his oath? Why?"

"Because he wants you to. You are fairly dense. Maybe what they say about Metal clan is true. What the people of Traier don't know won't hurt them. Well, Art's waiting. See you later."

"Art's your date?"

Jaine winked. "We have to keep it quiet because my dear brother keeps claiming me. I'm supposed to be chaste. I'm fairly anxious for his oath to finish. Of course, Jet's a bit more anxious about it." Jaine snorted and started on her way, but thought better of it and suddenly turned back and knelt close to Silver, brought her lips to her ear. Light perfume and ale and the woodsy scent of her clan—it made Silver gasp audibly to be close to the lovely woman, Jet's female counterpart.

Jaine cupped her hand around her mouth. "Our cousin, Mikalis—he's sweet on Jet. Get it? And he's done his best to convince Jet to be a lover of men. I don't think it works that way, but I wouldn't know. But here's the thing, Metal. You might want to keep open-minded, so to speak. In case our lord is *adventurous*, shall we say?"

"Adventurous? I don't understand."

"Jet picks only one woman, and he picks her for life. It's the way of our clan. You have no worries there. The bed might become a bit crowded in other ways, get it? And it might serve you well to open yourself up to it." Jaine backed away and grinned slyly. "I'd offer up Art, but only if I can watch."

"You'd watch your brother mate?"

Jaine shrugged. "He's the most beautiful man on Isla. Why not?" She made her way down the cobbled street, leaving Silver's mind reeling and heart racing.

❋ ❋ ❋

The lord's brand burned again, and Silver rubbed her wrist to ease the sensation. She watched him in the inner garden, walking idly from rose bush to lilac tree, inspecting blossoms, looking distracted. He wore a long, sleeveless tunic, open to his waist, revealing his muscular arms and chest.

He sensed her presence; she knew it, although he didn't turn to greet her. His scent wafted on the breeze, mixed with the sweetness of blossoms of every variety. Silver struggled desperately to push down the longing building hourly, whether she was with him or not. *Eligible. Did he know it? He must. But not worthy. Not wanted.*

Jet turned quickly and arched a brow, and raw male power and beauty brushed away her thoughts. "You are late."

"You may blame your sister, Lord. She detained me for a series of hints, warnings, and insinuations."

He laughed lightly and his eyes gleamed in amusement. "You have my sympathies. Imagine a lifetime of it." Grabbing her satchel and dropping it to the ground, he gestured for her to join him on a landing overlooking the town.

Her mouth went dry as she noticed the table set for two, candles and blossoms floating in a silver bowl. It looked romantic. *No. Put it out of your head.*

"You don't think me capable of a bit of romance?"

"Stop pulling at my thoughts. It's rude. And no, I don't think romance is your style. Nor would I understand the appropriateness of a romantic dinner between lord and bodyguard."

He pulled her chair out and sat near her, pouring dark wine into silver goblets. "We shall see."

The butterflies returned to her stomach as Jet propped his chin in one hand and regarded her seriously. A deep drink of wine did nothing to calm her nerves, and she finally stared back. *Seduce him? Do you want to seduce him? Oh, Mother, more than anything.*

"Is there something you want to say, Jet? Is there something you want me to say? You're making me very uncomfortable."

"Why?" He was close enough so she could see tiny flecks of silver and green in his midnight-dark eyes. Individual eyelashes, black as night, a tiny, scarred ridge marring one cheek, a small beauty mark on the other cheek— every detail called to her to reach out and caress, hold, own any part of him, if for a second. Looking away, she struggled to mask the ache for him clutching at her soul.

The sunset cast a pink glow on the rooftops of Traier. Silver concentrated on the town, spotting the dojo with its green and silver pennant flapping in the breeze. He remained silent, and she thought she might scream if he didn't move away, or touch her, or say something. A servant rescued her, bringing a tray of artfully arranged morsels of game, cheese and bread.

She concentrated on the meal, but his silence cut through her like a piercing scream.

I can't do this. She dropped her fork and folded her arms across her chest.

"What am I doing here?"

"You're eating." He waved a forkful of food in the air. "Although you aren't doing a very good job. By all that is holy, what ails you, Silver? Has it occurred to you a private meal with the clan lord is an honor?"

"Honor? You're taunting me."

"I am?" He looked truly confused. "I sensed you favored me. Fairly strongly, in fact."

"All the women of Traier favor you rather strongly, I'm sure. What's your point?"

A great sigh escaped from Jet and he leaned back in his chair, eyeing Silver carefully. "I don't know these games between men and women. And I can't blame the oath, because I haven't yet met the man who claims to

110

understand this ritual. What would you have me do? It might be easier if you stop shielding your energy. Let me in your mind if you won't open your mouth and fucking spit it out."

Silver started at his curse and sudden frustration. The air between them fluoresced briefly as his strong energy filled the air. *Oh, don't get this one angry, he's very powerful. Why hadn't he overtaken all of Isla? What control he must exert to always seem the calm, controlled master. There's a cauldron of heat bubbling beneath the surface.*

"I'll do whatever you want, Jet. I'll tell you what you want to know, but ask me outright. I'm confused. Jaine tells me things that may or may not be true and you treat me differently every time I meet you and I don't know my future or how you feel about me..." Silver winced at her words and clamped her hand over her mouth. He'd think she was soft, a simpleton.

"How I *feel* about you?"

A flush of humiliation flared in her cheeks and she bit at her lip and cocked her chin up in an attempt to maintain some ground, regain her pride.

He looked deeply into her eyes and all the world froze in time and space for a split second as their souls met. She saw his sudden intake of breath—he felt it too. *Oh, Mother, I'm lost to him, and he knows it now.* Absorbed in his own thoughts, Jet pushed his hand through his long hair and gazed out over his city, seemingly taking in nothing.

"How I *feel* about you?" He mumbled and rubbed at his palm, as if to scratch the Wu Xing symbol of his clan from his skin. "My feelings are not for your ears, not for anyone's. My desires are to be fulfilled, my orders followed, my leadership respected."

Silver bowed her head as a hand clutched at her heart. *You're stupid, Silver. Women are stupid.*

"It's not stupid to want, Warrior. I must put aside my attachments, keep my energy whole for my clan, but you have no need to put your desires aside. What do you desire?"

Facing her again, he suddenly put his palm to her cheek and brushed at her hair with his fingertips. "Look at me, Silver. Why are you crying? Tell me the truth."

With a shrug, she brushed away a tear. "My brother's dead, I am dead to my clan, I have no one, have nothing, am no closer to killing Cirin, and have gained nothing from trying an alliance with you but humiliation and heartbreak. I wish I'd never laid eyes on you, that I'd fled Belanor for the countryside. Is that what you want to know?"

"Have I humiliated you? Have I broken your heart?"

"No, I've done it to myself."

She stood and grabbed her satchel. "Tell your sister her trick was cruel. She led me to believe…"

"Ah, I see. Jaine hinted I might choose you as my mate."

Silver snorted in derision. "You have a very amusing family."

"I do."

"Well, run me through the back with your blade, Lord, because I'm going to defy your order to stay here. I'm leaving your service, leaving Traier. Please give my best to Pete." Her tears overtook her and she dropped her satchel and covered her face. "Tell him how much I liked knowing him."

He stood and moved towards her slowly, finally standing inches away and clutching her wrists.

"What do you desire, Silver?"

In one easy motion, he scooped her into his arms and strode into his quarters, dumping Silver on the pillows scattered about the floor. She sat up in protest and he pushed her to the floor. Blood pounding in her ears, burning for him to kiss her, she tentatively pulled away from his grasp.

"Silver, I'm irked. You ruined a perfectly pleasant dinner. My first romantic dinner, *ever*."

"Don't play with me, Jet. Let me leave Traier. First I'll tell you all I know—you have my word."

He pinned her arms over her head and hovered inches above her, nose to nose, angling his mouth over hers.

"I have no use for your knowledge. I can pull what I need from your mind. My spies tell me everything else of use. Do you want to leave me?"

Silver closed her eyes tightly, pressed her lips together. His strong probe delved into her thoughts, and she struggled fiercely to block him, but knew it was useless.

He grabbed her hair and her eyes shot open.

"I asked you a fucking question, Warrior, and you'll answer me aloud, *now*. Do you want to leave me?"

"Yes."

His dark laugh cut through her. The scent of Traier wafted from him—woods and spring air and spices. His long hair brushed at her breastbone, his hands burned into her wrists.

"You find this amusing?"

"I find you amusing."

He smirked and lowered his lips very slowly to hers, merely brushing his skin against hers. She struggled against his grip and kicked at his legs.

"Tsk tsk. Such insolence." Jet pressed his body along hers, crushing her beneath strong legs.

"Fuck you, Lord."

He winked mischievously. "In less than a week." Again he brought his lips gently to hers, this time pressing a bit harder, brushing side to side briefly. He let a low moan escape and moved his mouth to her ear. "I like it when you struggle."

In less than a week. In less than a week. His words pounded through her, a flair of hope racing with them. *No. He truly means to break his oath with me? But, he must choose one only...*

Releasing her arms, he laced his hands in her hair and moved his lips to her neck, whispering in an ancient tongue she couldn't understand. With each hot breath, she arched up to pull him in, aching to be closer, to be joined.

113

"A bit of practice, Silver. Perhaps my kiss?"

Shuddering under his hot breath, Silver pushed at his chest to stop him. "I won't help ready you to please another woman. I won't ready you for your mating. You can't ask this of me."

Yelling in frustration, he brought his hand to her neck and stared into her eyes, his smoldering with anger and lust.

"Enough. I can't announce my choice except before my clan. I won't. You've disturbed my peace, but you won't disturb my sworn duties. Now put aside this stupidity, this simpering and complaining. It annoys me, Warrior. It's beneath you, and you know it. I don't care how hard your life has been, how insecure you pretend to be. Use your instincts and tell me what you know in your soul to be true."

"I don't know what you mean. You're cruel." But she *did* know precisely what he meant. *He wants me. He's chosen me. Mother of us all, it cannot be true. But it is.*

His palm moved along her stomach and reached down beneath her leggings, pressing against her pelvis. She started in shock and quickly shuddered in pain as he burned his brand into her skin, as he had done the first night they met. The scorching pain dissipated quickly, and turned to pleasure as his spirit, his Ch'i, poured through her veins, filling every fiber of her body, mind and soul. He had claimed her again, but this time, he claimed her sex.

"Don't be a coward, Silver. Your brother Desmen was a coward. Kilé was not. Choose honesty, bravery. Claim your birthright as a proud warrior, a proud woman. Tell me what you know is between us, and stop pretending. You aren't an unwanted fetus in your mother's womb."

He pulled her up and they sat face to face, both with labored breathing, lips nearly touching. Her skin stung from his brand and her head spun, but she rallied herself to stare deeply into his eyes.

"Why did you brand me again? What does it mean?"

He simply arched a brow.

"No other man would touch me now with your mark on me."

A slow smile crept to his lips. "A man would need my permission to touch you now. There's a difference."

"Would you give permission?"

"Dear woman, you have no idea."

"I'm getting the picture."

"I doubt that very much. May I kiss you now? Are we clear on where we stand?"

He didn't wait for her answer, but broke the few inches between them, leaning in, pulling her by the neck to his mouth. His kiss was stunning, frantic, powerful, and it took Silver a moment to respond. His tongue probed at every bit of her mouth, and she sucked on his tongue and lips, aching to touch all of him, be touched everywhere.

"I'm falling in love with you, Jet."

"That's very convenient. Now quiet your mouth and your mind and give me what you promised."

"What did I promise?"

"To best Aileen's kiss of my neck. Don't you recall? I remember every word."

"You won't choose her?" Silver winced at his expression. He looked as if he wanted to throttle her.

"Give me a bit of credit."

"You were trying to make me jealous? Truly?"

"Aayee, stubborn. Yes, I was trying to make you jealous. And it worked. And now I'm fucking *here*, and you want me more than you've ever wanted anything in the world, and your chatter makes me want to jump off the parapets of Traier's high walls."

His tirade didn't completely cover a subtle smile, and his massive erection still pushed as hard as ever against her leg. Silver's heart bled a trifling more hope as she looked deeply into his eyes.

"I lied, Lord."

"Now what?"

"I'm already in love with you."

He leaned in for another desperate kiss, and they sparred and spoke wordlessly with their lips and tongues, breathlessly, endlessly. Jet lavished her cheeks and forehead and chin and neck with quick kisses, only to return to her mouth, more frantic each time. "Oh by all that is holy, you are more than I ever imagined a woman would be. I've chosen wisely. Keep your promise now. Take me, Silver."

Chapter Ten

The words were out of his mouth before he could call them back. *You asked her to take you, like a young girl. You've told her she's to become your wife. You broke your oath of intention. What will she think?*

The tears slipping from her eyes, her growing smile, the energy of relief and joy wafting from her spirit, all calmed his fears. Slipping away from him, she scrambled to her feet. He rose to hold her but she simply extended her hand for him to be still.

"Rid yourself of your tunic, Lord. I want to see my prize." Jet laughed at her urgent expression and pulled his tunic over his head. His laughter died as Silver slowly pulled off her blouse, kicked off her shoes, and unlaced her pants. He watched in wonder as she revealed a thin patch of silk covering her mound. His recent brand puckered her skin, and he longed to run his tongue across the willow branches etched in the creamy whiteness to soothe her pain.

But she only had eyes for his cock, hard beyond his memory, full and already weeping for her. *You can't take her now. Only a few days.*

"Show me, Jet. Show me what you do alone. Or do you perform for others?"

He nodded, knowing he didn't answer her, not caring. The throbbing of his cock spread through his body, his energy sliding into the air as he brought his palm to his shaft and spread the pearly liquid across the head.

"Jaine said you're hard for me, Jet. Are you?"

"Get your fucking mouth down here, Warrior."

"Does the oath allow it?"

She turned her back to him and wandered around his quarters, blowing out candles until only one burned, casting shadows on his torso.

"I cannot seed you."

Silver kneeled next to him and brought her lips onto his. She moved to his neck, scorching his skin with her tongue, licking her way to his chest, tweaking his nipples in her teeth.

Jet moaned in agony, sure he wouldn't survive the night, sure this woman would kill him with longing.

He barely heard her questions, uttered quickly between kisses. "Women have sucked your cock? No? I don't believe it."

"Didn't trust myself or others...the oath."

"And you trust yourself now?"

"I don't care."

Her mouth traced down his stomach with exquisite thoroughness. Her teeth nipped at his hips and her cheeks brushed briefly against his cock. Jet thought he would explode at the brief encounter, and pushed her aside.

"You care."

Her gray eyes drilled into him as she slid further down his body, breasts brushing his legs, lips puckered provocatively. When he thought she'd finally take him into her mouth, she licked at his sack, toying with each node, pulling it into her mouth and rolling her tongue along the skin.

"Oh, I had no idea..." He cried out when she finally moved her tongue along his shaft, pressing firmly and taking his head between her lips, rubbing her tongue across the sensitive tip, pressing inside, nibbling and toying. She sucked, and his conscious world gave way to sensation. All of Isla fell apart, broke into meaningless shards of reflective light. He saw himself clearly for the first time. Pleasure pounded to his groin, throbbed through his veins, and he knew he wouldn't last.

"Stop, Silver. I can't hold back."

"Hold back? Why would you hold back?"

Why? His last thought before dying of bliss in her mouth was that the oath was a lie. His energy moved quickly, more alive and real and powerful than ever before.

Jet grabbed onto her head and watched for as long as he was able before falling off the cliff into forever. His hot semen poured and poured as she lapped and sucked greedily, moaning in concert with him. When he was able to open his eyes, he saw a faint-green fluorescence fill the room. Silver fell onto him, clutching at his face and kissing him, giving him a taste of his own power. He rolled onto his side and hugged her tightly and whispered her name a hundred times.

Sweet surrender. When have you ever surrendered to anything, to anyone? He bit back questions and epithets and endearments, and caressed her hair. They lay staring into one another's eyes for an eternity.

A vision of her energy swept up his body to his heart. Her warm yang filled him with movement and light and quickness and the growing warmth of the spring. His heavy yin shifted to receive her, and with it came a new awareness, a stunning revelation. He spent his entire life working on wholeness, on becoming a complete force, but hadn't been complete for one day. Because he never allowed himself to receive, to yield, to accept the love others longed to shower upon him. He demanded attention, but longed for affection. And this woman longed to lavish it on him.

"My prisoner," he whispered.

"True enough, Lord."

❋ ❋ ❋

A fist of longing squeezed Jet's heart as he watched Silver eat, watched her drink, listened to her banter, her stories, her questions. Her breasts moved beneath her white blouse as she laughed, nipples rubbed into peaks. He smiled when he caught him staring at her breasts and she wagged her finger in warning.

She's happy now. Who is this happy woman?

Silver shocked him by offering him food from her fingers. He licked them clean and she pressed her eyes closed as if an orgasm washed over her. *With the touch of my lips, my mouth alone. It's because she loves you.*

His energy soared and rushed in continuous loops through his body, the thrill making him want to laugh, to cry.

She slid her palm up his arm slowly.

"Your touch is magic, woman."

"Jet? Tell me about the oath, the things Kilé never revealed. It's important to wait these final days?"

"I neglected you. I'll remedy that tonight." A wave of unfamiliar embarrassment swept to his cheeks. What had he been thinking?

"No, it's not that. Your place isn't to give pleasure. You're Lord."

"That's absurd. I've barely thought of anything else since Belanor, since first seeing you on the street there. Giving you pleasure."

"Ah, I've caught the great one in a lie. You pictured only your own pleasure, I saw it."

"Well, perhaps I can be forgiven, after all this time?"

Silver smiled and nodded briefly. "And you pictured another."

"Another?" Her question was valid, and he stalled, racing to explain he wasn't a man-lover. "Mikalis has...entertained me for years. With others. Perhaps one day he will entertain you as well."

Jet smirked at the blush rising to her pale cheeks. "Ah, wondering about that, are you? We'll see."

"Tell me about the oath."

"It's an ancient ritual, only excavated recently, since the masters foretold five of power would split into factions. I think they secretly hoped none would want the burdens of the oath. A lord must show strength, forbearance, and discipline—above all else—and demonstrate these to his clan and to himself. But there's another reason—at least the masters taught us as much—the Ch'i builds in a different way when there's no sexual release. For a man, it may build in a destructive way, so he turns on others, becomes a predator. For a man in control, it supplies power and knowing, deep knowing."

"And why do you think the oath is a lie?"

"Did I say that?"

"After a fashion. You said you felt whole, alive."

"Aloud?"

"No."

You're beautiful, Silver. Why can't I tell you?

"Did the oath give you power enough to fulfill your destiny? To lead all of the clans?"

I want to share it with her, he thought in shock. *How can you trust her? But you do.*

"My training was no small part. My entire life, spent dedicated to Wu Xing, to mastering the martial arts, to mastering my mind and spirit. The oath perhaps added to my mystery, perhaps gave me some appeal." He shrugged and stalled again, laying his palm on the table, avoiding her gaze.

"What is it?" Silver grabbed his hand and searched his face. *She thinks I'm straying from my decision to wed her. Tell her how you feel, what you want.* He silently cursed the masters, cursed their teachings, cursed the life that left him powerful and alone.

"No, put it out of your mind. I have no regrets about tonight." He laughed at himself. "It would be more accurate to say I have never enjoyed a night more…"

"Well, after ten years…"

"No, that's not all of it. I speak also of sitting here with you, eating, chatting. Remember? We spoke of it in Belanor. Might we have been friends in another time, another place?"

"And this is the time and place."

Jet took in a deep breath, calming his mind lest he cry out to her for solace. "As my sworn companion and my friend, you understand the sacred bond between us? Nothing I say can be repeated."

"Aaayee, Jet! Have I not thrown myself at your mercy—body, mind, and spirit? You read my every thought, you know my heart within the space of a few days. I am no longer Metal clan."

"You are. You are Metal. And you are Wood. And our children will reflect all of my hopes and dreams although I never intended to begin the revolution in this fashion."

"Revolution?"

"I will conquer the clans in order to lead them to freedom. To take power, and promptly hand it to them all."

"I don't understand." Her dark brows drew together in a frown and she pulled back her hand. "Give up power?"

"Metal and Wood are among the most benign of the clans, at least before Cirin killed Kilé. We don't torture our subjects if they have grievances. What do you know of history?"

"A good deal, actually. Metal warriors, all Metal citizens in fact, study a great amount of pre-Destruction history. I am particularly well versed in military tactics. I must say, Jet, this is rather serious talk coming right after our tryst in your chambers…"

"We've come together in a serious age. From your studies, you know of revolutions, of the strife they bring, the desolation. And, occasionally, the freedom. Perhaps not in our lifetime, but soon, the people will revolt against the destruction, against their clan leaders. What if I were able to hand the power to them before the revolution?"

Silver shook her head vehemently. "Chaos."

"Some, surely. But if planned properly, I would see a peaceful transfer of power from one individual to an elected government."

"The lords' armies wouldn't want to relinquish power, even if the lords agreed. And you don't know what cooperation you will find with Kilé's passing. I swear he would have stood with you."

"They would have no choice. If I become powerful enough to rule them all, I will be powerful enough to put down the generals and their sycophants. Do you notice the lack of intrigue at Traier?"

"It's quite peaceful. I don't detect threats towards you of any kind."

"I'd break up the trail of intrigue within other clans as well. You'd back me in my mission, stand by me?"

Silver stared in confusion, and he knew she struggled with many conflicting feelings. Perhaps he shared too much, too soon.

She finally nodded. "I don't believe it will work, but I'd do anything to see an end to this era of death."

"There are no guarantees, Silver. Trueborn, Elf and Were may always battle."

Silver placed her hand on Jet's arm. "Twenty years ago you sat next to my brother in the classroom, trained in the same dojo. I think the bedroom is the key. We'd be less likely to fight over bias if our races were mixed."

Jet shook his head with a deep sigh. "Surely you understand the war is over resources rather than race?"

"Of course I understand. All wars in the name of faith or racial purity have been fought for resources or power, even in pre-Destruction times. The leaders simply never admit it, although the people know it."

Jet leaned backed in his chair and regarded Silver with new eyes. How could he have asked for a better partner?

"I've spoken of this to no one."

"No one will hear it from my lips."

"And lovely lips they are." He looked out over Traier, wondering why he couldn't tell her his feelings.

"Lord?" She put her hand on his arm again and forced him to look at her.

"Am I to be a political statement, a merging of Metal and Wood?" Her hand shook as she picked up her wine goblet, and her cheeks flushed.

"Yes, I'm certainly sending a message by choosing you."

"I see."

"You know it's more. Don't irk your lord again." A tear rolled down her cheek, and he leaned in and brushed it away. "Would it be terrible? You want me, you've said as much."

"I had thought, hoped you might come to see me as more than a playing card."

A wave of shame broke through him and he thought of Master Guo, slapping his head to knock sense into him. He closed his eyes and took a deep breath, cleared his mind, and looked inside for the truth, beyond ego, beyond need, beyond greed.

"Silver, I thought we'd broken you of the habit to need assurance. All right, I'll try to be a patient, devoted partner. If you need reassurance, ask me. I've wanted you since the moment I saw you on the street where Belanor and Mashran Village meet, hiding in the shadows, waiting to ambush me with your seductive visions. You're more compelling every moment I'm with you. Is that enough, for now?"

She brushed away another tear. "It's probably more than I should hope for, but I won't stop hoping for more."

Ah, Silver, it's already much, much more. But I'm not powerful enough to admit it. And I don't know why.

"We're agreed, although I truly should not mention it, I'll name you as my mate?" He reached for her hand.

They both heard the cry and turned. Pete stood frozen, staring in horror at them. His cheeks flushed and he turned quickly and fled down the stairs.

"Pete, get back here!"

"Let me go after him," Silver pleaded.

"No, Pete is my duty. And I've neglected him. You'll have plenty of time to help me raise him."

Chapter Eleven

He'd come—he'd make it better, Pete promised the pain in his heart. *Tell me you won't leave me, Jet.* But the dojo remained empty, and Pete sat on the sand and worked not to cry. He took in a deep breath and let the familiar calm of the ancient practice ground seep into his spirit. The symbol of his clan, the ancient weapons covering the wall, Jet's colors of green and silver—they all softened the ache in his heart.

Suddenly Jet's essence drifted into the room and clenched at Pete's gut. Would he scold him like a baby? Certainly he'd want to know what was wrong. *How can I tell him? I don't know myself.*

"That's not much of a workout, Pete." Jet's voice, even hushed, echoed through the empty dojo.

"No, sir. Not even by my standards."

Jet's laughter stirred the air and Pete stood to face him. Jet's warm hand ruffled his hair, and Pete knew the lord sent the most precious of calming gifts through him. The essence of their clan—embodied in Jet's energy—meted out in tiny doses, usually only in emergencies. *Does he think this is an emergency?*

"Walk with me, Petrov."

Pete nodded in resignation. He'd get no scolding, but a serious chat. He wasn't sure which irked him more—Jet's harsh tongue-lashings or his well-meant lectures. But he welcomed the feel of his brother's warm hand on his back, was willing to listen to him for hours if it meant he would stay this close.

Pete inadvertently let a sigh escape as Jet pulled on his hand and led him out of the dojo, down the street that ran alongside and towards the clan shrine. They sat at the water's edge and Pete regarded the tiny, peaked building, situated a bit off center in a small lake. It always reminded him of a tiny kingdom, and more than once he imagined himself the leader of a clan living in the miniature fortress.

Jet pulled him into his arms and rested his chin on Pete's head as they both peered at the moonlight on the still water. *If only we could stay like this forever.*

"Did you fuck her, Jet? You didn't break your oath, right?"

His brother's groan vibrated through his body. "Jaine's right, your language gets worse all the time."

"She's one to talk."

"True. If you must know, and it seems as if you must, Silver and I came pretty close, Pete. But I haven't broken my oath."

Pete turned to take in his brother's expression. He looked calm and…happy. Jet looked happy.

"I wanted to keep her. We can keep her, can't we?"

"She not a pet, boy. But yes, I think we can keep her. I got the impression from Jaine you might want to keep her for yourself? Is that what upset you?"

"I'm not stupid, Jet, because I'm a kid. If she didn't want you, or you didn't want her, I thought maybe she might want me when I'm older. She's pretty. And she saved my life, you know. She seems to like me. Kinda figured she'd end up picking you, though. Heard about her talking to the birds."

"Why the dramatics, Pete? When you heard us talking about the mating? What were you doing up there anyway?"

"Spying on you. I do it a lot."

"I feel it. Why do you do it, Pete?" Jet pulled him in close and Pete heard him take in a deep breath. *You don't want to hear the answer, and I don't want to say you're all I have.*

"You'll marry her. Elsewise you wouldn't have kissed her and stuff like that, right?"

"Right. Now stop the evasive tactics. Why do you spy on me? Why did you follow me to Kor-Mashran and on to Mashran? You've made Jaine and Art sick with worry. It has to stop, and right now. Tell me."

No.

"Brother, I know you recognize an order when you hear it."

"Just like you to pull rank on me, Lord." Pete inched back a hair to feel Jet's chest against his back and his breath on his neck. "You don't worry about me, though."

Jet hugged him so tightly he thought he'd break a rib. "It kills me, Pete. How could you think I don't worry about you? Since Ma and Da died, you're my responsibility. In a way, you always were."

"How's that?" *Say it, Jet. Say anything. I don't know where I belong.*

"Hmnn. It's hard to explain, but I suppose it's our age difference. You're more like a son than a brother. And I guess…" His voice trailed off and his energy flickered a bit. "I guess I haven't been a very good brother or father."

The pain welled up and threatened to overtake him. "I spy on you so you don't get hurt, Jet. I have nightmares our enemies kill you and you leave me alone."

"You're worried I'll die like Da? It's grief, but grief passes, lessens. Do you understand?"

"I hated Da. I don't hate you."

"You loved Lue, and so did I. And whether you realize it or not, you loved Masur in your own way. Jaine and Art and I are here for you. You know that, don't you?"

Pete shrugged. "You might get busy or something. Like since they died. With the fighting and all. And with Silver around, you'll be real busy. Maybe you won't give me wushu lessons, or meditate with me, or read with me, or ride with me, or collect the crystals in the rivers…"

"Oh," Jet let out a long sigh. "Oh, I'm incredibly stupid." He squeezed Pete and ruffled his hair. "I love you, Pete. Look at me."

Jet's eyes caught the moonlight and Pete saw himself clearly, deep within his brother's spirit. *I'll look exactly like him.* He turned away quickly, embarrassed. The tears welled up, but he wouldn't let Jet see them.

"Let's go home, brother. Silver's waiting for us."

"She's waiting for you. She's your only bodyguard. Anyway, you don't need me anymore."

"You're wrong on all counts. Silver wants to see you. You're right, she's very fond of you. She cried about you tonight, worried she might have to leave Traier."

"She cried about leaving me?"

"You're still my best guard, the most gifted. And I'll need you for the rest of my life. Come on." Jet pulled him up and threw him over his shoulder like a sack of grain, as he did when Pete was a toddler.

"Put me down, asshole. I'm not a baby."

"Do you know what happens to someone who calls the lord an asshole?"

Pete giggled in glee. "You bring out the serpents." He squirmed from Jet's embrace and ran ahead, screaming.

"Here they come." Pete looked back to see Jet gaining on him, hands snapping at the air like striking snakes. *He hasn't done that in a year.* And he heard Jet mutter to himself, "I haven't done this in a year. You *are* an asshole, Jet."

❋ ❋ ❋

"Just in the neighborhood, my *ass*." Silver folded her arms and regarded Art and Jaine with amusement. *Lovers? What a pair—as different as...as different as Jet and I.* Art winked and she knew he caught her thoughts.

Jaine took Jet's empty seat at the table and drank from his goblet. "Metal, are you in the mood to share? Did you find the way to Jet's heart?"

"If you think I'm going to discuss our sex life with you…" She groaned. *Oh, Mother of us all.*

Jaine smirked and unexpectedly grabbed Silver's hand, gave it a brief squeeze. "Better you than Aileen."

Art make a tsk noise. "Woman, surely you can do better than that. Congratulations, my dear. You've captured a clan lord within a few days. The greatest lord of this or any age. Well, I suspect he will be. Your assassination attempt failed, but you are victorious, nevertheless." He leaned in and lowered his voice. "He's a good man, Warrior Atra. Help him become an even better man."

Jaine nodded a bit reluctantly. "A good man. It pains me to say it, Metal, but I believe you'll be good for him. And for Pete, if you're mindful of what I said to you."

"Pete seemed a bit upset when he saw us together. Jet's gone to find him."

The three stood when a bloodcurdling scream pierced the night air. Art ran towards the long, winding path leading towards lower town and Pete whipped by him, screaming still. He hid behind Silver, giggling hysterically.

Jet came up the stairs, two at a time, and gave Silver a quick wink as he dashed around her, playing cat and mouse with Pete. Finally, he scooped the boy into his arms and took a seat. "Stop squirming. I'm an old man, and you're wearing me out."

"Is she going to marry you? And have babies with you?" He pointed to Silver. Her heart pounded furiously as the full weight of her relationship with Jet fully sank in. *His wife.*

"Aye, although I make no guarantees about her skills as a mother."

"She'll do." Pete crawled out of Jet's lap and sat in Silver's. He rubbed her cheek with his small, calloused palm and his energy pushed into her, making her heart lighter. "But don't think that will get you out of your wushu lessons, Lady. In the dojo, I'm the boss."

"Yes, sir." Silver said seriously, meaning it. "It would be my great honor to have you as my Master Instructor."

129

"And I wouldn't mind having you for a…what will you be? Aunt?"

"Sister-in-marriage, although I don't think the lord wants us to discuss this. I'd prefer to think of you as my friend. I haven't had many of those in my life, Pete."

"Okay, I'll be your friend. As long as you don't nag me like *she* does." He pointed to Jaine.

"Well, aren't we all one lovely family now?" Jaine smirked, but peace and happiness poured from the young woman. *She's happy for Jet. Because of me.*

She found the nerve to glance at Jet. The candlelight highlighted the strong planes of his face, the sheen of his hair, the laughter in his eyes. He stared at her for what seemed like an eternity, and her blood raced with the thrill of the contact. *Is this hero, this legend, truly mine? Oh Mother of us all, thank you for saving my life, just when I thought it was pointless to live.*

Jaine started giggling.

"What's funny?" Jet scowled at her.

"You two. But I'll let it go for one night."

"I suppose I shouldn't ask when you and Art will marry?"

Jaine's jaw dropped and Art howled with laughter. He patted Jet on the back. "I think she's speechless for the first time in her life."

Pete giggled and pointed to Jaine, who flushed a deeper shade of pink with each moment. "Can you keep her quiet forever?"

Jet stood and stretched. "Time for sleep, all of you. We're less than a week's distance from Paulo's men. Tomorrow we'll sort out the plan. Art, bring the others with you. At sunrise."

Art stopped Jet with a hand on his arm. "Perhaps it will be a good time for us all to hear what Silver knows."

"Aye, and her plan to overthrow Cirin." Jet smiled at Silver and she forced a smile back.

Her plan. Her stomach rolled and her blood turned to ice water. Surely he'd dismiss her plan as folly. *You should have told him about Paulo sooner.*

Why did she think she could sacrifice herself to a loveless union with her former lover? Now, it seemed Paulo was knocking on the door of Traier. Surely Jet cared too much now to ask her to carry out her plan. She tried desperately to mask her thoughts as Jet held out his hand and led her and Pete to his quarters.

Pete quietly plopped onto the divan in the outer room. Jet caught Silver's eye, and she nodded quickly, understanding fully the small sacrifice he asked of her. He scooped the boy into his arms and carried him to his own bedchamber. Pete looked dead on his feet while Jet pulled off the boy's boots and tucked him into the huge bed. Jet held out his hand for Silver, who climbed into bed with him. She smelled their lovemaking in the room and yearned instantly to be back in his arms—to forget war and pain and her plan and everything, but the taste of his lips. Pete squirmed and finally curled up into a ball at their feet like a cat would.

Jet's warm arms pulled her close and he pressed his lips onto her forehead. "Is this all right, woman?"

"It's much more than all right, Lord."

But it wasn't, she thought. Because the lord wouldn't be happy to learn his fiancée had a past. And her past was marching to the gates of Traier.

❋ ❋ ❋

Cirin ordered for the servant to put the severed head of Paulo's messenger into a sack, and hand it off to a soldier to deliver to the Fire leader. The woman was a terrible lover, anyway, he thought, or he might have kept her for a bit longer. *What was her name? Senta, wasn't it? Wasn't that Paulo's sister's name?* Cirin dismissed the worry, concentrating on cleaning his blade of her blood.

Chapter Twelve

Spring in Traier blossomed like a fairytale and seemingly in one day—lush and colorful and warm. Silver wandered in Jet's private gardens, wondering where her new fiancé and his family met. Dawn, he ordered the night before, but the sun rose far above the horizon now. Perhaps she should try the dojo? *You're stalling, Silver.*

How to tell him about Paulo? It mattered not a few days earlier, when she sought Jet as an ally, when he lorded over her enemy clan. But now...*now you're in love with him.* Perhaps he wouldn't care about the indiscretions of her youth. Perhaps he'd send her away. The thought crushed her, and she searched frantically for a way to assuage the doubts and questions he'd no doubt have. Sister to one of his enemies, lover to another. Would he stop trusting her? *I would if I were him.*

She sat on a bench and turned her face to the weak sun, letting it kiss her skin. *Perhaps he'll send you away.*

"Good morning, Warrior. I'm a bluebird, I'm a bluebird."

"Hello. Bunky, is it?" The bird cocked his head and eyed her curiously.

"I'm a bluebird."

"Yes, I can see you're a bluebird. Quite a beautiful one at that. It's a pity you can't tell me where the Lord Jetre is this morning?"

"Beautiful bluebird. The lord awaits you in the dojo, Warrior SanMartin." Bunky flew into the trees.

Glory flagged Silver down as she made her way down the lord's path and onto the main street of the lower town. Silver suspected the woman had waited a long while for her appearance.

"Hello, Glory."

The woman pressed packages into her hands excitedly. "More clothes, Warrior. For the spring, lighter fabrics."

"Oh, Glory, I've no coin to pay you for these."

Glory looked hurt and shook her head. "Please don't say that again, Lady. You're my friend, at least that's what I've told the others. You invited me to see you, did you not? I came to your quarters, only to find you'd moved to the lord's chambers." Glory arched a brow meaningfully.

"Ah. Well, I can't comment on…"

"It's true. Blessed be the Mother of us all." The rotund woman hugged Silver so tightly she thought her ribs might break. Silver giggled despite herself, longing to share her newfound joy with this boisterous, friendly elf. But Silver reminded herself that joy might end quickly.

Paulo.

"I must go, Glory, I'm late for a meeting. I hope to see you again. Thanks for these." She hurried down the street and called over her shoulder. "I'll see if the lord will have you for dinner soon."

She heard the woman's squeal as she took the narrow street ending at the dojo. Jet's low voice carried through the clank of weapons and a dozen other conversations. Silver looked in tentatively and set her packages to the side as she took in the scene. Dozens of men and women trained under the direction of Jet, Pete, Art, and a few other men. Jaine sat on a bench, eating candy from a sack, and Silver moved quietly to join her, but Jet spotted her and smiled broadly.

He motioned for her to join him, and his students bowed and left the two alone. "I let you sleep, Warrior. You won't get this kind of treatment daily, you know." To her utter amazement, he reached behind her neck and pulled her in for a long, languid kiss that left her breathless.

133

The warriors ooed and aahed and giggled. A few clapped and yelled "Hear, hear!"

Jet's dark eyes glimmered with amusement at her surprise. "Something wrong?"

"Nothing wrong with your kiss, Lord. I didn't expect such a public greeting."

"We'll announce my choice tonight. It will be more fun if the clan knows in advance—give them a chance to get used to the idea, prepare a party for us."

"Give Aileen a chance to hear in advance you mean, Lord?"

"She's no one's favorite, Silver, but she has a heart and soul, and she's part of my clan."

He is a good man, and he deserves the truth.

"May I speak with you privately?" Her body quivered as she struggled quickly for the right words. But it had to be the truth, the full truth.

"Can it wait? I've postponed our meeting for an hour." Jet nodded towards Art and the men and women she presumed were Jet's other commanding officers.

"Aye, I suppose."

A stir ran through the crowd as a young woman scurried to Jet and saluted, hand to chest. "Lord, a woman, Metal, at the gate. She claims to come from Belanor directly."

"Metal? Seems Metal women are dying to get into Traier these days. Does she ask for me?"

"Yes, Lord. She is unarmed, and will not tell her name, but claims she comes in peace. We detected no subterfuge."

Jet motioned for Pete. "Take Art and a weapon. Look past any images she might use, dig past any blocks."

Pete and Art left and Jet cleared the dojo of all but Jaine and Silver.

"You send Pete on such a mission?"

"Ah, already the mother duckling? Pete's second only to me in skills, surely you realize that? You've a talented friend, Silver."

"You're serious about me, about us? No matter what?"

"Oh, Mother, what is it? Don't do this to me, Silver. You'd rob me of my fledgling peace?"

She wiped away the sudden tears and reached up to touch his cheek, to rub it with her palm in the affectionate gesture of his clan. "I hope it won't ruin anything, but I fear you'll hate me. I…"

"Go on." He was calm and ready for any pronouncement, but her legs went weak and her breath grew shallow.

"Jet, my plan was to offer myself to Fire clan Lord Paulo Ramirez, who has sought me for many years, since…"

He nodded for her to continue, one brow arched in question.

"Ramirez' men captured me and intended to use me as a bargaining chip shortly after the conflicts began. I was young, very young, and naïve. Paulo and I…we became lovers. But I never loved him, not the way he wanted, and I eventually escaped. My brother would have killed him given half the chance, so I never told anyone in Metal clan. Paulo continued to seek me out, sending messengers, letters… I rejected them. My plan…"

"To give yourself to Paulo and betray him to me. And with my power increased, to overthrow Cirin in revenge. You have a cold-hearted streak, Warrior." He leaned in and kissed her forehead. "Does the offer stand? You would still execute your plan?"

Her heart sunk. *He doesn't care. The war comes first, as it should.*

"If it's what you want, if you think it will bring about the peace you seek?"

Jet laughed and pulled her into his arms. "Silver, I thought you were brighter. Paulo certainly is. I have twice his force, but not twice his wits. He'd smell your plot the moment he laid eyes on you again. And do you think I'd give you up that easily?"

"I didn't know what you'd think about my past. I need your trust more than anything."

"I think your past is none of my business as long as it remains in the past, and I think it's a foolish plot. I won't be coming to you for help with strategy." Jet winked, wiped her tears and kissed her cheeks. "Tell me you don't want him, Silver. I only want to hear that. Speak the truth."

"I'm lost in you, Jet."

He sighed deeply, happily, and Silver thought she'd never heard a more lovely sound.

"I trained with Paulo, as did Kilé. You must know this. I've believed Paulo to be the likeliest ally of Wood clan. I'm interested to hear of the timing of this tryst of yours. The boy didn't keep his oath, did he? This does not surprise me. Ah, here is our visitor."

The woman knelt as Art pushed her gently to the ground. She pulled back the deep hood of her cloak.

Silver gasped as the sight of her old friend.

"Rise." Jet looked at Silver curiously but approached Jeannette.

Jeannette looked up and saw Silver. "You *did* survive. Oh, Mother, I prayed for your safety. How is it possible?"

Silver ran to her and fell to her knees, hugging her tightly. "Jeannette, what are you doing here? I am safe, but this is still your enemy lord."

"It might be helpful if our visitor would speak to me."

"This is Kilé's woman, Jet. His widow."

"Ah, evidently not loyal to Cirin. Presumably she has a plan of her own. Let's retire to council quarters and hear what she wants."

Silver helped the shaking woman to her feet and stayed by her side as they made their way to the Great House. A bell tolled from high atop the tower of the hall, and the council members assembled quickly, at least fifty men and women.

All stood until Jet took his seat before a semicircular arrangement of the council members.

Jeannette stood before him, head bowed.

"Speak, Jeannette. You didn't come all this way to show respect to an enemy."

She held her chin up, regarded Silver for a moment, and inclined her head to Jet.

"Lord Jetre. I come alone, representing myself only. I have no plan. I offer information."

"Why should I trust what you say?"

"I vouch for her." Silver's words left her mouth and at Jet's scowl she wished she could pull them back.

"Warrior Atra, you are not to speak again unless I address you. Is that understood?"

"Yes, Lord."

Pete held her hand and leaned in. "He doesn't want to sound mean, you know? But Council business is pretty serious stuff. Protocol, Jet calls it. What's protocol?" Silver brought a fingertip to her lips and nodded.

Jet motioned for Jeannette to continue. "Cirin is mad. Insane with the power he holds by a thread. Guntar recruits allies for a revolt that will throw Belanor into chaos within days. And Paulo will strike at that moment."

"My scout reports Paulo approaches Traier, and he's never wrong."

"No, Lord. Cirin slew Senta, Paulo's sister, and sent her severed head to him as a taunt. A thousand Fire warriors march on Belanor. I've no doubt with the chaos about to fall on Belanor, he will have an easy victory over Cirin. Paulo will rule a number greater than yours. He has near five hundred Fire Pterans ready as well."

Pete squeezed Silver's hand and leaned in again. "I hate those things."

"Me, too," she whispered back.

Jet stood and approached Jeannette, who backed up a step in fear. He held his hand a few inches from her forehead for a moment and returned to his chair.

"Why would you prefer I defeat Metal? Don't fancy serving Paulo?"

"Because of Kilé, Lord. Kilé was my life. He confided in almost no one, but he told me the day of his assassination his intent to approach you. It brought him no end of anguish—the thought of reaching out to you. But he was a good leader and wished to put the good of his people before his personal grievances with you. Kilé knew Metal clan was weaker than Wood clan because of your power. I don't understand this power fully, but Kile spoke often about the Cycles of Destruction and Creation, and said the latter was more powerful than the former. He believed you to hold the key to subduing all the elements, ending this misery. I suspect some of this he learned in his visions—in the deep knowing. And he knew you would come knocking at his door one day and wanted to save his clan from slaughter. You must *move quickly*, Lord, for I believe the decisive time is at hand. I want a quick end to this, as Kilé did."

Jet nodded absently at the woman and motioned for her to be seated with the others.

"The winds of change blow rather strongly and suddenly." And the fate of his people—no, all of Isla—would be settled within weeks.

He caught sight of Silver looking at him intently, and he knew she longed for him to share his thoughts, express his trust in her.

"Warrior Jeannette, you may stay in Traier, protected, until further notice. Jaine, take her to the guest suites and meet me at my quarters. Pete, Art, Warrior Atra, to my quarters." The rest of his commanders grumbled a bit and he silenced them with a glance. "Curb your tongues and put your energies towards readying your troops. We ride within two days."

He waved them off, including Art and Pete and Silver. "Art, find Mikalis. I'll join you presently."

The pounding in Jet's brain intensified, and he needed desperately to balance his energy, to think clearly, to plan precisely. Half of what Guo and Tsien taught him was nonsense. He knew it deep in his soul, had known it most of his life. They hadn't trained the boys to rule peacefully, hadn't given them the tools. *Why? What had the architects of post-Destruction Isla intended?*

Guo's words echoed in Jet's heart. "You'll either be the most loathed despot or the most benign leader…"

Walking from the Great House to the clan shrine, Jet waved off subjects who approached him, mulling through the past, his training, his view of the clans, of Wu Xing, of his world. Jet sat and studied the shrine, letting the crystal-clear breeze of meditative energy move through him. He reached back, far back, and found her, sitting on the dojo bench, smiling mysteriously.

"Master Guo. I've missed you."

Jet reached out his hand and rubbed her wrinkled cheek, longed to climb into her lap as he had long ago.

"You've waited a long time to call me, Jetre. You've come to a crossroads, and you want answers?"

"Yes, it's all in my hands, as I knew it would be. What was your intention for us? Why did you create the lords, train us, but not teach us how to achieve peace? You feigned disdain for the conflicts, but you ensured strong leaders would continue them."

"Yes? And was twenty years such a very long time to go from sure ruin for Isla to its rule by the one we chose?"

"You meant for all the power to come into my hands."

"Perhaps this is premature. The clan lords have not yet conceded to you."

"They will. And I will concede to the will of all the people of Isla. Is that what you intended?"

"It is what we hoped. It was the way of the ancestors, before the melting. But it has not been ours to orchestrate. You can change your destiny, Jet. You have free will. It is out of my hands."

Guo's sparkling image faded, but Jet pulled her back with his energy.

"Please, Master. The oath?"

"It was difficult after all, wasn't it, boy? You trusted me fully. I regret to tell you it was nonsense, created for show, to set you apart. You are the only one who kept to his vow. Tsien would owe me four gold coins on our bet if I were alive to collect."

"He bet for or against me?"

Guo stood and laughed lightly, leaning in to press a phantom kiss on Jet's head. *"Beware the one who appears to love you, Jetre. And follow your instincts. They are always accurate. The trick is in trusting yourself."*

Jet swayed a bit as he opened his eyes and adjusted to the living realm. An image of his young classmates filled him with poignancy—the boys who took the oath with him, the boys who returned to their clans, only to be raised to a status they never deserved, elevated to meaningless political stations. Each had broken the oath. He shook his head in dismay.

But it *had* worked, hadn't it? All the clans acknowledged him as the strongest, as the most elusive, as the most dangerous. And without the oath...would he feel this bond with Silver? Or would he have long since stopped yearning for a mate to share more than his bed, but share his dream as well. What was her part in the healing of Isla?

He took long strides up to his quarters, thinking about the family who waited there, what he would say, how they viewed him. Would they support him? Jaine and Art, always skeptical, always following orders despite their doubts. And Silver. A thrill pounded through him as he pictured her lovely, blue-gray eyes taking him in, whispering her love. Tonight, tonight he'd have it all. He stopped suddenly in the middle of the street at Guo's warning. No, surely she did not mean his new wife. But who? Who loved him, appeared to love him?

Please, Mother, not her. I cannot be wrong. She needs me, and I need her. I love her.

I've never needed anyone. Not Jaine, or Ma, or Art, or Mikalis, or Pete... And the lie rang in his ears just as the great clock of Traier struck the hour.

I need them all, he thought in wonder, as he reached his family, his friends, sitting outside on the landing of his quarters, sipping from steaming mugs. They looked at him silently and he knew the import of the moment, saw how his power made them tense as they waited for his pronouncements. And they trusted him at the same time.

And they *loved him.* It poured from them, and Jet wondered if it were always thus. You simply never let yourself feel it, did you? Jet sat and motioned for Pete to move to the seat next to him. The boy's eyes grew wide and Jet knew he yearned to ask a million questions, but exerted tremendous self-control.

"Petrov Artraud, I'll start with you. What would you have me do?"

"Me?"

"Yes, you. Do you see another Petrov at this table?" He heard Art stifle a laugh and flashed a warning glance his way.

"Um. Well, let's see." Pete propped his chin in one hand and cocked his head to the side, examining Jet seriously. "You must kill or capture Cirin, because he's big trouble—the sort who doesn't care who or how he kills. And he does deserve to die for Ma and Da."

"Go on."

"And you have Paulo to deal with, elsewise you might have him at your back while your front's crushing Belanor."

Jet nodded and tried to keep a smile from his face.

Silver put her hand on Pete's arm and gently shook it. "Elsewise isn't a word, boy."

"'Tis so. *Anyway,* as I was saying before I was rudely interrupted, I think you have one to get rid of—Cirin, and another to charm—Paulo. I'd see if Paulo wants to play nice, and join up with him and his damned Fire Pterans and beat the shit out of Belanor Metal idiots. No offense, Silver."

"What if Paulo doesn't want to play nice, then what?" *Come on, boy, show me I've taught you well, and you'll take my place someday.*

Pete concentrated, rubbing his forehead with a groan.

"The woman, Jeannette. She works for Paulo, doesn't she? She's part of his plan. You read her energy—she wasn't telling the whole truth. Come on, Jet, am I right?"

"Dead on."

Jaine slapped the table. "Paulo sent her, Jet?"

"His way of telling me his sword is for Cirin, not for me. And his way of asking for help without appearing weak to his clan. Perhaps trying to save face for himself. Not a surrender, however."

Silver shook her head. "That can't be right. Jeannette was devoted to Kilé, she doesn't even know Paulo."

"You sought me out, Warrior, and right under Cirin's nose. Don't you think Jeannette capable of the same?"

"But in a matter of days? To Kor-Tasrun and on to Traier, all the way from Belanor? I suppose it's possible. But what a risk. To throw herself at the mercy of two enemy lords?"

"Worse than living with a madman, the man who killed her beloved?"

"No, not worse. You'll spare her, Jet? She's a good woman, a good fighter in her day."

"Aye, I have enough blood on my hands. Soon I'll end the bloodshed."

Art looked taken aback.

"My general wonders where that leaves him?"

"I suppose I'll find something to do, although you already have a gardener. It seems we have use for the army a while."

"Indeed. The revolution may take longer than I imagine."

"Revolution?"

"Yes. We'll talk more of it later. For now, the horse master here must ready arms and mounts for the entire army, save those left to guard Traier. Any word on Water and Earth clans?"

Art nodded. "Mikalis left word—they do not stir. Ducking low under cover, waiting out the storm, hoping it passes them by."

"It will not pass them by. The revolution will come to their door as well. In my form. Where is Mik?"

"He said he'd be along shortly."

Jaine cleared her throat in an obvious fashion, pushed her chair back, and propped her boots on the table.

"Yes, Horse Master? Something on your mind?"

Jaine nodded towards Silver. "You're doing this all wrong. You're breaking your oath, breaking traditions, not explaining it to the people. They want to know *everything*, brother. They love you and want to know your business. They long for your happiness. And they must feel secure, especially before going into battle."

A ripple of shame washed through him. What kind of leader ignores such things—Jaine was right. How could he explain the coming revolution, his plans for a republic? It was too soon, the people weren't ready for an alliance with the other clans. They'd relied on bias for years now. He'd picked a poor strategy. How could he defy tradition without an explanation?

Jaine pointed a thumb in Silver's direction. "And much as it pains me to say it, this woman deserves better from you."

"What? I've chosen her as my mate. What more does she want?"

"Spoken like a true man. Brother, do you want to be her lord or her love?"

"Leave it be, Jaine, this matter is none of your business."

"Very well, but if Art treated me thus, he'd be looking for another to warm his bed."

Jaine stood and left the table, growling, leaving Jet to fume.

"Silver, explain this to me."

Art stood and pulled Pete to his feet. "Let's go, lad. Time to rally the troops."

"No. I wanna hear this."

"Trust me, you don't."

The air grew still and warmer and Jet knew Silver's tension increased as they sat alone. She stared into her mug and blew unnecessarily on the tepid brew.

Jet's heart sunk. Now what? "You must be joking with me, Silver. Something *else* is amiss? You came as an enemy, I let you live, I branded you, I made you my guardian, treated you like a queen. I kissed you openly before my clan, a clear pronouncement I will choose you."

"Jet, I have no grievance. Jaine is speaking as a woman for a woman, not understanding our relationship."

143

"What's to understand? You love me, and I've chosen you. I'll announce my intentions to the clan tonight."

She looked at him with misty eyes and shrugged. "As I said, I have no complaints. I am the luckiest woman on Isla."

"Spit it out, by the Mother! You've changed your mind? The lord isn't good enough for you now? You wanted me from the moment you saw me. We've shared...so much, already." He grabbed her arm and she pulled back.

No, please. I want you. I need you by my side now. I love you. What's happening?

"Nothing is amiss."

"I feel it. What does Jaine understand that I don't? What's this womanly complaint? I've a campaign to plan and the two of you criticize my courtship?"

"Courtship?" Silver laughed wryly. "Lord, many books remain from the last age, including dictionaries. I suggest you look up two words—'elsewise' and 'courtship.' One does not exist, and the other holds little relevance for our situation. I, for one, am falling out of shape and intend to spend the day on my training. If we ride to meet Paulo or Cirin, you'll need me as bodyguard more than as lover. Perhaps Pete will be free today to help guide me. You'll let me know when you're ready to break your oath? In the meantime, I'll be at the dojo."

He watched in amazement as she rose and walked away from him.

"Get back here! I'm not finished."

"I am."

"Not fucking likely." The rush of blood and fury pounded in his ears as he quickly strode to her side. When he spun her towards him and saw her smirk, the fury grew. Silver reached to her wrist and he knew his energy—his anger—coursed through her, rekindled the pain of her branding. She backed up a step and he put his hand to her throat and pressed lightly on her carotid artery, watching her grow a trifle dizzy and clutch onto his arm for support.

"What is it, Silver? When you snip at me, defy me, struggle against me? It stirs my cock along with my ire. No one walks away from me, woman." He heard his voice hiss and wondered who this man was, the one with his hand
144

around the throat of his beloved. Her eyes narrowed in anger to silver slits and she clenched her teeth tightly. And he thought he saw something else—amusement? Impossible. He was about to scold her again when she pushed her hand against his stomach and slid it down until it touched the head of his fierce erection. A subtle smile crept to her lips and she rubbed his shaft through his pants—long, hard strokes that nearly brought him to his knees. Blissful agony. He'd never been this excited, ready to spill out like an animal.

"I think the lord likes to control more than the Ch'i of a clan. Did you know that about yourself, Jet?" She choked her words out, gasping for air as she pried his fingers off her neck.

A vision of their first meeting pounded through him, the thrill of holding a blade to her neck, tasting her fear, tasting her longing for him. *What is wrong with you? When did you become a beast? I want to taste her life energy again*, he thought numbly. *I want a drop of her blood on my tongue. I'm a monster. It's the oath—it must be. I have to calm myself.*

But with each deep breath, the fury and energy and lust grew stronger, and his self-control slipped away.

He pushed her hard with one arm and she fell to one knee, looked up in surprise, hurt etched across her face.

"Leave, Atra. It's not time to break my oath. I'm not...myself."

"Yes, you are, Jet. You're arrogant, strong, and demanding. You want to conquer what's left of this world and do it your way. You're an egotist who thinks claiming a woman is the same as courting her. You don't want to hurt me, but you were born and bred to control. I don't mind that about you. I don't mind anything about you. I love you."

A hand squeezed at his heart, and all the longing of ten years ripped to his soul and screamed for this woman. The love was trapped, he thought, trapped deep inside, aching for release. *Well, I can find one kind of release.* Sweat broke out on his forehead and upper lip, and energy raced in fast circles through his limbs. The throbbing in his cock became unbearable, beyond painful, beyond desire.

He reached down and pulled Silver to her feet with one arm and pulled her by the hand, like a child. She stumbled a bit, trying to keep up, and he heard his own dark laugh at her whimper.

"Like this? Now?" She pulled at his sleeve and yanked him hard to stop. "Say something, Jet. You're breaking your oath now?"

He turned suddenly, cupped her chin and rubbed his thumb over her full bottom lip, the mouth that had given him more pleasure in a few moments than he'd encountered in a lifetime. Now he'd have other wet lips to suck him in.

"Silver, *not one more word.* Except when you scream my name. And you will scream."

The lust washed over her face and she closed her eyes and tilted her head back. "I'll do anything you ask. Anything."

"Shush."

He swept her into his arms and carried her to his quarters, suppressing a groan as she sucked at his neck, bit at his ear, kissed his jaw. He kicked his door open and dumped her unceremoniously onto his high bed.

"Undress." He watched her quickly pull off her clothes as he did the same. Her full, pale breasts rose and fell with her rapid breathing, her cheeks flushed in excitement. And she was smooth, all hints of hair whisked away since he last touched her. The sight of her bare mound thrilled him. The sight of his brand on her pelvis thrilled him. *Control, is she right? Is it wrong to want to own someone?*

"Mother," he muttered, biting his lip against a compliment. He stepped out of his clothes and moved to the bed.

"Here's your courtship, Warrior. Let's see how much you love your lord now." He pushed her onto her stomach and straddled her, pressing the head of his cock against her ass. She whimpered in protest, and he laughed. "You like your lord's huge cock, don't you?" He pushed the very tip into her soaking folds, crying out at the sensations coursing to his soul. "Oh, Mother of us all." Her muscles clenched around him, and he knew she worked his cock on purpose, trying to milk him, to pull him in.

Silver moaned and clutched the posts of the bed, spreading her legs further, arching the curve of her back. "My lord is a filthy oath breaker."

"I can stop."

"No you can't." Silver looked slyly over her shoulder and cocked a brow defiantly.

"I like your taunts, Silver. I like you."

"I think perhaps you love me."

"There's that, of course." He heard her intake of breath in time with his. He waited a moment to see if she'd speak, but she simply looked back again with a hint of a smile and a single tear escaping the corner of her eye. A truce—enough for now.

Clutching at the soft flesh of her hips, bringing his lips to the back of her neck, he pushed into her in one deep, hard thrust. Silver screamed his name, but he barely heard her, all sense and clarity succumbing to waves of contracting, wet heat. She clenched tightly and cried out again as he slid his slick cock out, luxuriating in the sublime friction.

Her whimpering sent his legs shaking. "Take me, Jet, I'm begging you. Don't stop."

Jet wanted to see her face, needed to watch her, and rolled her onto her back quickly. They stared eye to eye as he prodded against her pussy and she guided him, hand slick with her own juices.

He winked and pressed his lips to her forehead. "Be gentle. I'm a virgin."

Silver's laugh filled the room and he took the moment to claim her, thrusting in hard, crying out triumphantly. She laced her hands in his hair and pulled him in for a kiss as he moved slowly at first, deep inside, and pulled away, shaking, throbbing, fighting his release. She moved in a way he'd seen often in Mikalis' shows—a way he knew she would, a movement as primal and ancient as Isla. Their pelvises danced together in a rhythm that made him insane, set his entire body burning. Her walls caressed his cock with each stroke, her moans filling his heart. And when her moans turned to cries and she arched back and scraped at his back frantically—increasing the pace—he let go.

"It's done, my love." His whisper fell away into the room, drowned by the far away sound of his own cries of victory. He pushed harder, deeper, as his cock pulsed his seed deep in her womb.

Time stood still for a moment before he came back to life and rolled onto her, kissing her neck and pressing his face against her.

"Oath breaker," she whispered, and reached her palm up to rub against his cheek. "I'll have bruises on my hips from your grip."

"Perhaps I'll have you parade naked for all the clan to see."

"You're quite proud of yourself, aren't you? A big cock and the skill to use it?"

She smiled wryly and he laughed, tremendously happy to have her in his arms, to feel her warmth, the tingle of his cock, the calm in his soul.

"You're beautiful, Silver. I'm..." She pressed her finger to his lips to silence him, and he kissed it and kissed her lips.

Her tongue wound round his and invited him to sample more pleasure, to stoke the fire again.

"Was that the best?" He winced at his question. How could he want control and relinquish it in the same breath?

"No."

His heart skipped a beat. "Who? Paulo?"

"No, idiot. The best is yet to come. When you truly have your way."

"What are you saying? That I didn't enjoy myself?"

"You want more. Your thoughts screamed into the air, Jet. Your visions. Look at them."

Silver lavished his body with kisses as he took in her words, realizing in shock his fantasies were unfulfilled, realizing with excitement he loved a woman who wanted to make his fantasies reality.

"You'd welcome it? To be bound?" He took a deep breath, frustrated that he sounded embarrassed.

"And the rest. But I'll never watch you with another. It would break my heart."

"But you would be with me…and another? Man or woman?"

She nodded and smiled slyly. "I never took an oath, Lord. I have a few tricks up my sleeve."

"Ah, woman, tell me about them all. With Paulo? With a woman? Now, tell me every detail, I'm begging you."

"The great Lord Jetre begs?"

"Only this once."

"I detect a bit of excitement in your voice at the mention of your enemy, Lord."

"Ah, well, I'll have to see what kind of alliance I can make with Fire clan, see if Paulo has any interest in joining us."

His heart ached with happiness. Beneath every sentence, every caress and kiss, he heard her thoughts, her longing, her words. *I love you, Jet.*

"For now, we'll amuse ourselves alone." He rolled on top of her and kissed her neck, burying himself in the feminine scent and smooth beauty of her white skin.

A loud bang at the door jarred his nerves. "This had better be very, very important." Jet growled, threw Silver's clothes to her and pulled on his pants. Pete's excited energy filled the air. Jet opened the door to see the boy leaning against the entrance, smirking.

"All done?" Pete giggled and rushed past Jet, jumping on the bed near Silver.

"Not by a long shot, you monkey. What are you doing here?"

"Art sent me. He's dealing with the Council. Seems you upset them pretty badly, not consulting with them about your plans, kicking them out and such."

"Ridiculous."

"Well, they're all assembled at the Great House, waiting for you."

"On their own? They assembled without my order?"

Jet paced, furious. "Blazes. Tell Art I'll be there presently." He motioned for Pete to leave, but before he did, Pete whispered into Silver's ear and scampered out the door.

"What was that about?"

She shrugged nonchalantly, but he caught a glimmer of amusement in her eyes.

"You look like the cat who found the cream."

Silver winked. "Perhaps later, Lord, I'll have your cream running down my chin."

"Oh, woman, don't tease me."

Chapter Thirteen

Silver slid into the green gown, noting it felt cooler against her skin than when she first wore it, wondering if Wood clan could charm fabric into changing with the seasons. In the mirror, she caught a glimpse of Jet pulling his leather pants over his muscled thighs and buttocks. *I'm dreaming.*

She pulled a clean shirt for him from the closet and held it for him. He arched a brow and snickered. "Ah, the dutiful little wife. Charming." He suddenly caught her in a hard embrace, kissing her breath away.

"Am I truly your wife, now? There was no ceremony, no celebration."

"Ah, Trueborn rituals. This is Wood clan, wife." He pointed to the bed. "We had our ritual."

"I see. What a lovely wedding, Lord. In fact, I'm feeling the aftereffects, drunk on your wine."

"Drunk on love." He looked deeply into her eyes and the earth fell away from beneath her feet. He tightened his grip on her waist and sighed deeply.

"*I'm* drunk on love, Silver. I've said it. Satisfied?"

"Aye, Lord, very satisfied." The air rushed from her lungs and she pressed her face against his smooth, bare chest. "I love the smell and feel of you."

"How convenient." He laughed and pushed her away. "Now tell me why you wear that dress to a war council and what Pete said to you." Jet finished dressing, motioning for her to brush his hair.

"I'll never tire of this duty."

"That also is convenient. It does not, however, answer my questions."

"No. You'll wait for your answers."

He looked at her in the mirror and she stuck her tongue out at him. Finally she rested her hand on his shoulder. "Trust me."

"I do. Arm yourself. I've an odd feeling. Something coming our way."

I feel it too. Silver opened her satchel and pulled out her sai. "This is a little obvious." She held the weapons up. "They don't quite go with the gown."

"Bring them."

By the time they reached the Great House, the celebration was in full swing.

Jet inclined his head to whisper in Silver's ear. "Act surprised."

"You knew?"

He winked and nodded. Pete ran to them and Jet scooped him into his arms and kissed the top of his head. The three entered the Great House and a great cheer went up from the townspeople.

Pete laughed and clapped his hands. "This is for you, Silver. They know Metal clan has feasting before the mating. Jaine told them." He lowered his voice to a whisper. "They think you'll break your oath tonight. Are you going to tell them? Let me, let me tell them what you did."

"Shush. This is Jaine's doing?" Pete nodded and Silver looked around the throng to find her new sister-in-marriage. She sat in Art's lap at the main table.

"I guess the cat is out of the bag."

"The cat was never in the bag, Silver. The entire town has given her a free pass for a very long time. Art makes some very odd choices."

"You don't mean that at all."

"Hmnn. In any case, it looks as if our table is ready."

The citizens bowed less formally as the trio made their way to the main table. Many scurried towards them and hugged Silver or shook their lord's hand. Music filled the hall, sunlight cast rays through the haze of fragrant pipe smoke, and as before, the wine flowed freely. Once they took their seats, their guests approached one by one with small gifts—flowers, bits of crystal or a single pearl. Silver's eyes filled with tears at the realization these people were quite simple, quite poor, and gave all they could spare.

How had Jet built such a strong force with such a poor clan?

"Our horses, our spirit, our humor." He answered her unspoken question. "Don't underestimate the importance of our way with all beasts. They serve us in a way the Trueborn would never understand."

"My people…Metal clan understands all too well the strength of your cavalry. They know their only hope is on the ground, one on one."

"Lord," Art extracted himself from Jaine's embrace, "We've a bit of catching up to do, no? When do we meet Paulo?"

"In two days. Let them drink themselves sick today, repair and prepare tomorrow."

Art nodded. "I've ordered those outside Traier to ready themselves. Four thousand souls within the walls, five without."

"How many at Belanor, Silver?"

"Twenty thousand souls, at least. All will fight, down to the youngest child, if necessary."

Jaine slapped the table. "Time enough for strategy. Entertain your guests, Lord, and be quick about it. Art and I have a lot of catching up to do."

"Aye." Jet stood and Silver held her breath, wondering what he'd say.

"Thank you for coming here to feast with us. My wife and I…" The cheer broke out like a thunderclap and Jet couldn't finish—the crowd whooping and dancing and yelling and laughing.

"Damn." Pete snorted. "I wanted to tell them what you did." Jet ruffled his hair and pulled Silver in close. He kissed the top of her head and muttered, "They think I chose wisely, dear."

"You did."

Chapter Fourteen

"Your mind doesn't seem much on the coming battles."

Silver rubbed her hands vigorously to warm fragrant oil before making long sweeping strokes down Jet's impeccable naked body.

"Art has my orders. And we have tomorrow. Don't question me, and *do not* stop moving your hands."

"Roll over."

"I thought you didn't know energy work?"

"Who said anything about energy? Roll over."

Jet laughed and rolled onto his back. Silver moaned at the sight of his dark rigid cock, protruding nearly to his navel. She pulled up her skirt and climbed atop the table, ready to ride Jet into ecstasy.

She jumped as a tall, dark-haired man pushed through the door and stood, eyes wide, liquor bottle in hand.

"I see I missed only part of the celebration."

Silver climbed off the table and quickly threw a cloth over Jet's torso. Jet sat up and held his hand out to the man, who kissed his ring then leaned in and kissed him briefly on the lips. A few years younger than Jet, the man didn't have the lord's presence, but was still strikingly handsome—the man from his vision, the man Jaine hinted adored Jet. Were they lovers?

"Silver, this is Mikalis, my cousin, one of my generals, and my primary scout. And after Pete, this scoundrel is my likeliest successor. Mik, my wife, Silver."

"Yes, I heard."

Mikalis arched a brow, studying Silver carefully as he took a seat at the table. He set a bottle of Trueborn liquor on the table and poured himself a glass, held it up in toast, and continued to stare.

Jet pulled Silver in for a quick kiss. "Don't stop the massage. And I think I'd like some whiskey, too." Silver poured a glass for Jet, refilled Mikalis' glass, and found a third glass for herself, taking a stiff belt.

"It wasn't a massage, *as you know*, Lord. Perhaps a better time…"

Jet snickered and pulling the cloth off, lay back down on the table. To her amazement, Mikalis' arrival did nothing to diminish his mood, his cock still hard and ready. "Continue your *massage*."

"Jet, please. Not like this. I'll leave you to catch up with your cousin."

"I can take over there, Warrior SanMartin. Have a seat and relax."

"Very well." Silver sat at the table and folded her arms, matching Mikalis' dark, contemptuous gaze. *He hates me. It's true. He loves Jet.*

"Our lord must be relaxed to think clearly, to make best use of his Ch'i. I've certainly helped often enough to ensure he flows freely. Have you shared our stories with your new bride, Jet?"

Jet groaned in annoyance and rolled onto his stomach. Mikalis shed his cloak and kneaded Jet's shoulders, never letting his gaze wander from Silver's eyes. "I understand you know all about the lords and their needs? You were brother to one, lover to a second, and now married to a third. Quite an avocation."

"Mik." Jet's low warning seemed to sting Mikalis like a hard slap. "Don't take liberties. We're no longer children. Respect my wife."

Silver barely followed their discussion of the intelligence Mikalis and his men gathered on Paulo's movement, on their plans for the approach to Belanor. As she watched as Mikalis' strong hands knead Jet's bare flesh, Mikalis kept one eye on her response.

"Like watching this, Warrior? Jet, I think your woman has a fetish, but I'm not sure. Is it to see us fuck or for us to share you?"

Jet slapped away Mikalis' hand and gestured for him to sit at the table with Silver. He stepped into his pants and sat between them, his eyes narrowed to slits as he regarded his cousin.

Cocky bastard.

"Why, Warrior, whatever do you mean?" Mikalis tilted his head and regarded her with increased amusement.

"Stay out of my mind." *And keep your hands off my husband.*

Jet ran his hand through his hair and threw back a finger of whiskey. "Stop it, both of you. Mik, I have enough on me now. I don't need your theatrics—I need your support. Silver, you're playing right into his hands. It's best to ignore him."

"I'll ignore him, all right. Good night, Lord." Silver stormed into the bedroom, slamming the door behind her loudly, fervently wishing it had a bolt.

"Damn Elves."

"I heard that." Jet yelled from the outer room. Silver heard only the quiet whispers of the men and some laughter erupting occasionally. She pulled off her clothes and climbed into bed, hoping to fall asleep quickly, knowing she wouldn't.

An hour later, Jet climbed into bed with her and pulled her into his arms. "I know you're awake. The air is laced with your anger. Speak."

"It quite amused you. I was shocked at your exhibitionism in front of your cousin. He was trying to make me jealous."

"He was also trying to arouse you. Did it work?"

Silver sighed. "A bit. More to the point, did it arouse you? Am I to share you with him? Do I get to veto such an affair?"

"Of course. I will do whatever brings you pleasure, Silver, but sharing you with my cousin would not be my first choice. I've certainly made it clear enough to Mikalis that he and I will never...you know..."

"I don't much care for the man, Jet. I'm sorry to offend if the two of you are close. He seems…as if he's trying to wedge himself between us, literally and figuratively."

"We've shared a lot, Silver. It will be a while before Mik becomes accustomed to giving me privacy. I'll sort it out with him. I'm sorry that I let the teasing go on so long. I'm not used to this…"

"This what?"

"Caring. I care for Mikalis, but you are my priority."

"He doesn't respect me."

"But I do. I'll make it right, don't worry." Jet rolled atop Silver and kissed her deeply as he rubbed his erection against her thigh. She shivered as his tongue explored her mouth, making her ache for him, wet for him, despite her doubts and anger. Jet pressed the head of his cock into her ready folds and teased her, pulling away and pushing in. "I want to see you go wild. Insane with lust." He knelt and moved her into position with a slow, rhythmic thrusting that filled her near to tears with pleasure.

"We don't need Mikalis, Lord."

"No, we don't."

But her thoughts faded into nothingness as a wave of release carried her away, and she cried out her love for her new husband.

Chapter Fifteen

The second true day of spring dawned with mists dissipating in the fragile rays of the sun. Traieren citizens moved slowly through the cobbled streets, opening shops with bleary eyes, carrying their wares to the market with groans and grumbling. Silver wondered how late into the night the wedding feast lasted.

Everyone she saw was either elderly or quite young, and it struck her suddenly all the able-bodied warriors were elsewhere, preparing for the next day's march.

Glory fell into step with Silver, scurrying before her, bobbing in excitement. "We're terribly late, Warrior Atra. I wanted you to have this before we convene." Glory proffered a package, excited, holding it out like a precious treasure.

"You must stop doing this, Glory. I'll ask Jet for coin to pay you for these things…oh, don't tear up, now, I'm sorry. Well, I'll find some way to return the favor."

The fine parchment carried childlike images of beasts and battles, drawn no doubt by Glory's son. Silver carefully unwrapped the gift and gasped as the sight of the tunic, pale blue-gray, chosen to match her eye color exactly. Cut low, with the symbol of Wu Xing Wood clan embroidered in bronze and gold and silver thread.

"It's a masterpiece. How can I accept this?" Glory fell on her with a smothering hug and a sigh.

"Good enough for the Praeta to wear into battle?"

"The Praeta?"

"Our name for you now. You don't know of Praeta? The Warrior Queen who led Wood clan into the world of Trueborn in the ancient age?"

"Oh, Ling Huang?"

"Aye, she was a Trueborn outsider as well, from the land beyond the sunrise, now beneath the waters. She fell in love with the King of Wood Elves and bore his son. She taught the clan the skills of Wu Xing, and wrote her teachings down as well. Elsewise they might have been lost, mightn't they? She was Master of the sai, your weapon, so they call you Praeta, the chosen woman."

"I'm sure I don't deserve the honor."

"You're exactly like Ling Huang. You'll teach our lord some secrets and help bring us back to peace."

"I've nothing to teach Jetre, Glory, trust me."

Glory snorted and linked her arm in Silver's. "Ah, woman to woman, we know that's not true. The lord will bring us unification, but you unify the lord's family, the lord's heart. We cannot have peace without our lord's happiness. It makes him stronger."

"I've underestimated you." Silver looked more closely at the plump woman, who nodded in agreement.

"Aye. Don't fret. I do tend to blend into the crowd. The lord taught me the Wu Xing ways of hiding."

"The Lord Jetre taught you the martial arts? Ninjitsu?"

Glory cocked her head to one side, her blonde curls bouncing in the light morning breeze. "I am an empty-handed master, behind only the lord and lordling, and Generals Artier and Mikalis."

"Kara-te?"

The woman nodded cheerfully and extended a palm towards Silver, radiating energy she felt from inches away. Glory's brief touch of pressure points on her wrist sent Silver to one knee, arm tingling in agony. Glory lifted her back to her feet with one strong arm and smiled.

"Your Metal energy is very strong. It makes it quite easy for me to affect you with my Wood energy."

"It would seem so." Silver rubbed her arm as she leaned down to pick up the tunic. "As well as the most talented seamstress in the world."

"And your good friend, and your new bodyguard." Glory bowed dramatically. "The lord chose *me* to protect his beloved Praeta."

"Well I'll be..."

"Come on, I wasn't joking when I said we were late."

"To the dojo?"

"All the Wood warriors in the dojo? Goodness, woman, we're not wee folk." Glory winked and took the tunic from Silver, shaking it out and smoothing the fabric at they walked towards the edge of town.

"Glory, who will guard Traier while we march on Belanor? Surely not these aged ones or the children alone. I never understood why Kilé didn't strike when Traier marched on another clan."

Glory laughed and patted Silver on the back. "You'll understand, soon enough."

Jet sensed her before he saw her—the tall, lithe woman who now dominated all of his thoughts unless he worked for mental clarity. She stood high on the wooden battlement with Glory, staring down at him and his army.

What does she think of us? Of me? He knew her former clan thought the Wood Elves overly simple, somewhat naïve, perhaps even backwards. He watched as Pete broke rank and ran to meet her. She held out her arms and pulled him in for a hug.

Jaine groaned beside Jet. "She's disruptive."

"Shut up, Jaine. You like her immensely and you're not fooling anyone."

Jaine pressed her lips on his cheek, startling him. In front of the troops. The metamorphosis of his family in a few days—kissing in the open, hugging and proclaiming love, crying and speaking of buried hurt. All because of Silver.

161

Well, he had precious little time to take in hearth and home, he warned himself and motioned for Art to begin the battle preparations.

Art's voice rang across the huge courtyard, a loud, guttural cry that brought the thousands to attention. Another command, and they bowed as one. A third, and they assumed the Wood stance, as if riding a horse, with toes pointed out slightly. Art paced slowly along the front ranks and called out at a steady pace, and with each *kiai*, the troops executed a series of quick movements—punches, thrusts, parries, kicks, and chops.

The energy of the moving meditation of the clan rose into the air, shimmered slightly so that Jet and the most gifted saw it, and began a vibration of sound echoing through Traier. Jet held up his hand and, with one final cry from Art, the troops came to rigid attention.

He climbed to the battlement across from Silver and met her gaze for a moment, saw her appreciation, her pride in him and his people. Now her people. *Praeta*. He heard the whispers through town. They thought her the chosen one, the one to help their lord take over the world. If they only knew he intended to give the world back to them. They'd hate it, he thought in frustration. If only he could break through their fear, make them understand they were capable without the warlords, able to make their own decisions, rule themselves.

A whisper across the field interrupted his musings, and he saw Mikalis standing with Silver, Pete, and Glory. Very close to Silver, in fact. He pushed down a sudden urge to order Mikalis away from her, away from Traier. Jet waved his palm before his eyes, cleared his thoughts and cast his voice into the hearts of his troops.

"Kneel."

They dropped to the ground as one and sat back on their heels.

"Meditate." He reached out to each woman and man, touching their energy with his own, sending healing, strength, and determination. After many minutes, when he sensed total acceptance of his gift, he clapped his hands and they rose, bowed, and dispersed.

Jaine touched his arm and he looked down at her, surprised to see her eyes filled with tears.

"What ails you, Jaine?" He pulled her into his arms and set his chin on the top of her head.

He strained to hear her whisper. "My dreams, Jet. They're terrible, filled with death. I don't want to strike Belanor. Something awful awaits us."

"His name is Cirin. You have no faith in me? He's untrained, undisciplined, easily defeated, especially with Paulo's army alongside us."

"He's insane, willing to do anything to hold onto power. But my dreams are about Pete."

She pulled away and brushed at her tears.

"Pete stays behind, Jaine. I need Mikalis at my side because he knows Paulo well. Pete must stay at Traier, protected. If I fail…"

"Are you insane? He won't stay behind. We've been through this many times."

"He'll stay to protect Silver. She doesn't ride with us."

Jaine groaned. "Good luck. I'd love to be a bird on the windowsill when you break the news to her. Shit, Jet, you're going to get it from all sides."

"Which is why I do *not* need it from you. Don't you have work to do, Horse Master?"

"Fine." Jaine stomped off cursing him, and for once, it didn't amuse him. Jaine's dreams usually carried a modicum of premonition. Blazes. Was Pete safer at his side? Silver?

Jet wandered the streets of Traier alone, partly masking his presence with suggestion. When someone too strong to be fooled approached him with a bow, he waved them off, searching for a quiet spot, alone. The shrine would be busy, families gathering to pray and focus energy for the coming days. Useless to search for a quiet refuge, away from his quarters, away from his people. The town would be buzzing all day in preparation. He headed for the dojo, surprised to hear chatter coming from within. Silver's voice and Mikalis'. Tension gripped his stomach as he slowly looked around the entranceway.

Silver's graceful movements flowed impeccably as she demonstrated her sai form to Mikalis. How had Mikalis managed to patch the rift of the night before? Well, he was as smooth as any on Isla—that much was certain.

She finished with a flourish, flushed and excited. "These are the lord's sai."

"You're very accomplished. A tremendous addition to Wood clan."

Silver blushed a bit at what sounded like a sincere compliment and continued to toss the sai from hand to hand. "I've never held anything like them."

Mikalis smirked as he examined Silver's body in a way that made Jet's blood boil. *What's he up to?*

"And the lord himself, have you ever held anything like him?"

Silver frowned. "That's not open for discussion. My husband…"

"Your husband hasn't been with a woman for ten years. I'm simply intrigued. Perhaps I have a little voyeuristic streak."

"You're not interested in watching me, General, that much is quite clear. If you wish to see the lord, your cousin, engaged sexually, you must approach him."

"I *have* seen him thus engaged, my dear. Many, many times. He hasn't discussed what's between us, has he? What will remain between us? You can't possibly think our Jetre will satisfy himself with one lover for a lifetime? Certainly not one female." He snorted "You're to do the only thing for him I cannot—bear him children. He'll derive his pleasure elsewhere."

Jet was relieved to watch Silver deny Mikalis an emotional response. She merely shook her head in disagreement. Her hands clenched tightly on the sai. *She can't possibly believe him.*

Mikalis seemed annoyed and Jet knew he would prod further to get a response. *What is he after?*

"Perhaps you've fooled him, but you've not fooled me. I've been on the road a good deal more than Jet, Atra SanMartin. Your reputation precedes you. Does Jet know they call you the lords' whore? Paulo, Bourne, Eain, why, everyone but your brother Kilé. Unless, of course…"

"You're vile. No doubt Paulo started vicious rumors when I rejected him. Jet is my second only. And the last, I swear!"

Mikalis cast a quick glance at the doorway, and Jet thought his cousin might have spotted him, sensed his energy. He drew Silver closer, hissed at her lowly, but his voice still carried through the large hall. "My allegiance is to Jet. I love him more than you ever could. If I thought for a moment you could wound him, I'd kill you this instant. I warn you, Silver, I'm watching you closely. One misstep, and I'll tell him all I've heard."

"I love him—I'd never hurt him. You're *wrong* about me."

Mikalis grabbed Silver by the arm and she tried to maneuver away from him, readying to fight.

"Enough." Jet's own voice pounded through his head. He reached into his well of anger and channeled destructive energy through his palm. Mikalis fumbled back several feet as if shoved by a phantom and finally stumbled, dropping to his knees and clutching at his chest.

"Jet, stop it. You'll kill me."

Silver ran to Jet, trying to pull him into a hug. He firmly pushed her away. "Mik, what is this game?"

"It's no game, Jet. I'm looking out for your interests, as I've done my whole life. This woman has a reputation you're ignoring. You've broken your oath prematurely, making plans without the Council's input. It's not like you."

"It's precisely like me to do as I wish, and you fucking well know it. Leave, Mik. Meet up with Art and the others, and leave my sight. One more word from you—to her, about her, or behind my back, and I'll strip you of your rank and kick you to Paulo as a peace offering."

Mikalis pushed himself up and brushed the sand from his tunic. His jaw clenched tightly and he locked eyes with Jet for a full minute without speaking. He turned away and called back over his shoulder. "You'll live to regret this choice, Jet."

Jet wandered to the bench along the wall and sat wearily, massaging his temples to bring clarity back. He looked up at Silver, who stood before him, confusion, anger, and fear etched across her face.

Her voice was a mere whisper. "You don't believe him, do you?"

Jet shook his head. "I don't understand this. For the first time since we were lads, he's blocking his thoughts, hiding his purpose. I...we've been inseparable. Mik's talented, brilliant."

"Brilliant?"

Jet winced at the tone in her voice. She'd seen nothing of the man who was more than a brother to him. "I don't know what's gone wrong. He's a masterful martial artist, the most talented tracker on Isla. Mik is brave, a bit reckless perhaps—prone to excess in everything—drink, sex, battle..."

Silver sat and put rubbed her palm on Jet's cheek. He caught her hand and held it to his heart.

"Jet, look at me."

He hesitated, knowing what she knew, what she would say, not wanting to face the truth.

"You have not been lovers?"

"Not exactly. He certainly involved me peripherally in his exploits, but always as entertainment for my benefit, during the oath... But no, we've not been lovers. Perhaps in his mind, because of all we've shared..." *Oh, you fraud. You know precisely what happened, you feared it for months. And you let it happen, not willing to lose his love, his devotion.*

"Lord, a woman knows jealousy when she sees it. The man would like to slit my throat as I sleep."

Jet simply nodded.

"You care for him deeply. Nothing more?"

"No more. But I do care for him, and therefore, I've failed him badly."

"Because you let him think you returned his feelings?"

"No. I was clear. But I let him go on, let him hurt himself."

"Because he worships you, and it was welcome."

Jet pulled her into his arms, and pressed his lips to her forehead. *She's wondering if you feel the same about her. That you only want to be worshipped, you aren't willing to love in return. Are you?*

"Jet, thank you for believing in me. You know about Paulo, but I swear, the rest is a lie."

"I know. Now you must believe in me, Praeta. You will stay behind, with Pete, helping to guard Traier. I won't insult you by asking you do it to protect the boy. I intend to keep both of you safe."

Head shaking in disbelief, Silver stood. "I must be by your side. We ride to avenge the death of Kilé. Don't do this, I beg you, Lord."

"You are more a threat to me by my side. Both of you. What if Paulo or Cirin captured you? What would you have me do? Surrender my people in exchange for your lives?"

"I'm a warrior. I'm no more at risk than any of your troops. You think little of my skills…" Jet shook his head slowly and watched the truth of his order take hold, knowing she understood the danger, how she had come to mean everything.

Silver fell into his arms, trembling. "How will I wait for you? Oh Mother of us all, I can't be separated from you now."

"Only for days, Praeta, if destiny inscribed it on the stone of my time here."

"And if you are wounded? Killed?"

Jet laughed wryly. "How ironic, coming from a Metal assassin. If my horse returns riderless, your fate is to find a way to turn a brash young boy into the leader of a clan. Let's walk, Praeta."

Silver listened carefully as Jet pointed out each landmark building, each special shrine, every garden, during a serious hour-long stroll through lower Traier. As citizens approached him, each bowing quickly but reverently, he'd introduce them to Silver by name, amazing her with his recall.

Several of the Wood clan asked for Jet's opinion on topics ridiculous and deathly serious. One young lad asked how he should approach his love's father, who disapproved of the union.

"Why does her father dislike you?"

"I herd the swine, Lord. He says his daughter is not to lay down with the likes of my family. He's happy enough to eat our pork, though."

"That is not his grievance, lad. He does not want to lose his child yet. No suitor would be good enough. Tell the man to visit me."

"You would speak with him on my behalf?"

Jet slapped the boy on the back. "After we return from Belanor. Tell him it is my command."

Silver smiled at Jet and took his hand as they wound their way down a narrow alley.

"You are kinder than I thought possible."

"It's only a job, Silver."

"And you show me these things because we might lose you, because you want me to help Pete if need be."

"I show you these things because this is your home and you are my wife. And when all is well, you can assist. They will approach you as well."

"What can I teach them?"

"They don't want to be taught. They simply want someone to care, to make them feel secure. You'll understand in time."

"Lord." An ancient man called from his window, where he sat sipping tea.

Silver heard Jet's low groan. "Hello, Mort. How is the chill in your bones?"

"Some terrible, Lord Jetre. Some terrible. The cure you gave me last month didn't keep. I'm not asking for more, mind you, know you're a busy fella."

Silver suppressed a grin as Jet squeezed her hand. "I think we have a moment to try again." They ducked into the dark, low, single room, every corner crammed with carved wooden trinkets.

"Oh, these are lovely. You did these, Mort?" She picked up a delicate sculpture of a small bird on a tree limb.

"Aye, Praeta. But the chill hurts my hands." Jet kneeled before Mort's chair, rubbing his hands vigorously and clutching them to his own chest, eyes closed, breathing slow and deep. Silver watched intently as a faint shimmer surrounded his hands when he clutched at Mort's gnarled fingers. The man winced in pain and then a look of relief relaxed his face, his whole countenance.

"There, perhaps that will take."

"Aye, Lord, it did the trick, I'm sure of it."

"For a week," Jet whispered to Silver.

"Praeta, please take the sculpture if it pleases you. As a wedding gift."

"Oh, I couldn't."

"She'll be delighted to accept. We must be on our way, Mort. Take care of Traier for us when we ride tomorrow."

"Aye, Lord. May the Mother protect you."

As they walked up the stairs towards Jet's quarters, Silver examined the sculpture.

"That's a month's wages for him—one of his more popular themes."

"A month's wages? And you let me take it?"

"Would you insult his pride? He'll brag about it for the next year, I guarantee it."

"You wanted to show me your life. That's what this walk is about, isn't it?"

Jet didn't answer, didn't have to.

"Your days are different than I imagined."

"And this day will be different than any day of my life."

"Why?"

"Because I intend to spend every hour of it giving you pleasure."

Silver laughed, but she saw the sudden smolder of his eyes and knew he meant to be true to his words. With each step closer to Jet's quarters, her heart beat faster.

"What will we do?"

He ignored her question.

"Jet, come on, tell me."

His silence excited her. By the time they entered his bedchamber, Silver longed to strip him down, possess him, beg him to take her. But he would have none of it.

"Undress."

While Silver stripped, he poured wine into two goblets. She was naked when he offered one to her, and he surveyed her carefully as he sipped his wine.

"Your turn to undress, Lord."

He shook his head and slowly moved towards her, a bit of a sly grin pulling at one side of his mouth. From his pocket he pulled two long strands of leather and dangled them before her off one finger.

"Oh no you don't."

Jet pushed her to the bed and in a swift movement, pulled her arms behind her and bound her wrists. She struggled briefly, biting back a smile, knowing he wanted her to fight a bit.

"I would have liked a bit more fight." He rolled her onto her stomach, pressing a knee into the small of her back as he bound her ankles and secured them to her wrists, leaving her lying helpless on her side. He stood back to examine his handiwork, breathing rapidly. Silver eyed him, feeling more vulnerable, more excited than she expected. She watched as he pulled off his clothes, ready for his cock, ready to get on with it.

"Jet, you're beautiful. Come here."

"Shuush." He leaned in and kissed her briefly. "Not another word."

"Oh, well, that's like asking…"

Silver squealed at sting of Jet's flat palm slapping her buttock. He rubbed the sting to tingling warmth with his palm, only to strike again.

"Ow! Now you never said anything about…"

"You're a slow learner, wife."

After a third slap, he ran his mouth along her sensitive flesh, licking away the pain, torturing her with a different kind of heat. Silver bit at her lip as he moved to her breast, suckling each into hard peaks, tweaking her nipples between his teeth. Her juices flowed down her legs, the throb for him growing with each suck of his lips.

She caught her breath when he moved his mouth slowly down her torso and prodded at her pussy with his finger, gently teasing her labia, wiping her juices from his finger into his mouth, brushing it along her lips. *Please, please let me feel your mouth on me.*

"Wife, we will do this all day, so you may as well stop fretting."

After minutes of toying with her folds, he pressed his mouth to her and feasted like a starving animal. The first stroke of his hot tongue made her entire body shudder and her pussy clench to hold onto him, but she was empty, aching. Side to side he rolled her labia as she bucked beneath him, desperate to hold him, unable to do anything but receive, and feel. And cry out his name in curses and endearments.

"Dear Mother, you'll kill me."

His low laugh was muffled as he sucked at her clit, rubbing his full lips over the pearly nub, abandoning it to press his tongue inside.

"Fuck me, Jet, I'm begging you. Please stop."

"Stop?"

"Don't stop, damn it."

Jet grinned and kissed her nub again, this time rubbing his tongue in a circle of endless torture as he pressed his fingers into her, exploring every secret spot, listening for her reaction. The wave of release broke fiercely, suddenly, and Silver screamed his name as her womb clenched at his hand.

"Was it good?" He wriggled up to kiss her lips.

"Blazes, untie me."

"Unlikely." Laughing, he straddled her head and pushed the tip of his cock into her mouth. Silver sucked desperately, aching for him to join with her. He came quickly, groaning in pleasure and pulsing his seed over her breasts, then licking his essence from them. And with that, began his trail of torture all over.

"You can't mean to keep doing this?"

"We have hours."

"I'll die."

"I think not. And Warrior, take heed. If someone knocks at the door, and they will, I will open it."

"No. Untie me."

"And if you're a very lucky citizen, Artier will be the first to come calling. He brags of his ways with women."

"Jaine would kill me."

"Jaine would insist on watching."

"What the hell kind of place do you rule, Jet?"

"Shush. Don't make your lord angry again."

Chapter Sixteen

The lights of Traier twinkled into life, one by one, giving the town an eerie predawn glow. The warriors no doubt hugged their families, bidding one another words of undying love and uttering fervent prayers to the Mother for victory and safety.

"Some of you will die." Jet gazed over the streets, wondering which doors would bear pine wreaths of mourning in the coming days.

"Maybe you will die, Jet."

Pete's agonized voice pierced his heart, and he turned and gestured for the boy to sit on his lap. Pete hesitated briefly before throwing himself into Jet's arms in tears.

Jet thought of reassuring Pete, but hesitated. For he *would* die one day, and Pete would have to carry on. How could he teach the boy to think of the world without him? The frustration overwhelmed him. *No one tells you how to be a father figure, how to teach the children about pain and suffering. At least my father did not.*

"You're strong, Pete. Stronger than I was at your age. You must be strong for Traier, for I'm putting it in your hands with all my trust." *What nonsense. He's only a lad. An orphan once, and perhaps again.*

"And I'm counting on you to care for Silver."

"Why?" Pete brushed his tears away and rubbed Jet's cheeks with his little palm. "You stopped loving her, didn't you? Why doesn't she ride with you?"

"Spying again?"

"She took a pteran dart for me. She's stronger than you know."

"I know she's strong. I know you are, too. The point is to keep my wife and the heir to Wood clan safe."

"I don't like it, Jet. You can't make me like it."

"No, you have the right to your feelings. But pay attention, Pete. There will come a day when you won't have the right. When all you feel and think and do has to be for the clan—for the good of Isla. Do you understand?"

"When you're dead, you mean?"

"If I die before the clans unite. You'll always have a very powerful role to play on Isla. To begin your role, I'm leaving the Calling to you this time. Can you manage it?"

A stroke of brilliance, Jet thought proudly, as Pete's eyes gleamed in excitement, distracted from his worries.

"Yes. Yes, I can do it. May I call the most ancient masters as well? Praeta?"

"Aye, I believe we should have Praeta this time if she agrees. The others will certainly be willing to guard Traier. You must begin soon."

Pete's eyes narrowed and he shook his head glumly. "You do this to distract me—I feel it. Why do you treat me like a baby?"

"I do it to distract us both, boy. The truth is, if I fall in the coming days, you must be able to do this on your own. No one else has the strength." Jet leaned in and kissed Pete on his head, taking in the scent of his youthful energy, wondering if anyone had ever loved him as much as he loved Pete.

He yearned to speak with Silver, to see her loving eyes, but he didn't trust himself to leave her behind. *I wish she could be by my side every waking moment.*

"You won't say goodbye to her?"

"Stop reading my mind. Let's go." Jet stood and pulled his cloak around him tightly, feeling an ominous chill. He walked to the ancient bronze gong of his clan and handed the hammer to Pete, who took it quickly and bowed his head in meditation. Jet joined him in meditation, sending Pete strength and all the ancient energy of the clan.

Silver threw open her window as a gong echoed through the streets. The call to battle, she thought. The Wood clan kept to the ancient ways. One by one, the doors on her street opened and from each a warrior or two emerged, each carrying their weapons, a satchel of food, and a canteen of drink.

She reached for her cloak and stepped onto the street, anxious to catch a glimpse of Jet before he rode into battle. A new pain hit her suddenly, took her breath away. What if it was to be her last glimpse of him?

No. He's too strong, too wise. Please, Mother, I'll never ask for another thing. Even if he would turn away from me, don't let him fall.

Inevitably, Glory fell into step beside Silver and laced her arm in hers. "I miss this battle because of my duties to guard you, Lady."

"That irks you, does it? Well, two of us are miserable, so we'll be good company."

Glory looked at her curiously but remained silent as they made their way to the edge of town, following the flow of warriors.

The gong still sounded, each beat louder than the one before, each reverberating through Silver's heart and soul. "How long will this racket continue?"

"Until our lord has summoned spirits enough to guard Traier. As well as the beasts in the forest—at least the ones large enough to attack invaders."

Silver opened her mouth to ask what Glory meant and stopped in awe at the sight before her. Dozens of warriors knelt at the end of the street, where a shimmering blue figure in full armor brandished a phantom sword.

"Oh, Mother of us all! What is it?"

"One of many of Wood clan who has gone before us, Silver. One of many hundreds the Lord calls."

"I don't believe it."

Glory took her arm and pulled her down the street, pointing out the ancient ones, all armed and ready for battle, as they shimmered into view.

"No wonder the clans avoid Traier, even unguarded. I'd heard of the lord's demon magic, but thought it a fairy tale, or Kilé's excuse to cover his fear of Jet."

"We honor our ancestors, and their spirits respond to our prayers. There are *some* advantages to practicing the ancient ways and in having a lord who understands them."

Silver was too awestruck to respond, shocked at the full power of her husband.

When they reached the town wall, they climbed to a high turret to watch the warriors mount or join ranks on foot. Silver scanned for a familiar face—but found none, not even Art or Jaine or Mikalis.

"Stop looking for him, Silver. He rides as a common warrior, you won't recognize him." The huge wooden gates were opened and the warriors rode out of Traier, eight abreast. Amidst the first group to leave, one tall man peered up at the stars, as if to speak to the sky.

"You're wrong, Glory. I do recognize him."

Jet, come back to me.

The man turned and pushed back the hood of cloak. Even from a distance, Silver saw the passion of battle already flaming in his eyes. But they softened for a moment as he stared at her. Without a gesture for her, Jet pulled his hood back up and rode forward—out of Traier.

I love you, Lord.

❄ ❄ ❄

"Ready?" Pete threw a saddlebag onto Silver's bed and she sat up and wiped her tears.

"Oh no, you don't. Don't even *think* about it, Ugly. You're in my care."

"Actually, you're in my care, but I won't chop words."

"Mince words. Think, Pete. If something happens to Jet..." She shook her head, willing away the pain the thought brought. "You're his successor. Traier needs you."

"Silver, you're pretty stupid for a smart woman. I don't have a prayer if Jet dies. He knows it, I know it, and most importantly, the other lords know it. I'm here because he doesn't want me to die in battle. I guess he cares a lot about me or something."

"He loves you more than life itself, Pete. Don't defy him."

"I'm going with or without you. You aren't strong enough to stop me."

Silver ran through a list of arguments and knew they would all fall on deaf ears.

"What can you do out there for him? You'll be another worry."

"I can watch his back. I can keep him safe, like I've done since Ma and Da died."

"You were there at Mashran, weren't you, when I first met him?"

"Aye. I didn't like him letting you go, and I would have killed you if you would have tried anything. He shouldn't have branded me his guard if he didn't want to be guarded."

Silver paced and saw the glimmers of first sunlight hit the walls of her room. Wood clan would be miles away by now, perhaps halfway to Kor-Tasrun, soon to meet up with Paulo. Silver uttered a silent prayer Paulo wasn't laying a trap. And perhaps...no, Jet would see through any plot of Mikalis'.

"Pete, what do you think of Mikalis? Is he trustworthy?"

"Mik is family." The boy sat on the bed and a frown crossed his face, brows drawn in deep concentration. "Why do you ask this?"

"There *is* something. Tell me."

"Dunno." Pete shrugged. "He's been asking me a lot about you."

That didn't help, Silver thought. Mikalis might simply be protecting Jet in his inquiries. But what if *he* were the spy for Paulo, or even Cirin? Was he capable of betraying his lord simply because Jet spurned him? Perhaps Jet did need someone watching his back.

Pete must have picked her thought from the air, because he nodded seriously.

She stroked the boy's cheek, thinking how precious he'd become to her, wondering desperately the right course for them both. "There's nothing I can say to change your mind?"

"Nope. Leaving now. On a fast horse, I'll catch up with them in an hour, if Jaine left any beasts worth riding in the stables."

"And no one will stop you?"

Pete frowned in derision. "I'm second-in-command, Silver. They wouldn't dare, not even the spirits."

Silver picked up Jet's sai, tucking them into her belt, and pulled Pete into her arms. "They'll be hell to pay when he learns we've disobeyed him."

"He has to live to get angry at us. I'm willing to risk it."

"I am too, Ugly. Let's go." A sudden thought made her pull Pete back. "Where's Glory? She could be a problem."

"No problem. She's sleeping like a baby. Asnrieroot tea."

"You knew I'd come with you."

"I know you love him."

Silver sighed. "We ride to meet him?"

"No. We spy on Paulo and make sure he's going to play nice."

Her stomach clenched at the thought of seeing the Fire Lord. "Well, Pete, we're in luck. Because I can find out quicker than anyone if Paulo intends to play nice." Surely Paulo's anger had subsided through the years. *Or he may kill you on sight.*

Chapter Seventeen

Jet tried to smile at Jaine as she took the reins of her most treasured mount, an unnamed white stallion.

She blew an errant strand of hair from her eyes and scowled. "Don't ride him hard in this heat. I want him to make it home to sire a full stable."

"What heat? It's beautiful. And we've barely outpaced the foot soldiers. What do you want to scold me about now?"

"Bah! It's not worth my time." Jaine turned and led the horse to the stream to join dozens already drinking greedily.

Art joined Jet, opening a satchel and offering him sweetbread and nuts. "Sit with me, Lord. We're close to Paulo. What's the plan?"

"We wait for Mikalis. I can't make a move without his information. I should say I won't *yet* make one. Another half-hour."

"He was to meet us at sunrise. We've already come too far for Traier to be a refuge, caught between Kor-Tasrun and Belanor like fish in a barrel."

Art stared at him curiously, and Jet knew he bit back a dozen questions, trying to show restraint and respect.

"What do you think of him, Art? Permission to speak freely. Get it all out in the open, once and for all."

"Talented. Ambitious. In love with you, no doubt."

"I've wounded him."

"Nonsense. He fell on his blade unaided. Have you declared your undying lust and love to him, Jet? He knew you'd choose a mate, and he knew damned well it would be a woman. Has he spoken to you on this subject?"

"I nearly killed him in anger. He may be a threat to Silver."

"Surely not. He may be wounded, but…" Art looked stunned at the possibilities. "Was he truly disturbed? You know I loathe the man, but capable of murder? Betrayal?"

"You called him ambitious. Ambitious enough to try to topple my claim to Wood chair?"

Jet opened his canteen and drank deeply of the cool spring water, wishing it could wash the bitter taste of doubt from his mouth and his mind. Mik? He closed his eyes and let the sun warm his face, the gentle breeze run through his hair, the smell of the heat on the pine trees fill his nostrils.

"I love the coming of summer. Someday we'll all enjoy moving freely about the countryside, not worrying what territory we enter, whether the sky is plagued with Pterans, or assassins hide behind the next crest."

"What romantic talk for a warlord."

"Didn't you know? I'm quite the romantic according to Silver." *Silver. I miss you already. I wish you were at my side.*

Art slapped Jet squarely on the back. "Mooning over your new wife. That's a good sign, Jet."

"I see nothing good in it."

"It's the most normal thing in the world. Cheers my heart."

Jet groaned. "You talk like a wise old crone. You're a few years my senior."

Art pointed to a low ridge. "Mikalis approaches."

Jet shaded his eyes to watch the rider who crested the hill a quarter mile away. Mikalis lay close to the horse, digging in his heels and riding like the wind, his long black hair flying behind him. "And he certainly has news."

And it's not good news. Mik's cheeks were flushed from his efforts, and he was covered in sweat and dirt, small cuts marring his face—no doubt from hiding in the trees or crawling on the ground. Jet noted his eyes, anguished, worried.

He dismounted and ran to Jet, who stood and offered him his canteen.

Mikalis waved off the water and caught his breath. "It's off. The plan is off. It's Silver, Jet. She's with Paulo."

His heart pounded furiously and his mouth went dry. He went to speak, but couldn't find the words. *Silver?*

Art grabbed Mikalis' arm gruffly. "Explain this. Did you hear this, or see it with your own eyes?"

"I saw it, Artier, I swear. That's what took me so long. When the ranger came to me with the news, I decided to confirm it myself. I saw her enter his tent."

"As a prisoner? Perhaps she's trying to help in her own imbecilic fashion?"

"It didn't seem so, Lord. She was accompanied, but wasn't treated as a prisoner or enemy."

"And no sign of Petrov?"

"None."

Jet leaned against a tree, legs trembling, head swimming.

Art approached him and whispered lowly. "What does this mean, Jet?"

"Paulo has signed his death warrant."

Mikalis paced, running his hand through his hair in frustration. "You *cannot* mean to approach him now. She will have told him everything."

"What's there to tell, Mik? He knows we're here. He knows I intend to take Belanor."

"We'll ride directly to Belanor?" Mikalis nodded, already sure he knew Jet's plan. It annoyed Jet immensely, and he wanted to test the man, but held back.

"We will ride directly to Paulo and I will collect my wife."

"Your wife? The lovely Praeta? His lover, you mean, and a traitor—a whore."

Jet stood quickly and took two strides to Mikalis, whose eyes flared in fear as Jet pressed his hand against his neck. "Why do you seem pleased to tell me this news, Mik? If this is a trick, I swear, you won't live to see sundown."

"I...I..." Mikalis squeezed his eyes shut and clutched at Jet's hand.

"Not one more word," Jet spat out and pushed his cousin to the ground with one arm. "Art, fifteen minutes. Sound the horn."

Paulo's tent smelled subtly of the filthy pteran he prized. Warriors of every clan whispered the Fire Lord had taken to riding the beasts through the air—had acquired enough power to subdue the animals that were once merely his allies.

Thin slivers of bright sunlight carved yellow into the otherwise black interior of the tent. A huge guard pushed Silver onto a cushion and stood at the entrance, barring her exit. He held her weapons in one hand.

What were you thinking? Paulo's no longer a lovesick boy. Please, Pete, get far away from here.

Paulo's strong energy preceded him, and Silver squeezed her eyes shut, fearing his reaction at the sight of her. His chuckle startled her and she looked up into his black eyes.

Paulo bowed mockingly, a smirk pulling at his lips, the tiny bells and darts woven into his long black braids jingling. Handsome as ever. No, more handsome—a powerful man now, not simply a pretty youth.

"Ah, the mistress of the grand Lord Jetre. I cannot imagine to what I owe this extreme honor."

"I am not his mistress. I'm his wife."

Paulo threw his head back and laughed. "Indeed? I'll remember to offer Jetre my congratulations. He succeeded where I failed. Or do you intend to leave him under cover of darkness as well?"

Silver stood and Paulo surveyed her head to toe.

"Do we have to go through this, Paulo? I was a girl."

"A girl?" Paulo spat at the ground and signaled to the guard. "I've a bad taste in my mouth, Joshua, bring wine." The guard bowed deeply and backed out of the tent.

"We're alone, Paulo. Get it off your chest, everything you've waited to say to me."

"I've nothing to say. I am, however, all ears. For surely you have something to say to me. Where is your *husband?*"

"I don't know where he is. I'm here on my own. To make peace with you."

"To make sure I don't intend to trick Jetre with my probes for an alliance. Very touching. He understands I offer to take on Belanor at his side, use my warriors, my Pterans?"

"Indeed."

"How did you plan to warn your lord should you learn I aim to kill him? This isn't much of a plan, Atra. Who lays in wait outside my camp?"

"I came alone. I came..." Silver looked away as Paulo stripped off his shirt and wiped the sweat from his muscular torso. Memories of endless nights of youthful passion flooded her senses. The feel of his skin, the feel of the first time...

"Yes, I remember, too."

Silver met his eyes and saw his expression soften. *I broke his heart.*

"For years, I thought of you every day. Do you know why?"

Silver nodded. *Because you were in love with me.*

"No. Do not flatter yourself. My anger was misdirected. I hated the world. For hating me and Fire clan. For fearing the brown-skinned lord, one of the remaining Were, waiting in fear to learn if we could revive the old ways and turn into horrific beasts of lore. For detesting our alliance with the Pterans, and fearing my growing power. I thought you left me for those reasons. Now I know I left myself."

"I don't understand?"

"You simply didn't love me. Why?"

"I'm sorry, Paulo, I don't know. I never knew."

"Exactly. It had nothing to do with my heritage or my clan, did it? You simply didn't love me. But I spent my youth blaming everything that went amiss on the clan. I couldn't accept a woman might not love me."

"In that respect, you lords are very similar. Kilé and Jet have said the same."

"Ah, Kilé. I regretted his death. Cirin is foul. To assassinate an unguarded lord in his sleep demonstrates extreme cowardice."

"And to assassinate the elderly parents of another lord and blame it on Kilé?"

"Blazes, it was Cirin? I suspected as much. Jeannette would not say."

"Jeannette is safe with Jet."

"She's of no consequence to me and makes her own choices. Come, sit with me, Atra, tell me how you came to marry Jetre. I'm mystified by your life choices."

"As am I, Lord."

The guard brought wine and bread and Silver sipped cautiously at Paulo's side, wondering when Jet would arrive. And what he would think of her if he saw her breaking bread with another lord.

Paulo ran his finger along Silver's jaw and sighed. "Why are you here, woman? How did you possibly think you could help Jet this way?"

"If you planned to kill him, I was going to offer myself in his place."

"With what bargaining chip? I'd have you both."

"I planned to offer myself as your mistress."

Paulo snorted. "I've mistresses enough, Atra. Relax, you need fear neither my ardor or my weapons. I plan to ride on Belanor at Jet's side. And evidently, at the side of his new wife."

"And his younger brother?" Silver winced, hoping desperately she made the right choice.

"The Lordling Petrov rides with you? The happy little family." Paulo sighed deeply. "Aye, signal him in—I'll do him no harm."

Silver whistled through her fingers, the sign the way was clear for Pete. She repeated the call several times, standing at the tent opening, searching the edge of the camp frantically for him. There was no response.

"Paulo, something's terribly wrong. Pete's gone."

"Not by my hand. Are you sure he didn't leave you here?"

"Never."

"Ah, the Lord Jetre isn't going to like this at all. Not a good way to start the campaign."

Pete woke in a dark room, head splitting in agony. He reached to his forehead and gently probed the growing lump, looked in shock at the blood on his fingers. *Stupid, stupid, stupid.*

Absorbed in the sight of Paulo, in the safety of Silver, he'd ignored his own vulnerability. The last thing he remembered was lying on the ground high above Paulo's camp, squinting to watch Silver enter the lord's tent, and hearing a snap of twig from behind. He'd left his weapons out of reach, and… *Shit. Jet's going to kill me. Unless they kill me first.*

This must be Belanor. Trueborn heroes involved in epic battles covered the walls of the small room. A grand map of the world, with each Clan's territory painted in a different color, covered one huge wall. He'd never seen the likes of it. Pete pushed himself up on an elbow to study the map more carefully, although he had to fight against blurred vision and his aching head. The painting detailed the ore-rich caves south of Belanor, the great pine forest surrounding Traier, the ragged coastline guarded by Water Clan at the easternmost edge, and north, the fertile plains and valleys of Earth clan.

No wonder Paulo wants an alliance. Fire was surrounded by plenty, but had to steal or barter with enemies to feed the clan. Pete stumbled to the map and ran his hand along the Western edge, where blue now covered the ancient world. For the first time, he wondered at the loss of the expanse of dry land, the variety of animals, and foods, and cities, and grand places that had always been simple fairy tales.

Vertigo claimed his senses and he lay back down, willing away nausea and chills.

Please let Silver be well. Please, Mother, I beg you. Jet needs her.

A faint scratching at the door brought him back to clarity, and he watched in terror as the door slowly swung open. An older man, hair pulled back in a queue in the manner of Metal warriors, put a finger to his lips and Pete nodded uncertainly.

He hurried towards the bed, bowed his head briefly in respect, and examined the goose egg growing on Pete's head.

"No doubt you feel unwell. Do you think you can walk, perhaps even run? Or must I carry you?"

"Who *are you*? Where am I, and where are we going?"

The man nodded seriously and pulled on his beard. "Yes, of course, Lordling. Sorry. I'm Guntar, a general of the deceased Lord Kilé."

"And you serve Cirin now?" Pete's heart lurched in his chest and hope waned quickly.

"I'm lordless, boy. All of Metal waits for your brother to arrive, to free them of the madman who terrorizes us and kills our children as sport after abusing them."

"You'd surrender to Jet?"

"Aye, and word has it he's forming an alliance with Paulo. I harbor a hope…"

Pete nodded quickly. "Jet harbors the same hope. What's harbor mean? Never mind, I get you."

"Aye. Here's the problem, Lordling. If Jetre learns Cirin holds you captive, he'll likely raze Belanor to the ground if he can't find you. And he may not find you if Cirin decides to cut you into small pieces for sport. Don't judge the Metal clan by one devil. Can you understand, Master Petrov? Kilé intended to speak with Jetre on the topic of an alliance before Cirin butchered him."

"And my parents."

Guntar nodded. "Aye, that's truly tragic for you."

"Jet's none too happy about it either, and Silver isn't tickled her brother was killed, and she had to come running to Wood clan for help."

"It is true. Silver is among you?"

"She is my new...she's Jet's wife."

Guntar squinted one eye and regarded Pete curiously.

"Never mind all that, General. What should we do?"

"We must get you safely out of Belanor, which is no small task. Cirin no longer trusts me. I have a few guards on my side, a number of troops, but not enough to stage a coup. Cirin is very well protected, and though his powers aren't near those of the true lords, he does easily detect threats against his life."

Pete sorted through the information, trying desperately to think as Jet would. Could he trust Guntar? Did he have any choice?

"You want to smuggle me out and come with me to meet up with Jet and Paulo before they kill all the Metal clan."

"That's right."

"I think it might be best if I kill Cirin."

Guntar snickered. "That would be lovely, boy, but highly improbable. I told you..."

"Yes, I know, his guards. But if your men can take care of his guards, I have the power to fight him."

"Only a lord may kill a lord in fair battle. I won't sanction another vile assassination."

"You'll simply have to make me Lord of Metal. Tell those loyal to you. I'll turn things over to Jet when he arrives. I might even let him in the gates."

Pete smiled as Guntar's expression changed from one of disdain to thoughtfulness to amusement.

"I heard you were a bright lad. Can you pull this off, boy? It's about as risky as it comes."

"No problem." Pete forced down the wave of nausea welling up again, wondering how the hell he would kill Cirin before Cirin killed him. *For Jet. And for Ma.*

Chapter Eighteen

Jet exhaled deeply in the clear deep knowledge the proud Lord Paulo approached him as an ally. The tall warrior wore a bit of a smirk as he pulled his sword from its scabbard, turned the grip towards Jet, and dropped to one knee before him.

Jet took the heavy weapon and handed it to Art. Anxiety poured off Silver, but he wouldn't meet her gaze, not yet. *A moment you've planned for months, that will change life for us all, and you care only this woman loves you. When did you grow weak?*

"Hello, Paulo."

"Jet. Seems you've grown a bit taller since last we met."

"If you'd fight beside your warriors instead of flying around on your ugly pets, you would have seen me in recent years."

"Droll. Not different from my arrogant classmate."

"No. Not so different, Paulo."

"I understand congratulations are in order." Paulo nodded towards Silver. Jet knew he was sincere. Silver openly declared her love for him to her old love?

"And I understand condolences for your sister Senta."

Paulo nodded briefly, expression unchanging.

"We all have grievances with Belanor. More precisely, with its cowardly, would-be lord."

Silver approached slowly and Jet met her eyes, saw the anguish in them. She placed a hand on his arm and her energy chilled him to the bone. When he placed a hand on her cheek and she broke down, he pulled her into his arms.

Paulo groaned. "You have more of a grievance than you know. Your brother is missing. I assume unless he met with an accident, he is captive at Belanor, or worse."

Silver wiped her tears and clutched at Jet's hand. "I'm sorry, Jet. He wouldn't stay in Traier, no matter how I threatened to stop him. I couldn't let him come alone. His plan was to ensure Paulo was sincere about this alliance. Our goal was to keep you from harm's way."

Pete. Anything else. Jaine's premonitions rang in his ears. Anger and guilt assaulted him. *Pete, my love. Silver, why didn't you protect him?*

"And you found Paulo sincere?" Jet winced at his own tone. *Tell me you love me alone, that this man means nothing to you. Help me rescue my brother.*

Her pale eyes grew wide and she reached to touch his lip. He repressed a shiver at the feel of her skin on his, if only briefly. "I was ready to lay down my life to keep you safe. I'll do the same for your brother."

Paulo patted Jet on the back. "Lord, the woman is true to you. We were very young, and those days have long since faded, as if a dream. She came to me to assure my allegiance to you. Let it go."

"Why have you told tales of her exploits? Of her courting all the lords, looking for power? Tell me, Paulo."

Paulo arched a dark brow and frowned. "I cannot fathom your reference. I've had no time or desire to tell such lies. Her life was simple enough—at least when I knew her. Our warriors captured the young sister of our enemy Lord Kilé, we became fond of one another..." He shrugged. "Perhaps I fonder than she. She escaped, I felt the fool, and as far as I know, she lived in Belanor until finding her way to your arms. I've spoken to no one about it, and certainly no one has dared point out to their lord he was abandoned by a woman."

Jet turned and walked a few paces to Art's side. He nodded towards the men. "Find Mik. Put him in chains until I can question him."

"Aye."

"And do not smirk. Do *not* let Jaine learn of Pete's capture."

"Or death, Lord."

"Oh, no, he's alive. In Belanor. Paulo, you will excuse me while I speak with Silver? Art, please introduce Paulo and his guards to our men, discuss our plans."

Fear gripped Jet's gut. *Pete, can you hear me?* He walked quickly away from the camp. Silver hurried behind him, trying to keep pace but staying back in uncertainty.

"Fucking idiot. I'll kill him if Cirin hasn't."

"You don't mean it."

"Shut up." Jet turned and grabbed Silver's arms so tightly she winced, and another day flashed through his mind—a day when the harsh embrace excited him. He shook her and she cried out, struggling to break free.

"You were to keep one another safe. Why did you betray my order?"

He let her go and sat against a tree, watching light dance off a tiny stream winding past a green hillock. She knelt next to him and pressed her hand to his face.

"Jet, look at me." She pulled his chin to force him to look into her eyes. "Don't send me away. I can't bear it. I must be with you to find Pete. I must be with you always."

"Why?" *Say it. Make me believe you.*

"I'm your wife. You chose me. You love me. Tell me, Jet, tell me you love me."

"I don't know what it means to love."

The hurt in her eyes pulled at him, brought him nearly to tears.

"Keep me as your mistress, only don't push me away. I can't lose you. My life has been nothing but war and loss and pain. You're the only joy I've known. And Pete."

"Joy?" *Why does joy feel like pain?* The truth washed through him and he let out a deep breath. *You're fighting it, Jet. Why does she frighten you? Because it would hurt too much to lose her, too.*

He lay back in the grass and watched the clouds move slowly in a pale-blue sky. Silver lay beside him and he pulled her into his arms, taking in the rich scent of her, feeling her flesh warming his, warming his heart, his groin.

"Aye, Silver, you're my wife. And it irks me to say it, but I don't want to be without you."

Her tears soaked his shirt and he rolled her onto her back and pressed his lips on hers. "Help me save my brother." He hated the weakness of his plea, the neediness in his own voice.

"I love him, too," she whispered.

"Time to leave. We'll reach Mashran before sundown, Belanor by midday tomorrow."

"Jet, what about Mikalis?"

"Art will see to him, extract the truth. I don't want to lay eyes on him. You'll stay by my side today and tonight. At least we'll have tonight. Tomorrow, our lives will become very, very busy."

"Aye, tonight."

Jet forced a smile. "The lord will need something to take his mind off his woes. Think up something pleasant for me, wife. Perhaps we should invite our new ally?"

"Paulo? Oh, Jet, that's not wise, not now."

"I'm joking. Tonight I need you alone. Come on." He stood and pulled her into his arms, pressed his lips on her forehead, and muttered a prayer for his brother.

❋ ❋ ❋

"This isn't right, I belong with the warriors, as do you." Jet threw back another finger of whiskey before filling Paulo's glass.

Raimondo scurried to the table and warily set a second bottle down. Paulo drained his glass quickly. "You worry too much, Jetre. Your man Artier and my own generals have it under control. Live a little, it could be your last day. The next assassination attempt could be around the corner."

"The last one was. About three miles from this tavern. My wife, in fact."

"A unique way to meet women."

"Paulo, you took the oath when I did. You never honored it?"

"Blazes no! Why would I do such a fool thing? Oh, friend, please don't tell me you stayed away from women for ten years? Didn't Masters Guo and Tsien tell you it was simply ceremonial?"

Jet groaned.

"Ah, the brilliant gifted, obnoxious child became the disciplined master of us all. I suspected one day you'd either wipe out my clan or we'd sit as we are now, discussing the future."

"Which brings me to your position, Paulo. I don't intend to rule alone. In fact, I don't intend to rule at all. I'll create a council, and ultimately, those council members will be elected by all the clan members."

"Chaos. Impossible."

Jet held up his hand to ward off more objections. "Give me a chance. There are precedents, and I'll explain them in due time."

"Don't you think we'd best defeat Cirin, and then turn to Water and Earth? This isn't over, not by a long shot."

"Agreed, but I want your word you'll support my council?"

"What choice do I have, Jet? I've surrendered to you rather than see you destroy me and my people."

"I want you at my side because you want to be there, not out of fear."

"Guo underestimated you."

"She may have underestimated us all."

"I'll take that as a compliment."

Jet inclined his head.

"Aye, I'll stand with you, Jetre. Now, there's a plump, little pointy-eared warrior who fancies the enemy lord, at least her eyes roamed up and down long enough. Artier will no doubt help me locate her. Hopefully she'll be willing to return to my camp, although you Wood clan are quite sensitive to the smell of the pteran. I suggest you join your wife. She's besotted with you, and no doubt waits anxiously for your return."

Jet smiled and stood. "Not in the least bit jealous, Paulo? That's difficult to believe."

"You're still an arrogant bastard, Jet."

"So I'm told."

Jet stepped from the tavern into the warm night air and opened his shirt to let the gentle breeze kiss his skin. He pulled his hair back with a leather cord and glanced up as a street light flickered on. He preferred the dark streets of Traier, the smell of spices and herbs and wood, the gentle slopes of cobbled streets, the twinkling stars overhead. Metal clan worked hard to capture some of antiquity in their towns of Mashran and Belanor. Street lights, paved walkways, angular buildings. Sterile, out of touch with Wu Xing, he thought.

He rounded a corner and froze, sensing her only a few paces behind him, waiting. Two metal throwing stars in one hand, his sai in the other. He turned slowly and grinned.

"Another assassination attempt, Warrior Atra?"

"You forget you branded me as your guard? Tonight, I guarded you."

She approached him with a smirk, pushing her stars into her pocket and belting the sai.

"Well, guard, I remember the last time we met here you tried to lure me with sex."

"I think it was the other way around." Silver ran her hand along his chest and brushed her palm across his nipple, working it with her fingertips. Fire coursed through his veins.

"I'm not convinced." Jet tried to close his mind to thought of Pete as his body responded to Silver's caresses.

"I'm sorry, Jet, I see it in your eyes. This isn't a good time." Silver pulled her hand away and he grabbed it quickly and kissed it.

"I don't know what tomorrow will bring. This may be the only time."

Silver knew Jet wanted something from her, and she struggled desperately to understand it. She watched as he brought a candle to life in his tent with the energy from the palm of his hand. His back towards her, he pulled off his shirt, pushed it into his saddlebag, and pulled out a small pouch.

"My mother's." Without ceremony, he handed the pouch to her. She opened it gently, pulling out a stunning ruby on a gold chain. The light of the candle set the ruby on fire, and something stirred deep within the gem.

"I don't understand this. Something's moving inside. What is it?"

Jet sat near her on the bedroll and held the gem to the light. "My mother claimed the clan's energy could be found within any of the ancients' possessions. This is the only object known to have belonged to Ling Huang, the Praeta. My family guarded it for centuries. Now it is yours."

"Surely this should go to Jaine, or one of your clan."

"It's mine to give, Silver. Along with my heart." Jet took the necklace from her and clasped it around her neck. The warmth of the stone pulsed against her breastbone. Jet pulled her shirt aside and kissed the skin around the necklace, sending chills through her limbs. His hot tongue ran along her collarbone and to her neck, where he kissed and nibbled, drawing moans from deep in her being.

Silver winced, knowing she put off the inevitable. "Jet, I'm sorry. I am having my woman's course. But I can pleasure you…"

He pulled away and smirked. "You think I don't know? I can feel your body weep. It draws me."

"Because you know I won't become pregnant?"

"You'll become pregnant when I allow my energy to send living seed to your womb." He arched a brow. "We have a lot to learn about one another."

He fell back onto her, pulling her shirt away as he ravaged her mouth, his long hair falling onto her skin, filling her with his spicy scent.

Silver tried to lose herself in him, but dreaded the disgust he'd feel when he stripped her down and saw the blood. *He doesn't understand, he hasn't experienced this.* She remembered hearing the male Metal warriors talk in disdain of women and their moods and messes.

"Enough. You don't think I know my own mind?" Annoyance flared in his eyes as he pulled her pants to her knees and kissed her belly. He worked her underwear down over her hips and she squirmed to free herself. Jet growled and reached for a cloth and wiped her soft folds dry, rubbing the blood away, and rubbing her into ecstasy at the same time.

"Jet, no, please. Oh Mother, that feels wonderful."

"Stupid Metal clan. No respect for any kind of nature."

He held his hand over her mound and her cramping eased, fantastic warmth pouring into her womb. She basked in the heat and relaxation and watched as he stripped off his leather pants, leaving his hard cock jutting out beyond her reach. Her womb ached differently as Jet tossed his hair aside and straddled her, rubbing his palm over the plum head of his erection, circling his thumb. His intake of breath thrilled her and she found herself mesmerized by the strokes of his hand along his shaft. His eyes narrowed, dark lashes made midnight by Elven kohl pressing against his cheeks, full lips parted slightly, stomach muscles rippling as he moved above her. Silver slid down so he hovered right above her face. He moaned in anticipation, and cried out as she flicked her tongue against his sack, darting back and forth along his smooth, silken skin, pulling each globe into her mouth.

"Let me suck you, Jet." He moved back and she guided him onto his back. He seemed far away, lost in his lust, submissive, out of character.

"Do what you want, my love. But do it quickly. This ache will kill me."

"I'll ease my ache with you." Silver leaned in to kiss him and he caught her head with his hands, running his fingers through her hair, pulling her mouth closer, desperately pulling at her lips, at her tongue.

She edged her hips up and slowly lowered herself onto his cock, moaning loudly as he filled her deeply. His eyes shot open and he grasped at her hips, moving her up and down with his strong arms. "Oh Mother. You are so wet, your blood so hot. So hot." He gasped as Silver squatted and rode him. "I'll never tire of you, Silver."

He ran his hands up her torso and grasped her breasts, arching up to fill her further. Dying to hear more, to tell him how she felt, Silver could only pant his name breathlessly as a wash of bliss filled her and her vision clouded over. A moment later, the pulse of Jet pouring into her extended her orgasm, and his husky voice cursing and moaning warmed her heart.

Jet pulled her into his arms and rocked her gently, kissing her head and whispering her name. "I'm not lonely any more, Silver. Don't worry about me."

"Yes, you are, Jet. I don't know why, and I don't know how to fix it. I wish I were enough for you."

She longed for his protest, but his silence filled the tent as their cries had moments before. *He needs Pete.*

Chapter Nineteen

Gunter proffered a vial to Pete, who regarded it suspiciously.

"Why would I poison you, Lordling? You're my last hope. Come, drink up, it will clear your head and send warming energy to your wounds."

"I'm adverse to increased yang—all Wood clan are, General. This won't help me."

Guntar groaned and pushed the vial in his hand.

"Blazes, all right." Pete downed the syrupy potion and heat instantly warmed his limbs and cleared his head. He nodded.

"What's the plan?"

The old man pulled on his beard in concern. "It took some convincing, but my men are willing to accept your claim to the Metal chair, willing to call you Lord. They want assurance your brother and Paulo will show mercy on Belanor."

"We'd better hurry. Jet's not a patient man. How do I challenge Cirin? I've no weapons."

Guntar reached into a long leather bag and pulled from it a metal staff—ends capped in blades—and threw it to Pete.

The weight felt good, felt perfect, in fact, and he twirled the staff expertly. "I feel energy in this weapon."

"That is because Lord Jetre gifted it upon Kilé at the oath taking ceremony. It belonged to Ling Huang."

"He gave the Praeta's staff to the enemy?"

"Kilé gave a precious book to Jet, the only one of its kind. They all exchanged gifts, even though it was clear the clans grew more segregated, and violence between them was inevitable."

Pete remembered clearly an image of Jet, candle burned to a nub, hand pressed reverently upon the ancient book, struggling to decipher the foreign script.

"I dislike books immensely. Too much work."

Guntar chuckled. "I care right now more about your skill with the staff."

"It's adequate, trust me. How will we work this?"

"He's called for you. I'm sure he doesn't intend to kill you outright, but instead use you as a bargaining chip against Jet. The problem is, he's insane enough to forget that and to kill you for sport."

"What's his skill level? What weapon does he use? How am I supposed to hide a staff?"

"He's skilled enough in long sword to do mortal damage. You'll have to disarm him. He's a large man, Lordling, don't underestimate him. If you challenge him outright, you won't have to hide your staff. I warn you, he's not above lowly tricks."

A large man with a long sword. Spectacular. He sorted quickly through the tactics Jet taught him for bringing down a large armed opponent. There weren't many.

"Well, General, the bigger they are, the harder they fall. Let's go."

Guntar pushed open the door and they stepped over the bodies of two of Cirin's guards. Guntar nodded to four of his men, and they wound their way through the halls and stairways of the cold stone mansion.

"This place is nasty. Cold. Lifeless. How can you bear it?"

Guntar put his hand on Pete's back. "We have different ways, Petrov. I would like to see Traier one day. I understand you live among the trees and animals like wild creatures."

"You're not serious? I'll throw a big party for you in Traier, General, if you get me out of this mess alive."

"That's the goal." Guntar motioned for the men to stop and listened at a large door. "He's within. There's nothing for it, but to face him head on. Or to hide you and wait until your brother arrives. The choice is yours."

"Wish I had a choice. But I want Jet to find Belanor free of this scum." *He'll be proud of me. He'll never leave me behind again.*

Pete took in a deep breath, calmed his nervous stomach, pushed away the jitters making his hands shake, and pictured his family. The face of his mother, tucking him into bed, kissing his forehead, whispering her love.

This is the man who ruined your world. And immediately he heard Jet's admonishment, "In battle, anger is your second enemy. Anger causes supreme errors in judgment. Seek calm. Seek wholeness. Trust yourself."

Pete kicked through the door and laughed at the shocked expression on Cirin's face. The man was a giant, but not as fit as Pete feared. His belly sagged over his pants, and he looked unwell—Pete noted with relief a pallor of disease on his cheeks. His pale-gray eyes shone unnaturally against the yellowing of the whites. What did Jet call it? A liver imbalance, quite deadly.

He approached Cirin, who stood from behind his desk. "I understand you sent for me. Here I am." Pete twirled his staff casually.

"What's this, Guntar? You arm the brat?"

Guntar bowed his head slightly. "He claims to be the next Lord of Metal clan, Cirin, and would challenge you."

Cirin exploded with laughter and fell into a fit of coughing. "The great Jetre sends a child to do his work? Or is he dead as well, like your parents, Lordling?"

Pete inhaled another calming breath, closing his eyes, praying for patience.

Guntar pulled a short sword from his belt. "The army acknowledges the Lord Petrov as their new ruler, Cirin. He is here to prove his worth. You must fight him."

"Bah! The army is faithful to me, old man."

Guntar strode to the balcony of Cirin's quarters and threw open the tall doors. Cirin peered out and gasped at the sight of at least two thousand warriors, weapons thrown on the ground in defiance.

"That is *not* the full army. My other generals, my guards…" Cirin broke off unsurely, sweat beginning to bead on his brow.

"Some are dead. Others wait in their homes to see the outcome of this coup. The warriors below risk their lives to show you what a foul coward they believe you to be. They were loyal to Kilé, but not to his murderer. You had no right to claim power as a lord. One who has the skill and the blood of a lord in his veins challenges you. You're out of time, Cirin."

"I do not accept the challenge. It's preposterous. He's a child. I'll take my chances with Jetre. Guards, lock these two away."

The guards stood like statues, ignoring him. Pete watched in amusement as red suffused Cirin's puffy cheeks. *Let him grow angry. Let him make the mistakes.*

"All right, onto the field with you, Lordling. When your brooding brother arrives, he'll find you hanging from the gate of Belanor. Of course, he may not make it to Belanor, as part of my force circles behind him led by one of your own."

"Who? Name the traitor." Pete knew in his heart Mikalis' betrayal far surpassed all their suspicions. "You no doubt promised Mik the Wood chair once you killed Jetre? What a fool. You can't even hold onto this chair. I can't believe Mik would be that stupid."

Guntar groaned. "Mikalis Artraud has had grand aspirations since boyhood, Petrov. And some axe to grind with Jetre."

"He's a dead man now. Come on, Cirin, let's go. I'm tired and hungry. Here's your chance to cut my heart out like you did my parents. And my sister-in-marriage's brother."

"Your sister-in-marriage's brother? What's this babble?"

"Never mind." Pete moved to the balcony and took the winding stairs to the enclosed field below where the army stood in wait. He realized with anxiety the men and women bowed their heads as he descended the steps,

201

acknowledging his claim to lordship. *Well, I guess you'd best kill Cirin. Elsewise you'll look the fool, and Jet will throw a fit.*

He stopped midway and cleared his throat. "Hey Metal warriors. Um, I'm going to kill Cirin and become Metal Lord if my brother Lord Jetre lets me. I think he's interested in ending these battles. That's what you want, right?"

A mighty cheer went up and Pete's heart lightened. Maybe this ruling stuff wasn't difficult after all. Or maybe he was a natural. He shrugged and hurried to the field, spinning his staff impatiently, waiting for Cirin. The man slowly descended, long sword in hand, eyeing the field of warriors with fury and disdain.

Guntar called the challengers to the center of a square marked off in chalk and bid them bow to one another. Pete saluted and bowed. Cirin leaned on his sword with a smirk.

Guntar spat. "No true practitioner of the arts would ignore a command to bow, Cirin. You are arrogant. It has proven your downfall."

"No one has gone down, yet, Guntar. I certainly won't fall to a boy with a stick."

Cirin took a defensive stance, sweeping his long sword high over his head with a fluid, practiced motion.

Don't underestimate him, Pete. It would be a grand mistake.

Guntar held up his hand. "At my command, combat begins. To the death." He threw down his hand and called out with a guttural yell.

Cirin circled Pete slowly, like a cat, leaning one way and the other, brandishing the heavy sword like it was a feather. *He wants me to strike first*, Pete thought, reminding himself to stay patient. It didn't take long before Cirin growled in frustration and leaned in low, slashing at Pete's feet.

Pete dug one blade end of his staff in the ground and leapt over the Cirin's sword with feet to spare. They continued the pattern for minutes, Cirin thrusting, turning, slicing, and Pete ducking or leaping from harm's way.

"We can do this all day, Cirin. You're ill. You'll never outlast me."

"Don't try taunting me, boy. You have no idea what you're dealing with." Cirin turned his back, waiting for the strike, but Pete wouldn't take the trap, and leaned on his staff. The warriors gathered close by snickered and clapped, and Cirin's fury grew with the taunts.

With a great cry, he rushed at Pete, slashing furiously in every direction, backing him out of the square. The man's eyes were wild, and Pete felt truly threatened for the first time. He took in a quick breath and spun away, as he had practiced many times in Jet's presence. This would have to be perfect, or be his death. One, two, three leaps, the final a perfect airborne circle, he came down on Cirin's head with his heel, and disarmed his blade with the staff. He heard the warriors' cheers as if from far away, the blood rushing in his ears, heart pounding furiously, as he pressed the tip of his staff's blade against Cirin's throat.

"For Lue. For Kilé. For my brother…" *Do it, Pete, you can do it.*

"Halt!" Jet's voice filled the air and Pete automatically stepped back, years of training taking over. He looked over to see his brother, Silver, Jaine, Art, and a dark-skinned warrior Pete knew must be Lord Paulo Ramirez staring in wonder at him. Jet stormed to his side and pulled him away from Cirin. The Metal warriors fell to one knee in respect and Jet nonchalantly motioned for them to rise as he grabbed Pete's sleeve.

"I'm damned happy to see you alive, Petrov. Damned happy."

"Let me kill him."

"No." Jet's brow furrowed and his eyes flared in intensity, and Pete knew it was hopeless.

"I've earned this. They're calling me Lord of Metal."

"You've earned the right to kill a man?" Jet kneeled and pulled Pete into a tight embrace, nearly smothering him, and finally pushed him away and stared at him intently. "Listen to me, you brave little idiot. The kill means nothing. Nothing. You know this, Pete. You've no blood on your hands, and I'm going to do everything in my power to make sure it stays that way. It's hard to sleep at night when you see the faces of men and women you've killed in your dreams. Not my boy. There are other ways."

"Damn it, Jet. He killed Ma."

Jet subtly reached down and put a hand on the staff lying at Pete's side. Their eyes met and Pete suddenly sensed it too, the threat behind Jet, the hatred welling up from the fallen would-be lord. Pete rolled out of the way as Cirin charged at Jet, who hit the ground and quickly sprung to his feet, staff spinning with blinding speed. Cirin stepped back, fear etched across his face as Jet whirred the blades towards him.

"Surrender." Jet's voice was low, and Pete thought he might have imagined it. But Cirin heard it and shook his head.

"I should have been trained with you, Artraud. Guo and Tsien picked the wrong boys. I can beat you."

"Nonsense."

Jaine ran to Pete's side and pulled him by the hand to watch the battle with his family. She placed her hand on his shoulders and squeezed tightly, and despite his disappointment at Jet taking his place, he loved the safety and warmth of her arms. He glanced up at Silver, who reached out her hand, but had eyes only for Jet as Cirin prepared his attack. Silver gasped as Jet spun the staff one last time and threw it to Pete.

Unarmed, Jet closed his eyes and pressed his palms together at his heart. Pete groaned, knowing the difficulty of Jet's plan, how risky.

"What's he doing?" Silver's voice shook, and Pete squeezed her hand.

Jaine hissed at her to quiet down. "Don't you believe in him? In the power of his Ch'i?"

Cirin appeared confused by Jet's curious move, but stepped back when Jet finally opened his smoldering eyes and extended his palms towards him. Pete saw the tiniest glimmer of energy flowing from Jet's hands, knew he must be alone in his ability to detect the undetectable. As Pete expected, Jet's strike threw Cirin back several feet. He crumpled to the ground in pain and shock, his blade abandoned. Cirin scraped against the soil, but Guntar kicked him squarely in the stomach, and he rolled to his side.

Jet climbed the balcony stairs and extended his hand to the crowd of warriors, now a throng pressing forward to hear him. He bowed his head respectfully and motioned for Silver to join him. Pete watched proudly, heart bursting with love for his brother. *He seems older today.*

"Here is Kilé's staff." Jet extended the weapon for the warriors to examine. "I gave it to him ten years ago when many of you were, like me, very young. The energy of Wood clan flows freely in it, and I give it to Guntar as my gesture of peace to you.

"Here is Kilé's sister, Atra SanMartin. My wife of three days. My wife forever." Jet pointed to Paulo. "There stands Paulo Ramirez, honored Lord of Fire." Paulo waved nonchalantly and Jet snickered. "He is my ally."

"The Cycle of Creation can begin here, now. It's in your hands. I'll lead the revolution, or you can choose another."

The cry started with a few, and soon all joined in, chanting "Jetre, Jetre, Jetre" until the noise became deafening. Jet bowed again and motioned for silence.

"Go home to your families. Enjoy your freedom from the tyranny of the lords. On the day of the next full moon, send ten of your clan to Traier, to sit on the council of Wu Xing. Elect them as you will, but take heed. You must carry on peacefully, or Fire and Wood will combine against you, and force our peace down your throats.

"Do what you will with Cirin. I've enough blood on my hands."

Pete turned and hugged Jaine, who rubbed his hair and whispered the baby names she used to call him. She shuddered, and he looked up to find her crying.

"What's wrong with you, Jaine?"

"I'm simply happy you're okay, Pete."

"I could have beaten him. I did beat him."

"Yep, we all saw it. You're lord material all right. But it looks like we won't be having any more lords."

Paulo snorted. "I always thought it would come to this. I dearly hope I get to keep my lovely house."

"And your pet Pterans?" Pete smiled at the huge warrior.

"Would you like to ride one, Lordling? We can race." The man ruffled Pete's long hair.

"Uh-uh. Hate those smelly things. Keep 'em away from me, would you?"

"Whatever the staff master wants. Can't afford to make you angry." Pete saw him wink at Jaine and turned away. *They're making fun of you, still treating you like a baby. What do I have to do?*

"*Ella*, Petrov!" Jet gestured and Pete walked to him glumly. *Another lecture?*

"Yes, Lord Jetre?"

Jet smiled serenely. "I want you to stay close."

"That's pretty hard when you ride out of town without me."

Jet picked him up, rubbing at his cheek. "That will never, ever happen again."

"Do you promise, Jet?"

"I promise, Pete."

"Let's go home. Paulo, we'll see you at full moon."

"Aye, Lord, you will."

The men clasped arms. Pete looked back over Jet's shoulder to see two warriors pulling short blades from their belts, leaning down towards Cirin, who fainted at the sight.

Chapter Twenty

Two days. I can't bear it. Two days without a moment alone with him. Silver paced in the lord's quarters, desperate to understand why Jet held her at arm's length, rode alone, slept alone, walked for hours in solitude. He answered her gentle probes with half-hearted claims of headaches and preparations for the coming council meeting.

Perhaps he stopped loving me. Perhaps he never loved me. I should be at his side, helping him.

She opened the shutters of his study to let the daylight and smell of sweet flowers fill the room. A spear of blue darted through the gardens, and she held her hand out, calling him as Jaine had done.

Bunky lighted on her hand, whistling happily. "Hello Warrior."

"Hello Bunky. You're my only friend these days. You and Glory."

"Glory Glory Glory. I'm a bluebird."

"Aye. I don't suppose you know what ails the Lord Jetre?"

"I'm a bluebird."

Silver swept her hand in the air, watching Bunky take flight over the colorful trees, now in full bloom.

"Hello, wife." Her heart raced at the sound of Jet's deep voice. He looked exhausted, older, in pain.

How stupid you are, Silver. He's weary, torn up over Mikalis' betrayal, with all of Isla riding on his choices.

"Where is Mikalis?"

Jet shrugged as he gently laid a book on the table he clutched under his arm. "I don't know."

"He escaped?"

"No, he did not escape. I set him free, but he's not to come within miles of Traier."

"Set him free? You can't be serious, Jet. He's a danger to you. Something's terribly wrong with him…"

Jet held up a hand to signal her silence.

"We have no crime in Traier—no theft, no murder, nothing save a few drunken brawls now and again."

"What does this have to do with Mikalis?"

"We've no system of justice. No way to judge him fairly."

"I don't understand. He's a traitor, a spy, and worse."

"So were you." Jet arched a brow. "I didn't kill you either. Of course, I didn't set you free."

Silver sat at Jet's desk and rubbed her hand across the book. *He's struggling with his decision to make these changes. He's writing history each day, the future of us all.*

"I think I understand."

A glimmer of light flashed to his eyes as he took a deep breath. "Do you? I fear no one will respect the choices I make now. They are hard ones."

"What is this book, Jet? May I see it?"

"Aye, take a look. The gift of your brother to his enemy, ten years ago to the day. A Trueborn relic. Do you understand how old it is, Silver? That is real paper, made from trees."

Silver examined the spine, but couldn't read the faded, golden letters. She gently opened the cover and squinted at the first page. "*The United States of America. Volume I.*" Silver looked up. "It says there are twenty volumes."

Jet watched her silently as she leafed through the pages. A flattened, golden leaf marked one page, and she ran her hand along the text. "'*We the People of the United States of America, in order to form a more perfect union...*' I know these words. From the ancient land that ruled the West for several centuries. You seek a model for a government? Why one that failed?"

"They all failed. But the idea isn't flawed—at least I pray it is not. I do worry about the part regarding God. Some who don't worship the Mother might take issue with it. But the council will have a say. This is simply a place to start." She hadn't seen him so unsure, every statement a veiled question.

"Oh, I can't imagine anyone would care about such a minor detail. This is a good enough place to start. May I read on?"

He first looked startled, then immensely relieved. To her great shock, he fell to his knees, resting his head in her lap. *He's holding back tears.*

Silver set the book aside and stroked his hair until he relaxed under her caresses. He looked up, smiling. She kissed away the one tear sliding down his cheek.

"Whatever is wrong? I can't bear to see you hurt this way. Is it Mikalis?"

"Nothing is wrong. Everything is absolutely right. You'll help me? I've no one else..."

"You were truly destined for this, Jet. Don't doubt yourself now. Of course I'll help. Remember, I'm the history expert." She brushed her hand on his cheek and he caught it in his and kissed it.

"I knew there was something I liked about you."

"I thought you liked me for my skills as a warrior."

"There's that as well." He pulled her into his arms. "I love you, Atra SanMartin. Please love me back."

She tried to think of something clever to say, but couldn't utter a word. She brushed away her own tears.

"I sent for Paulo. I want him at my side before the rest of the council arrives. I...I need him."

"What of Earth and Water?"

"We'll make them a very generous offer."

"Lay down their swords or die?"

"Aye." Jet brushed his lips on hers and pushed her down onto the divan, hovering an inch over her. "Kilé gave me two great gifts—a fine book and a lovely sister. He was brilliant, far brighter than I even pretended to be. I was all noise and show. Do you think he could have possibly meant for me to take this book seriously? Could he have imagined my need for it one day?"

"Yes."

"Perhaps he'll bless our mission from his place in eternity. Whether he'd bless this union is another matter."

"We'll ask him when the opportunity presents itself. Don't you think it's time to break your oath again, Lord?"

Silver reached down to run her hand along his stomach.

"Patience, Praeta. Don't want to wear me out, do you?"

"I certainly want to try."

"Good answer."

Silver started as Pete banged through the door. Cheeks flushed from running, he ran his hand through his hair nervously.

Jet knelt near the boy and placed both hands on his shoulders. "Tell me."

"A runner from Fire clan. The Lord Paulo."

"What about Paulo? Dead? Hell, Pete, spit it out."

"Kidnapped and taken to Logan. Lords Eain and Borne demand you attend them, or they'll kill him."

"Bring this runner to me." Pete nodded and left Silver and Jet to regard one another seriously.

"Fools. The revolution will have to wait a while it seems."

"You mean to go, don't you? Well, at least you'll let me go with you this time?"

"Aye, Warrior. We stand together, through everything."

About the Author

To learn more about Ciar Cullen or to send her an email, please visit www.ciarcullen.com. Join her Yahoo! group to chat with other readers as well as Ciar. http://groups.yahoo.com/group/CiarCullen

Deep in the Mayan jungle, a brooding archaeologist searches for the lost tomb of a Jaguar King, but finds more danger and erotic passion than in his wildest fantasies.

Mayan Nights
© 2006 Ciar Cullen

Deep in the Mayan jungle, a brooding archaeologist searches for the lost tomb of a Jaguar King, but finds more danger and erotic passion than in his wildest fantasies.

In the wilds of the Yucatan among the Mayan ruins lays the tomb of Shield Jaguar, once King of Pacal. Professor SinJin Twaine is a dark mysterious man, a renowned archaeologist who has spent years looking for the tomb. And at long last, he seems to have succeeded.

Tamara Martin jumped at the chance to work with SinJin, jokingly known as the Ivy League Beast. Expecting a white haired, eccentric old man, Tam isn't prepared for the sexy, compelling, complicated young man she's been hired to assist. As the pair uncover the secrets of the tomb, the "curse of Pacal" seems to be more truth than legend-is the enemy sabotaging the dig real, or otherworldly?

Tam and SinJin fight their hopeless attraction for one another in a battle of words and wits, until Shield Jaguar himself unites the couple from his eternal vantage point.

Available now in ebook and print from Samhain Publishing.

"Rosa!" SinJin found her pulling fresh bread from the oven and hugged her tightly, laughing at her expression of surprise.

"What smells so wonderful?"

"Since we have company, so I thought I'd make your favorite, Pibil chicken. Did you have a good day on the site?"

"Awesome! Asombroso! Perhaps the best day of my life! I may have found what I'm looking for at Pacal—the tomb of Shield Jaguar. We'll see. Alberto will be here tomorrow or the next day, and he'll stay for a few days, at least."

"Professor Ramirez will come from Mexico City? Then this is terribly important!"

"He has to provide me with a permit to excavate further. I only had a partial nod from the government to do preliminary exploration of that section of the site. Understand?"

Rosa nodded enthusiastically.

"Rosa, where is the woman?"

"Tam. Dr. Tamara Martin. I have not seen her for hours. She went exploring, I think. Perhaps a swim in the cenote."

SinJin frowned. She couldn't have gotten far on those wounded feet. It wouldn't be very safe to swim in the sinkhole alone under any conditions, much less at night. He hurried to the back of the house and saw the light in the workroom.

"Son of a bitch!" His body tensed with fury as he strode to the hut and looked in.

She didn't hear him, but continued to work, glasses pushed down far on her nose, sweat dribbling in beads down her sundress. She sighed and stretched, then put down her tiny glue brush and gently rotated the wooden plank she had placed under the pot. SinJin watched in shock as she examined the exquisitely restored piece—a small cacao cup, one meant for a king. She read the turquoise and coral painted symbols aloud, almost reverently. "Spear Jaguar, son of Shield Jaguar." Then she pushed her chair back and sighed deeply.

Stunned, SinJin waited to hear if she'd say more. Could it really be the cup of Spear Jaguar—it meant he might be right about the tomb. If the son were at the site, would the father be far away? How had she put it together in one day? He had been putting off the job, sure it would be at least two days' worth of backbreaking work. How had she read the glyphs so easily? He would have needed to call in an expert. He rubbed his hand through his dusty hair as he watched her sketch busily in his notebook.

She stretched again, and this time, a different shock ran through him. He hadn't taken the time to really look at her this morning. Her legs went on forever, barely covered by her short dress. Her full breasts were falling out of her dress as she bent over the table, thinking herself alone. Her pale hair brushed her bare shoulders…She's a bombshell, as beautiful as in the dream.

"Damn it!" He pushed the metal door wide so it creaked loudly.

"Oh! You scared me! I didn't hear you."

"How dare you touch my notebooks? And my artifacts! Who the hell do you think you are?"

She sighed and rubbed her eyes. "All right. I took a chance, and it didn't work. I called you an asshole. Well, you are an asshole. A brilliant one," she indicated his notebooks with a sweep of her hand. "But an asshole, nevertheless. It doesn't matter how brilliant or hot you are. Nothing could make up for that horrible personality. I hope you choke on your King, Señor Suave."

"Which King?"

"Nothing else matters to you, does it? I know your type. Can't say I blame you, actually. Spear Jaguar, son of Shield Jaguar. Is that what you want to hear? You were hoping for the father, I see." She shoved the chair back under the workbench. "Lovely cup. Don't worry, I won't tell anyone. Congratulations—you've found your tomb. Will you give me a lift to the road tomorrow? My feet are still killing me."

SinJin saw her fight back tears—were they tears of anger or disappointment? Probably both. He didn't move from the doorway.

"How did you do that?"

"What?"

"Put that together so quickly? And read it. Are you sure of what it says?"

"Positive."

He pinched the bridge of his nose and squeezed his eyes shut.

"Tamara, is it?"

She nodded.

"You're fired."

"I know." She looked at the floor and hobbled toward the doorway, crying openly now. She didn't leave him any option but to move aside or be slammed with her body. He didn't move. She nearly bounced off him, but he grabbed her arms and steadied her. She took in a quick breath and looked into his eyes.

"I resigned from Princeton today." He laughed at her shocked expression. "You can't imagine someone doing that? They've instructed you to return immediately. Did you call me hot?"

"Resigned? But why now, when you might have found Shield Jaguar?"

"I might have found Shield Jaguar." SinJin let the thrill of the words sweep through him, then pulled himself together at the sight of Tamara's tears and confused expression. "Today seemed like a good day to let the Mexican Government know what I have down here. My friend, Ramirez, is in charge of all Mexican antiquities." He didn't elaborate, seeing she recognized the name. "I've accepted his offer of employment, as a Professor of the University of Mexico. He won't make me teach, thank God. Just some dog-and-pony shows, fundraisers and such. You said I was hot, I'm sure I heard it."

"Princeton's been pressuring you to come back and teach?"

He nodded.

"That's so short-sighted."

"Agreed."

"Won't Princeton make a claim on your finds?"

"They can't touch it. Not a dime of the funds came through them, and they don't hold the permit. They know the Mexican Government owns anything I pull out of the ground and they can't afford to piss off the Minister of Antiquities here, who happens to be my good friend. I don't want anymore politics. Ramirez is a straight-shooter, at least I think he is."

"I see. You can let go of me now, mate."

He moved his hands to her hips, wondering if she'd slap him, or respond.

"I don't think I want to let go of you."

"Listen, Professor, under any other circumstances, I'd be sweeping your precious finds off that table and giving you the time of your life. But I'm not much in the mood, after getting fired. So get your fucking hands off me now."

SinJin let go. She slipped by him and hobbled towards the hacienda.

"Shit."

She wouldn't consider it, would she? No, she was young, her entire career ahead of her.

He caught up to her in a few strides and grabbed her wrist.

"Dr. Martin."

"Fuck off."

SinJin put both hands on her shoulders and turned her to face him.

"Curb your foul language and listen to me."

Tam opened her mouth, as if to protest and he clamped a hand over her lips. They stood in near silence for a moment, and as if to fill the empty space, the cicadas sang out in rhythm with the gentle warm night breeze.

SinJin took in a deep breath and searched for the right words, the perfect words. "You have a choice. You can put that suit back on and take up your duties at some college, teaching the unappreciative urchins all about the wonders of the ancient world, probably never putting your full talents to use. Or, you can have a piece of Pacal, as a contributor. Not as a co-author, mind you. My assistant. Same pay as Princeton, but only one weekend day off. The work continues straight through the rainy season, inside the storerooms. You've only been here a day, so you don't know how isolated we are, how hard we work. It's no picnic, and Cozmano isn't the Plaza. I suspect I know your answer already, but I'll give you the night to think of a nice way to refuse my offer."

He tried to ignore the movement of her breasts beneath the thin fabric of her dress as she panted under his grasp. She was so close, the scent of her light perfume filling the air, heated by the warm night air. Her brilliant blue eyes grew huge, and she looked very confused. He slowly removed his hand and let it slide down her arm, taking a final opportunity to feel her smooth skin. It shocked him to realize he hadn't touched a woman since Laura, except to hug Rosa.

Doctor Martin, if you could read my mind, see my dream, how you'd be cursing me now.

Regarding him carefully, silently, she slowly pulled her arm away and stepped back. He saw her swallow nervously. It didn't seem in character, and he waited for the barrage of insults. They never came. Instead, she simply nodded.

"What does that mean?"

"I called you hot."

A sly smile crept to her eyes and he felt a tremor of hope and life stir in his gut, a sensation he never expected to feel again.

"I thought so. But I can't compete with Princeton."

"I came here for Pacal, for the tomb. Not for Princeton. I hate teaching the 'urchins', as you call them. And we'll see about that co-author clause, Professor."

"It's non-negotiable."

"Everything's negotiable, SinJin."

"Then you'll throw in that lap-dance, along with long hours sketching glyphs and restoring pottery?"

"Before the season's over, I'll throw in a lap dance." She turned her back on him and headed towards the house. Rosa stood on the veranda, motioning for the pair to come to dinner.

Before the week's over, if I have anything to say about it.

An alternate dimension…demons…
a dangerous game…will fiery passion be their only defense?

Lord Night
© 2006 Jessie Verino

Temp agency owner Shannon Miller likes to play video games, but she never expected to find herself *in* one, let alone with a sexy scientist who makes her body melt with desire.

Physicist Damien Richards is blind—and not only in matters that concern his sight. Despite the accomplishments he's achieved in creating an alternate dimension, he still believes he is unwhole due to his physical impairment.

When a lab accident propels the two into an experimental, alternate dimension, they find themselves playing a dangerous game, unable to return, fighting demons as well as a passion that could consume them both. Will they be able to face their personal fears and win the game of love?

Available now in ebook from Samhain Publishing.

Enjoy the following excerpt from Lord Night...

"Allow me to satisfy all your hungers this evening."

He led her inside, closing the doors behind him. She settled on the plush rug, leaning provocatively against silk pillows before the warmth of the fire. The little gold clasp of her robe winked at him, inviting him to explore the secrets it hid. But he wanted to go slow and savor the rest of the evening. *Enjoy Shannon.* He backed away from her before he acted on carnal impulse, and turned his attention to the champagne.

The loud pop brought an explosion of bubbles over the lip of the bottle and sprayed his chest with the cold liquid, helping him maintain control.

After he placed the two flutes filled with the sparkling wine on a silver platter, he added a little taste of everything, and two personal fondue bowls brimming with warm melted chocolate.

The mirror above the mantle reflected his nude image bearing the large tray. Rather like a male slave of ancient Greece servicing his mistress. He smiled at the thought of playing the meek role before turning the tables and dominating the unsuspecting mistress with his dark passions. The thought had him hard and throbbing.

He placed the tray beside her on the floor. "Mistress, my humble offering."

He watched her gaze move from the tray to his rigid cock. Her tongue moistened her lips. "Not so humble a feast at all."

"Champagne?" he offered.

She took the flute and held it high, never looking away from his midsection. "To feasts. May they always be...bountiful."

He held the other glass to hers and answered. "May you always have your fill."

She bit on her lower lip. "Everything looks delicious. I don't know where to start."

He settled on his knees next to the tray. "Allow me," he said and reached for a plump strawberry. He bit into the succulent fruit, releasing the sweet red juice. He traced the fleshy morsel over her parted lips, tempting her, before allowing her to take it into her mouth.

Sweetness burst on her tongue when she sank her teeth into the berry.

She watched in anticipation as his fingers hovered above the tray, but he didn't choose another strawberry. Instead, he produced a small red mask from the tray. "I have a few surprises myself. This will make the experience more…tantalizing, more daring."

Her stomach quivered at the thought, and a delicious shiver ran from her hardened nipples to her swollen labia, releasing a scintilla of moisture. She leaned back into the pillows when he moved to straddle her, and she stretched languidly, rubbing her legs together, trying to increase the sensation.

He placed the mask over her eyes. "Turn over," he commanded.

She felt the tug of the mask as he tied it into place. When she rolled onto her back, she opened her eyes, testing it, but couldn't see even a speck of light through the thick red silk.

Even sensing his movements, she still gasped in surprise when the next strawberry touched her lips. Warm, creamy chocolate coated the fruit and it spread over her tongue as she ate. Oh yeah, she could get used to this.

"I need another sip of champagne."

The brush of his fingers against her bare skin tickled, but the light caress didn't linger. He grasped the amethyst and pulled gently on the chain. "You didn't say please."

She arched her back and lifted herself to her elbows, careful not to let the slight tension lesson. "Please?" The word escaped her in a breathless supplication.

The cool rim of the flute coaxed her mouth open, and he allowed her one sip of the sparkling liquid before denying her another.

Her frustration mounted as he played with her this way. Each time she felt the tug of the chain or the taste of sweetness on her lips, she begged him to satisfy her, or end the torment. He refused to do either.

He sucked her firm nipples, holding them taut with the chain, until she cried out from the agonizing pleasure of it, only to be rewarded by the caress of his breath across the wet buds and nothing more. She squirmed beneath him, trapped between his strong thighs and the chain, helpless to do anything but whimper in pleasure.

When he finally unfastened the gold clasp of her gown, it fell away, exposing her fully to his gaze. The head of his shaft played against the skin above her mound. The little droplets of moisture he left behind only heightened her fervor.

"Do not move," he commanded. The weight of the chain lessened and he placed the amethyst between her breasts.

She had begged for relief from the sweet torment earlier, but now the loss of it made her crave it all the more. The heat of his breath caressed her bare stomach when he crouched low over her, like a predator stalking her scent.

She fisted her hands in the plush rug underneath to keep from moving and held tight when he nipped the sensitive flesh below her navel. The sensation of his love bite stayed even as he backed away until she couldn't feel any part of him touching her.

"Spread your legs for me."

The skirt of her gown feathered over her legs when she opened for him. She held her breath in anticipation, fully aware of his gaze on her. She felt his triumphant smile when her juices surged and flowed over her swollen labia.

He nestled between her legs, and she clenched her hands in an effort to keep from raking them through his hair and pulling him closer. An eternity passed, but she lay motionless as he had instructed, refusing to beg him. Every muscle in her body trembled, taut with expectation.

She squirmed beneath him, exposing more of herself to his mouth. The moist warmth of his tongue penetrated her swollen flesh, sending waves of ecstasy through her. He kissed her opening, plunging into its hot depths. Her muscles tightened around him.

He pulled out before she came. "You have a greedy little pussy, Shannon. Fortunately, I'm a generous man."

Suffering from lack of completion, a low cry of frustration escaped.

"I'm going to kiss you again. Sample your sweet nectar until I'm drunk from it. Don't come until I allow you."

Her breasts swelled and ached. She moved her hands to massage them, but he caught them and placed them back at her sides. "Every part of you is *my* pleasure." His strong fingers found her nipples and squeezed as his tongue delved deep inside her once again.

Samhain publishing, Ltd.

It's all about the story…

Action/Adventure
Fantasy
Historical
Horror
Mainstream
Mystery/Suspense
Non-Fiction
Paranormal
Red Hots!
Romance
Science Fiction
Western
Young Adult

http://www.samhainpublishing.com

LaVergne, TN USA
10 August 2010
192737LV00004B/45/A